# KING of
# ATHELNEY

# By

# H A Culley

## Book two of the Saga of Wessex

1

# Published by

# oHp

Orchard House Publishing

First Kindle Edition 2020

# Text copyright © 2020 H A Culley

3

# Place Names

*Note: In my last series of novels I used the modern names for places in Anglo-Saxon England as some readers had said that my earlier novels were confusing because of the use of place names current in the time about which I was writing. However, I had even more adverse comments that modern names detract from the authentic feel of the novels, so in this series I have reverted to the use of Anglo-Saxons names.*

*The only exception is Athelney itself. The Saxon name for it was Æthimgæg but I felt that calling this novel 'King of Æthimgæg' would resonate with few readers.*

Ægelesthrep - Aylesford, Kent
Afne - River Avon
Basingestoches - Basingstoke, Hampshire
Baðum - Bath, Somerset
Berncestre - Bicester, Oxfordshire
Berrocscīr - Berkshire
Cantwareburh - Canterbury, Kent
Cent - Kent
Cilleham - Chilham, Kent
Cippanhamme - Chippenham, Wiltshire
Cocheham - Cookham, Berkshire
Cynuit - Countisbury, Devon
Dyfneintscīr - Devon
Danmǫrk - Denmark
Dofras - Dover, Kent
Dornsæte - Dorset
Dumnonia - Cornwall (also called Kernow)

Dyflin (Viking name) - Dublin, Ireland
Ēast Hlenc - East Lyng, Somerset
Ēast Seaxna Rīce - Essex
Eforwic - York, North Yorkshire
Escanceaster - Exeter, Devon
Fŏsweg - The Fosse Way (Roman road)
Freumh - Frome, Somerset, also the River Frome
Glestingaburg - Glastonbury, Somerset
Glowecestre - Gloucester, Gloucestershire
Hæfen Kernow - Porthcurno, Cornwall
Hamtunscīr - Hampshire
Hamtun - Northampton, Northamptonshire
Hamwic - Southampton, Hampshire
Hreopandune - Repton, Derbyshire
Irlond - Ireland
Legacæstir - Chester, Cheshire
Lindesege - Lindsey District, Lincolnshire
Lundenwic - London
Orkneyjar - The Orkney Islands
Oxenaforda - Oxford, Oxfordshire
Neen - River Nene

Norþ-sǣ - North Sea

Pedredan - River Parrett
Pegingaburnan - Pangbourne, Berkshire
Poole Hæfen - Poole Harbour, Dorset

Portcæstre - Porchester, Hampshire

Readingum - Reading, Berkshire

Sæfern - River Severn

Scirburne - Sherborne, Dorset
Silcestre - Silchester, Hampshire
Somersaete - Somerset
Stanes - Staines-upon-Thames, Surrey
Sudwerca - Southwark, South London

Sūð-sǣ - English Channel

Sūþrīgescīr - Surrey
Suth-Seaxe - Sussex

Suttun - Plymouth, Devon
Swéoland - Sweden
Sveinsey - Swansea, South Wales
Temes - River Thames
Thon - River Tone
Tomtun - Tamworth, Staffordshire
Wælingforde - Wallingford, Oxfordshire
Wealas - Wales
Werhām - Wareham, Dorset
Whitlond - Isle of Wight
Wiltunscīr - Wiltshire
Wintanceaster - Winchester, Hampshire
Ytene - River Itchen

# List of Principle Characters

*Historical figures are in bold.*

Ædwulf – A former thrall rescued from the Danes, later one of Jørren warband

**Ælfred** – King of Wessex

Ælfnoð – Abbot of Cantwareburh

Æscwin – The elder son of Leofflæd and Jørren, also the name of Jørren's eldest brother, the Thegn of Cilleham in Cent

**Æthelflaed** – Eldest daughter Ælfred and Ealhswith, later Lady of the Mercians

**Æthelhelm** – The late King Æðelred's elder son

**Æðelred** – Mercian nobleman, later Ealdorman of Mercia

**Æthelwold** – The late King Æthelred's younger son, a contestant for Ælfred's throne

Acwel and Lyndon – Two of Jørren's scouts

Ajs – Steward at the ealdorman's hall in Cantwareburh

Alric – Jørren's other brother

**Asser** – Bishop of Wintanceaster

Bjarne – A former ship's boy on a longship hailing from Swéoland, now a member of Jørren's warband

Brennus – Thane of Athelney

**Burghred** – King of Mercia

Cei – A former slave belonging to Jørren's family, now one of his warband

**Ceolwulf II** – King of Mercia after Burghred, puppet ruler installed by the Danes

Cerdic – A Mercian rescued by Jørren, now an outlaw

Cináed and Uurad – Two young Picts enslaved by Vikings, now part of Jørren's warband

Cissa - Ealdorman of Berrocscīr after Jørren

Cuthfleda - Jørren and Leofflæd's elder daughter

Drefan – Ealdorman Odda's youngest son, a member of King Ælfred's gesith

Eadda – Hereræswa (war leader) of Wessex

**Eadward** – The elder son of King Ælfred and the Lady Ealhswith

Eadwig – Master shipbuilder at Hamwic

**Ealhswith** – Ælfred's Mercian wife and Lady of Wessex

Ecgberht – The brother of Leofflæd, Jørren's wife

Eafer – A feral boy who became Jørren's body servant

Eadred – Ealdorman Odda's eldest son and successor

Eomær – The son of a charcoal burner; later one of Jørren's warband

Erik – A Dane captured by Jørren, now captain of his warband

**Ethelred** – Archbishop of Cantwareburh

Galan – A monk from Glestingaburg Monastery

Glædwine – Ealdorman of Cent

Godric – Jørren's body servant

**Guðrum** – A Danish jarl who joined Halfdan with his army. Later they split and he became ruler of the Danelaw

Håkon – Oscatel's captain

**Halfdan** – One of the leaders, with his brothers Ívarr the Boneless and Ubba, of the original Great Heathen Army. Later King of Northumbria

Hilda – Jørren's second wife

Hrodulf and Oscgar – Mercian thralls rescued from the Danes, later scouts for Jørren

Jerrik and Øwli – Jutes enslaved by the Danes, now members of Jørren's warband

Jørren – The protagonist and narrator, initially Ealdorman of Berrocscīr

Leofflæd – Jørren's wife

Nerian – Ealdorman of Somersaete

**Odda** – Ealdorman of Dyfneintscīr

**Oscatel** – A Danish jarl and one of Guðrum's lieutenants

Oswine - Jørren's stepson

Redwald – The son of a poor farmer who was the first to join Jørren and Cei

Rinan – A young member of the fyrd who saved Jørren's life at Ethundun

Sæwine and Wealhmær – Bernicians who had joined Jørren's warband

Stithulf – Port Reeve of Hamwic

Wolnoth – One of those who joined Jørren's warband in Northumbria

Tunbehrt – Ealdorman of Hamtunscīr

**Ubba** - Halfdan's brother and one of the leaders of the Great Heathen Army.

Ulfrik – Danish jarl who pledged his loyalty to Jørren

Wilfrið – Captain of Jørren's skeid, the Saint Cuthbert

**Wulfhere** – Ealdorman of Wiltunscīr

**Wulfthryth** – King Æðelred's widow and Ælfred's sister-in-law

Ywer and Kjestin – Jørren and Loefflæd's twin children

# GLOSSARY

## ANGLO-SAXON

**Ætheling** – literally 'throne-worthy. An Anglo-Saxon prince

**Bondsman** – a slave who was treated as the property of his master

**Birlinn** – a wooden ship similar to the later Scottish galleys but smaller than a Viking longship. Usually with a single mast and square rigged sail, they could also be propelled by oars with one man to each oar

**Burh** - fortified settlement

**Byrnie** - a long (usually sleeveless) tunic of chain mail

**Ceorl** - Freemen who worked the land or else provided a service or trade such as metal working, carpentry, weaving etc. They ranked between thegns and villeins and provided the fyrd in time of war

**Cyning** – Old English for king and the term by which they were normally addressed

**Ealdorman** – The senior noble of a shire. A royal appointment, ealdormen led the men of their shire in battle, presided over law courts and levied taxation on behalf of the king

**Fyrd** - Anglo-Saxon army mobilised from freemen to defend their shire, or to join a campaign led by the king.

**Gesith** – The companions of a king, prince or noble, usually acting as his bodyguard

**Heræswa** – Military commander or general. The man who commanded the army of a nation under the king

**Hide** – A measure of the land sufficient to support the household of one ceorl

**Hideage** - A tax paid to the royal exchequer for every hide of land.

**Hundred** – The unit for local government and taxation which equated to ten tithings. The freemen of each hundred were collectively responsible for various crimes committed within its borders if the offender was not produced

**Sæ Heræswa** – Commander of the King Ælfred's navy

**Seax** – A bladed weapon somewhere in size between a dagger and a sword. Mainly used for close-quarter fighting where a sword would be too long and unwieldy

**Settlement** – Any grouping of residential buildings, usually around the king's or lord's hall. In 8th century England the term town or village had not yet come into use

**Shire** – An administrative area into which an Anglo-Saxon kingdom was divided

**Shire Reeve** – Later corrupted to sheriff. A royal official responsible for implementing the king's laws within his shire

**Skypfyrd** – Fyrd raised to man ships of war to defend the coast

**Thegn** – The lowest rank of noble. A man who held a certain amount of land direct from the king or from a senior nobleman, ranking between an ordinary freeman or ceorl and an ealdorman

**Tithing** - A group of ten ceorls who lived close together and were collectively responsible for each other's behaviour, also the land required to support them (i.e. ten hides)

**Wealas** – Old English name for the Welsh

**Wergeld** - The price set upon a person's life and paid as compensation by the killer to the family of the dead person. It freed the killer of further punishment or obligation and prevented a blood feud

**Witenaġemot** – The council of an Anglo-Saxon kingdom. Its composition varied, depending on the matters to be debated. Usually it consisted of the ealdormen, the king's thegns, the bishops and the abbots

**Villein** - A peasant who ranked above a bondsman or slave but who was legally tied to his vill and who was obliged to give one or more day's service to his lord each week in payment for his land

**Vill** - A thegn's holding or similar area of land in Anglo-Saxon England which would later be called a parish or a manor

## VIKING

**Bóndi** - Farmers and craftsmen who were free men and enjoyed rights such as the ownership of weapons and membership of the Thing. They could be tenants or landowners. Plural bøndur.

**Byrnie** - a long (usually sleeveless) tunic of chain mail

**Helheim** – The realm in the afterlife for those who don't die in battle

**Hersir** – A bóndi who was chosen to lead a band of warriors under a king or a jarl. Typically they were wealthy landowners who could recruit enough other bøndur to serve under their command

**Hirdman** – A member of a king's or a jarl's personal bodyguard, collectively known as the hird

**Jarl** – A Norse or Danish chieftain; in Sweden they were regional governors appointed by the king

**Mjolnir** – Thor's hammer, also the pendant worn around the neck by most pagan Vikings

**Nailed God** – Pagan name for Christ, also called the White Christ

**Swéoþeod** – Swedes, literally Swedish people

**Thing** – The governing assembly made up of the free people of the community presided over by a lagman (*q.v.*). The meeting-place of a thing was called a thingstead

**Thrall** – A slave. A man, woman or child in bondage to his or her owner. Thralls had no rights and could be beaten or killed with impunity

**Valhalla** – The hall of the slain. It's where heroes who died in battle spend the afterlife feasting and fighting

## LONGSHIPS

In order of size:

**Knarr –** Also called karve or karvi. The smallest type of longship. It had 6 to 16 benches and, like their English equivalents, they were mainly used for fishing and trading, but they were occasionally commissioned for military use. They were broader in the beam and had a deeper draught than other longships

**Snekkja** – (Plural snekkjur). Typically the smallest longship used in warfare and was classified as a ship with at least 20 rowing benches. A typical snekkja might have a length of 17m, a width of 2.5m and a draught of only 0.5m. Norse snekkjas, designed for deep fjords and Atlantic weather, typically had more draught than the Danish type, which were intended for shallow water

**Drekar** - (Dragon ship). Larger warships consisting of more than 30 rowing benches. Typically they could carry a crew of some 70–80 men and measured around 30m in length. These ships were more properly called skeids; the term drekar referred to the carvings of menacing beasts, such as dragons and snakes, mounted on the prow of the ship during a sea battle or when raiding. Strictly speaking drekar is the plural form, the singular being dreki or dreka, but these words don't appear to be accepted usage in English

# Chapter One

## WESSEX

## Early March 874 AD

My name is Jørren and I was born the son of a Jutish ceorl in Cent. I was his third son and, in normal circumstances, I would probably have been lucky to become the tenant of a smallholding eking out a bare existence from the soil. But then the Great Heathen Army invaded and our peaceful world was turned upside down.

My father and his brother, the Thegn of Cilleham, were both killed in battle against the heathens. My eldest brother, Æscwin, survived and became thegn in our uncle's place. I suppose I could have done nothing and I would have no doubt taken over our family farm when I was old enough, but my other brother, Alric, had been captured. He and I were close and all I could think about was rescuing him. Like the idiot I was at the age of thirteen, I set out with just one of our slave boys to do just that.

God was with me; no doubt about it. Not only did I manage to rescue Alric, but I gathered a warband of young misfits and orphans on the way. Over the next eight years I made a name for myself as a warrior and a leader. I was lucky enough to come to the attention of Ælfred the Ætheling and, despite the enmity of many of the nobles of Wessex, he favoured me. When his brother died and he became king he made me

Ealdorman of Berrocscīr. By this time I had married one of those who had joined me – a girl called Leofflæd – and we had two children: a daughter who we called Cuthfleda and a son who I named after my eldest brother, Æscwin.

Sometimes I think she resented our children. She wasn't like most other girls; she loved riding to war and was as skilled an archer as anyone I knew. Pregnancy and childbirth had prevented her from staying at my side in the past, but now she was dressed in tunic, trousers and a warm cloak ready to go hunting with me.

It had been a hard winter with deep snow, bitingly cold winds and frozen ground for months. Now at last the thaw had started but game was scarce and our larder needed replenishing. I therefore organised the hunt as soon as my scouts found the tracks of deer near Readingum, where my family and I had our hall.

The past few months had been spent hearing complaints, passing judgement on felons and administering the estates that I now owned, but it had all become extremely tedious with little to look forward to each day, except spending time with my family. Even that was losing its charm as Leofflæd was even less able to deal with the claustrophobic confines of the hall than I was. We were at each other's throats at the end and both of us were eagerly looking forward to riding out hunting once again.

However, it was not to be. It was still cold and the breath of both people and horses condensed into a cloud that looked like steam in front of our nostrils.

The sun shone down on us but it was early March and there was no warmth in it. As we rode through the gates in the palisade surrounding Readingum a mud splattered horsemen appeared out of the forest and made his way towards us.

He looked to be no more than a youth but it was difficult to tell as his face was smeared in the same muck that coated him and his horse. The melting snow had left thick mud along the tracks and roads of Wessex. Evidently he had had a hard time of it reaching us, to judge by his blown horse and his weary appearance.

'Lord Jørren, I bring greetings from King Ælfred,' he began, his voice sounding as weary as he looked.

My heart sank. If it was necessary to send a messenger all the way from Wintanceaster with the roads still nigh on impassable, then the matter must be serious.

'Come up to the hall. Whatever Ælfred wants can wait until you've had a chance to clean up and have some refreshments. Leofflæd, my love, you carry on with the hunt.'

'No, let Erik take over,' she responded with a frown. 'I want to hear what the king needs you for just as much as you do.'

I sighed. I had a nasty feeling that whatever it was, there would be a certain amount of danger attached to it; there usually was. I would far rather that my wife stayed at home, but once she knew what was afoot there was little chance of that.

†††

'Lord, the king has a mission that he would like you to undertake on his behalf,' the messenger said once he'd had a wash and borrowed a clean set of clothes whilst his were being laundered.

I had offered him bread, cheese and mead and he sat at the table across from Leofflæd and me munching away as he spoke between mouthfuls. He looked familiar to me and suddenly I realised why. I had never been told his name but I recalled that he was the third son of Odda, the Ealdorman of Dorset. He had been a ten-year-old page when I'd last seen him. He was the boy who had taken us to see Ælfred the first time I had met him. At the time I had been seeking to buy the vill of Silcestre using silver taken from Danes we'd killed in battle. Now the boy was a young man of perhaps sixteen but, because of his association with my rise in status, I'd always remembered him.

'You're Odda's son!' I said with a smile.

'Well remembered, lord. You've done well since becoming Thegn of Silcestre,' he said grinning back and looking around him at my hall.

There were few halls constructed of stone in Wessex at the time but mine was one of them. The only others I knew of were the king's hall at Wintancaester and that of the archbishop at Cantwareburh. The walls were lime washed to make the place brighter, but this was slightly countered by the shields and banners displayed on them.

'My name is Drefan,' he said turning his attention back to me. 'I have a letter from the king but all it says is that he wants to see you as a matter of urgency.'

I frowned. Drefan meant trouble and I had a feeling that that was exactly what the young man's arrival presaged. I broke Ælfred's seal and read the letter.

*To my trusted and well beloved Ealdorman Jørren, greetings*

*I need you to act for me in a matter of some delicacy. I must ask you to come to Wintanceaster so that I can explain the situation to you. There is the utmost urgency so, despite the state of the roads, you need to set out as soon as you read this.*

*Ælfredus Rex*

The letter was curt to the point of rudeness, but that only emphasised the need for haste. I cursed. Erik and most of my warriors were out hunting and were unlikely to return before dusk. If the situation was as dire as the king said it was, I needed to set out without delay. Drefan was in no state to return with me and so I sent him away to get some rest first.

'Which of my warriors remain here?' I asked my reeve as Leofflæd went to get the servants to pack for us.

'Only those on watch, lord,' he replied nervously.

He was an excellent reeve but he was always fearful of doing something wrong. I assumed that he was now worried that I would blame him because of the lack of men to escort us.

'Very well. Thank you.'

I went outside the hall to see who the sentries guarding the door were. I smiled when I saw Lyndon and Ædwulf half asleep, leaning on their spears and looking bored. They had joined me at the age of thirteen as scouts; now they were eighteen and experienced warriors, in addition to being skilled trackers and bowmen.

'I have some good news for you,' I told them, making them jump. 'Relax,' I told them as they pretended that they had been alert all the time. 'Get your kit together; you're coming with us to Wintanceaster.'

†††

It was another hour before we were ready to leave. We were a small group: Leofflæd, Lyndon, Ædwulf, me and my body servant. He was a Saxon who had been sold into slavery when he was eight years old. His father was a ceorl who had killed another man in a drunken brawl. As he was unable to pay the necessary wergeld to the dead man's family, he and his family had been sold as slaves to clear the debt. I happened to be in Taceham when the slave market was held and I had bought the boy on a whim.

I had never had a body servant before, preferring to look after my own needs, but an ealdorman was expected to maintain a certain style. He was very young to be a personal servant but I demanded little of him. However, his mother had taught him to cook – an unusual attribute in a young boy – and I therefore ate better on campaign than most men. He also looked after my armour, weapons and my horse. Over the years he had become invaluable and now I wouldn't want to be without him – at least when away from my hall.

His name was Godric and he was now twelve. Recently he had asked me if he could train as a warrior when he was old enough and I had told him I would think about it, but the truth is I didn't want to lose him as a servant. Even if I'd freed him, without land or any other way of earning a living, he had little choice but to remain in my service.

I had decided to teach him to fight with sword and spear when he became fourteen, but only if he continued to look after me. I hoped that would satisfy him. However, I knew that he had already persuaded some of my warriors to teach him how to use a knife.

We took the same route that Drefan had. There was a good Roman road from Silcestre to Wintanceaster. They had a better surface that the normal roads, which would be fetlock deep in mud, and so we could make much better time. However, first we had to get to Silcestre and the road there was a quagmire.

Thankfully the vill belonged to me and we were able to clean ourselves up and change our clothes in the hall at Silcestre. I also collected three more warriors to bolster my small escort: Wealhmær, Sæwine and Swiðhun. All were Bernicians from Northumbria who had been members of my warband for years.

They had joined me with another, Wolnoth, when they were boys. Initially, they had been employed as scouts but now they were fully-fledged warriors. Redwald, the reeve, would have liked me to take more men as my escort, but I was conscious that he had few enough experienced fighting men to defend the settlement as it was.

It was close to dusk by this time and so we stayed the night at Silcestre. At some point Drefan rode in and he joined us at dawn when we set out the next day at a good pace along the ancient cobbled road built by the Romans centuries before. It wasn't perfect, but even in the places where the cobbles had disappeared – taken for use elsewhere or just eroded over time – the underlying hardcore was a much better surface than mud.

The day was almost spring like. Mist had hung close to the ground initially but, as the sun rose higher, it dispersed and the bright blue sky lifted my spirits. For a time I even ceased to fret about why the king wanted to see me.

It was thirty miles from Silcestre to Alfred's capital and we arrived there mid-afternoon. As soon as we rode into the compound surrounding the palace a page came running up before I had even dismounted. He looked very much like Drefan when I had first seen him and I glanced at the latter, reflecting how much he had changed in the last six years.

'Lord Jørren, the king awaits you in his private chamber,' the boy said as he skidded to a halt in front of my horse.

Despite the high, clear treble voice there was an air of command about his statement. Evidently I wasn't to be allowed to wash the dust of the road from my face and hands before attending the king.

Leofflæd and I divested ourselves of our weapons as soon as we'd dismounted and the page made off in the direction of the entrance to the king's hall. It wasn't a hall in the normal sense; more a labyrinth of corridors and cloisters around the central audience chamber. The king lived in a series of chambers on one side of the complex. In addition to his bedchamber and office, there were cells which accommodated Bishop Asser and the various priests and monks with whom Ælfred surrounded himself.

His wife's accommodation lay on the far side of the complex, which also housed her ladies and their maids. A guardroom for the sentries on duty, a pages' room, several guest chambers and the kitchens made up the rest of the complex.

The latrines, which I was dying to use, lay some distance away next to the stables and the kennels. All were downwind of the prevailing westerlies. However, when the wind changed to the east the stench was distinctly unpleasant. Despite the page's insistence that I follow him, Leofflæd and I set off in the direction of the latrines. I had a feeling that the meeting might last some time and I wasn't about to suffer the discomfort of needing to piss during it.

I finished what I had to do and re-joined the impatient page just as Leofflæd came out of the women's latrines. We both washed our faces and hands and then followed the hurrying boy into the hall complex at a leisurely pace.

Although the summons was for me, my wife wouldn't be deterred from accompanying me. I knew that would displease Ælfred's wife, the Lady Ealhswith, who had a very different view to mine on a woman's place in society, and I prayed that she wouldn't be present. I was doomed to disappointment. She sat like a broody hen in the corner, present no doubt because she was a Mercian noblewoman and, as I was about to discover, it was the situation in Mercia that was troubling the king.

I felt Ealhswith bridle with disapproval as soon as Leofflæd appeared. Apart from her long hair and lack of a beard, her appearance was similar to mine. She was wearing tunic and trousers, stout riding boots and her hair was bound in pigtails instead of being hidden under a wimple. Like most women, and many men, Ealhswith felt that it was unseemly for a married woman to display her hair.

No doubt the king felt the same, but he knew what a good warrior my wife was and tolerated her because of that. Bishop Asser, who was also in the room, shared Lady Ealhswith's disapproval and, if possible, was even more antagonistic towards her – and consequently to me.

The fourth person present was Eadda, the Hereræswa of Wessex, who commanded the king's army. He was jealous of me and apparently felt that I coveted his position. I didn't. I wasn't even sure that I wanted to be an ealdorman. I looked back with fondness on the days when my small band of boys and I were free of the cares of adulthood. All we had to worry about in those days were the Danes.

With a start I realised that the king was speaking and I dragged myself back to the present day.

'How much do you know of the present situation in Mercia?' he asked.

I thought quickly. I knew that Halfdan and his Viking horde had retaken Eforwic from Rigsige, the King of Northumbria, and re-established control over the southern part of the kingdom. Rigsige had retreated to the fortress of Bebbanburg on the edge of the Norþ-sǣ and continued the rule Bernicia, that part of Northumbria north of the River Tes, from there.

All this had happened the previous year and now Halfdan and Guðrum, the other main leader of the Vikings, had moved south of the River Hymbre and were encamped at Torksey in Lindesege, part of Mercia.

'The Danes are in winter quarters at Torksey, cyning,' I said, puzzled by the question.

'Not any more they're not,' Ælfred replied grimly. 'According to my agents, they left Torksey several days ago and are headed south west into the centre of Mercia.'

'What is King Burghred doing to oppose them? Should we march to assist him?'

'That's the problem. I gather that Burghred is at Hreopandune, but he hasn't called out his fyrd, nor even assembled his nobles and their warbands.'

I was aghast. What could the man be thinking of? Evidently my reaction showed on my face because the king nodded and continued.

'Yes, you understand the problem. If the Mercians do nothing to oppose the heathens, Mercia will fall and Wessex will be isolated.'

'What can we do Cyning? We can't go to Mercia's aid if they have no army for us to support.'

'Quite. That's why I want you to ride north and try and convince King Burghred to oppose the Danes. If he calls out his army, I will march to join him. Together we can defeat Halfdan and Guðrum.'

'And if he won't be persuaded? After all, time isn't on our side.'

'Then try and get the ealdormen of western Mercia to fight. At all costs we must stop the heathen army from facing us across the River Temes. From there they could strike into Wessex anywhere along its length. Time is of the essence. You must ride to see Burghred immediately. Bishop Asser will give you letters appointing you as my emissary. Take only as many men as you need to protect you. I calculate that you have less than a week before the Danes will reach Hreopandune at their present rate of progress.

I was going to ask Ælfred 'why me?' but I already knew the answer. If I succeeded, all well and good. If I failed none in the royal court, save the king, would mourn my death. I was willing to bet that Ealhswith or Eadda, or possibly both, had suggested me for this mission.

# Chapter Two

## MERCIA

## March 874

The nine of us were a small enough party but nevertheless I sent Lyndon to scout ahead and Sæwine covered our rear just in case we were being followed. However, we encountered no one apart from lone travellers and a group of monks until Hreopandune hove into view. I stopped the monks to ask them if they had seen any sign of the Danes. They looked at one another and their leader shook his head, but I had the distinct impression that he wasn't being completely honest.

When I asked where they were bound they said that the monastery at Hreopandune had a daughter house ten miles away: a farmstead where they bred horses. The abbot had tasked them with moving the stock further away to prevent the Danes from stealing them. Perhaps there weren't any Vikings nearby at the moment, but it was evident that the abbot knew only too well that they were on their way.

Hreopandune lay on a small hill just to the west of the River Earþ. The settlement wasn't large but it was dominated by the Benedictine monastery and the king's hall, both in the same compound. I knew that, unlike the settlement itself, it was defended by a palisade but that didn't pose much of an obstacle.

There was no ditch and no rampart, just a fifteen foot high timber wall. The only towers stood either side of the main gate.

We rode cautiously through the streets of the settlement, which were unusually quiet. There was an air of despair and desolation that hung over the place. The only people we saw kept in the shadows or disappeared up narrow alleys as soon as we approached. I suspected that all who could afford to flee had already done so; only the poor and the infirm remained.

We were stopped by a nervous looking sentry at the gate into the compound that housed both the king's hall and the monastery.

'Who are you and what do you want here?' he asked belligerently.

'I'm Ealdorman Jørren, the emissary from King Ælfred to King Burghred,' I replied as amiably as I could.

Having an argument with the warrior guarding the gate wasn't going to help matters. The man still looked at me suspiciously. Then he saw Leofflæd. There was no mistaking her for a man, despite her male attire. His eyes widened in surprise.

'This is my wife, the Lady Leofflæd,' I said impatiently, 'now let us pass and inform the king's chamberlain that we have arrived.'

'Yes, lord,' he said uncertainly. 'Wait here and I'll let the chamberlain know.'

My wife realised that my temper was rising and put a cautioning hand on my arm. I bit back the acid response I was about to make and nodded.

The sentry's companion, a youth barely old enough to grow hair on his face, was sent to summon the chamberlain whilst we sat on our horses. A minute after the lad had disappeared I felt a raindrop on my face. I looked up as the rain began in earnest. The sky had turned an ominous shade of dark grey and a jagged fork of lightening lit up the sky several miles away. A few seconds later we heard the thunderclap.

'I'm not sitting here waiting to get soaked to the skin,' I barked at the sentry, kicking my heels into the flanks of my horse.

He leaped forward, knocking the unfortunate man out of the way and I cantered into the compound.

Leofflæd grinned and led the rest of the group through the gate, ignoring the foul-mouthed curses of the sentry.

I pulled up outside the hall as two more Mercians pointed their spears at me. I swore in frustration, wondering what to do. In retrospect I should have kept a rein on my temper and resigned myself to getting wet. However, it wasn't just me that would have got drenched; so would my wife and my men.

Thankfully the lad from the gate appeared out of the hall at that moment followed by a portly man in an expensive looking robe. He frowned at me and then his face cleared and his expression changed to an insincere smile.

'Lord, it is a pleasure to welcome you to Mercia,' he said pompously. 'If you would like to follow me, I will escort you to your chambers where you can refresh yourself and get cleaned up. I will, of course, let the king know of your arrival and I'm sure he will want to hear King Ælfred's message as soon as it's convenient.

'This man will show your men the way to the stables and the warriors' hall,' he added dismissively.

'Thank you. But my wife and Drefan, my fellow emissary, will accompany me. I need to see the king urgently.'

The chamberlain looked at my men and his eyes widened in surprise when he saw Leofflæd.

'Of course, lord. All of Mercia has heard of the exploits of the brave Lady Leofflæd.'

He bowed his head briefly in acknowledgement but not before I noted the scowl of disapproval on his face.

'However, the king is busy at the moment. I'm sure that he'll grant you an audience as soon as possible.'

Drefan edged his horse closer at that moment and whispered in my ear.

'The Danes have got here before us,' he said, nodding towards a sizeable hut across the courtyard.

Two warriors stood in the doorway out of the rain. They were unmistakeably Vikings, presumably part of the escort for Halfdan's own embassy. The two men studied us with interest before retreating back inside the building. Now I knew why the monks we'd met on the road had seemed so shifty.

I had thought that my task would be difficult; now it seemed that, not only was it impossible, but extremely hazardous as well. If I had had any sense I should have turned and galloped back through the gates before it was too late. But I didn't. Some part of me still hoped to be able to persuade Burghred to fight the invaders.

I dismounted and, accompanied by my wife, Drefan and Godric with our baggage, I followed the rotund chamberlain into the hall. Meanwhile the young Mercian sentry shouted for the stable hands to come and take our horses before leading my men off to their accommodation. The die was cast.

✝✝✝

The interior of the hall was unremarkable. Rough-hewn tree trunks had been laid horizontally to make the walls and then the gaps filled with daub. Windows had been cut in several places and then skins scraped until they were thin enough to admit light had been nailed to the frames. At least the walls had been lime-washed to brighten up the dimly lit interior as much as possible. It seemed a mean place to house the King of Mercia but, of course, it wasn't his main residence; that was at Tomtun.

There were two central hearths on which spit boys were roasting a sheep and a boar respectively, ready for tonight's feast. The smoke rose into the

eaves and out through two smoke holes in the roof.
The three of us made our way past the hearths to the
far end of the hall where King Burghred sat at a table
in earnest conversation with two other men, whilst
his wife – the Lady Æthelswith, Ælfred's only sister –
sat with a downcast expression.

The two men couldn't have been more different in
appearance. One was in his early forties, clean-
shaven and dressed in a long robe of fine wool dyed
green with gold embroidery at the hem, neck and
ends of his sleeves. The other man had carefully
groomed fair hair and a beard to match, but the effect
was ruined by the human finger bones which had
been tied into his bushy facial hair.

That alone told me he was a Viking, though
whether Dane, or Norse I couldn't say. He was
wearing a finely made byrnie over a leather tunic and
bright red woollen baggy trousers, bound up to the
knee with wide black ribbons. From his appearance I
guessed he was a jarl, possibly even one of the
leaders of the heathen host. Behind him stood
another Viking, a large man who stared at me
unblinkingly. It was slightly unnerving so I tried to
ignore him.

The Mercian in the green robe was arguing with
the seated Viking whilst Burghred was trying, and
patently failing, to mediate between them. I expected
them to break off their discussion so that the king
could greet me but, as I approached with Drefan and
Leofflæd - now dressed in an expensive embroidered
mantle over a linen kirtle, they carried on their
heated dispute regardless.

34

'I'll be damned if the king will meekly bow the knee to you heathens,' the Mercian noble was saying. 'If you want Mercia, you'll have to fight for it.'

'You know we'll win and all that will achieve is to inflict heavy casualties on your army. Your ceorls are no match for our Viking warriors. Be sensible and bow to the inevitable. In return we will allow the king and his family to go into exile instead of being killed or sold into slavery.'

'I'd rather be dead than allow you to take our land without a fight,' Æthelswith said with some heat.

'Be quiet, woman,' Burghred said, turning to her. 'This is about what's best for Mercia and our family, not about supporting your brother.'

'What if King Ælfred wishes to support you, cyning?' I asked.

A deathly hush descended on the hall as the eyes of the four turned their attention to me.

'Who are you, who dares to interrupt our discussion uninvited?' the Mercian noble asked, glaring at me.

'Oh, but I was invited. King Burghred's chamberlain informed me that he wished to see me immediately in the great hall, and here I am,' I said with what I hoped was a disarming smile.

'Ah,' said Burghred, 'you are Ælfred's messenger. You wanted to see me, I believe; not the other way around.'

'His emissary, Ealdorman Jørren of Berrocscīr; yes cyning. May I present my wife, the Lady Leofflæd and my fellow emissary, Drefan, the son of Ealdorman Odda of Dyfneintscīr?'

35

Burghred looked uncomfortable whilst the jarl waved his hand dismissively. In contrast, both the Mercian lord and Æthelswith looked relieved at our arrival.

'May I be so bold as to ask the names of the others with whom you confer,' I continued with another smile. 'The Lady Æthelswith I know, of course.'

'This is my close adviser Ealdorman Æðelred and this is Jarl Oscatel, cousin of Guðrum, one of the two leaders of the Danish army. The man behind him is his captain, Håkon.'

Æðelred nodded to me and was kind enough to say that my reputation as a warrior was well known. Oscatel, on the other hand, spat into the rushes on the floor by my feet and put his hand on his sword. Håkon sneered and continued to glare at me.

'This brat is no warrior,' Oscatel shouted venomously. 'He ambushes Danes and uses arrows from hiding like the coward he is. King Halfdan and Jarl Guðrum have put a price of ten pounds of hack silver on his head!'

I was impressed. That much silver represented well over a thousand silver pennies: a fortune to most men, and a sizeable sum for many nobles too. I sensed a change in Æðelred's attitude towards me and I wonder just how far he could be trusted. Perhaps the jarl wasn't the only enemy I had in this place.

'What message has the King of Wessex sent me?' Berghred asked, ignoring the reaction of the others to my identity.

I looked at him in amazement. Did he really expect me to discuss the matter in front of Oscatel and Håkon?

'Perhaps we could talk somewhere privately?' I suggested.

'You are among friends here,' he declared with a frown. 'We all want what's best for Mercia.'

'The Vikings don't,' I said bluntly, trying to keep control of my temper. 'All they want to do is rampage through your kingdom unopposed, raping, slaughtering and pillaging your monasteries. When they have done that, they'll drive out your nobles and take over the land for themselves.'

'He's right!' Æðelred declared. 'Cyning, surely you must see that.'

'No,' he said, shaking his head. 'I have the oath of Halfdan and Guðrum that they will respect our people if I abdicate. They will let me and my family leave and live in exile in Rome with a generous pension.'

So that was the bribe that the Danes had offered. Burghred would be allowed to live the rest of his life with his family in the Saxon Quarter of Rome, all paid for by the pillaging of his kingdom. However, I doubted if he would receive any sort of pension once he was safely out of the way. My mission here was doomed to failure from the outset. It was all but a done deal.

'And who will rule Mercia once you've left, Burghred,' I sneered. 'Guðrum?'

I couldn't bring myself to give this miserable excuse for a king his royal title. He'd betrayed his people and, as far I was concerned, he deserved less

37

respect than the lowest of his slaves. He glowered at me and for a moment I thought he would reprimand me for my lack of respect for his position. Only his closest friends would dare address him by his Christian name.

'No, I have Guðrum's word that the Witenaġemot will be allowed to choose a successor, advised by King Halfdan and Jarl Guðrum, of course.'

'A puppet king!' I sneered.

Burghred flushed with anger, or perhaps it was shame.

'Enough!' he shouted, banging the table. 'What was Ælfred thinking of, sending me an insolent puppy to insult me!'

'Perhaps he was under the mistaken impression that we could negotiate an alliance to drive these dogs back into the sea,' I said gesturing at Oscatel and Håkon. 'It seems that my king was mistaken.'

Without being told to leave, I turned on my heel and the three of us marched back down the hall and out of the door.

'Go and tell the others that we are leaving, would you please Drefan?' I said as soon as we had retrieved out weapons.

Leofflæd and I went up to our chamber and told Godric to pack. Leaving him to follow us, we went down to the stables just in time to see Drefan and the rest surrounded by a mixed group of Mercians and Danes led by Æðelred and Håkon. My men were outnumbered by three to one but it looked as if they were defying an order to lay down their arms.

I was in a quandary. I had assumed that we would be allowed to leave peaceably; it seemed that wasn't the case.

'What do we do?' Leofflæd whispered in my ear, 'fight our way clear?'

I shook my head.

'No, that would just cost lives unnecessarily, and to no purpose. We're trapped here.'

I stepped out from the doorway and called to Ealdorman Æðelred.

'It's me you want, presumably? Let my wife and my men go and there'll be no trouble. If you don't agree, you and the Danish swine with you will lose a lot of men before you overcome us.'

'This is isn't my doing, Lord Jørren, but I'm bound to obey the orders of my king.'

'But he won't be your king much longer,' I called back. 'He has abdicated and abandoned his people. Your oath of loyalty to him is null and void.'

'Perhaps, but it is Oscatel and his Vikings who are in control now.'

He was clearly unhappy at the turn of events. He was lost in thought for a moment and then seemed to make his mind up.

'Very well, order your men to give up their weapons and they and the Lady Leofflæd may leave unharmed. They have two days to quit Mercia. I don't want them hanging around for some foolhardy rescue attempt. Oscatel would kill me if that happened; he might still for releasing the rest of you.'

Håkon had been following our conversation closely and now remonstrated with Æðelred. However, the ealdorman stood his ground and, as soon as his warriors threatened to join mine in opposing his, Håkon stalked off to find his jarl.

'Quick, lady, you and your men must leave before Oscatel orders the gates closed,' Æðelred urged.

For a moment I thought that she was going to refuse to leave me but thankfully she nodded her assent and a few minutes later she and the rest of my retinue cantered out of the compound and headed south through the settlement. I watched them go with a heavy heart. It was only then that I realised that Godric hadn't gone with the rest.

I was disarmed and even my servant was made to give up his eating knife. Then we were escorted back to my chamber and locked in.

✝✝✝

'What do we do now, lord?' Godric asked as soon as we were alone.

'I have no idea,' I replied, running my hand through my hair despairingly.

One thing I did know. They were only keeping me alive so that Halfdan or Guðrum could have the pleasure of killing me personally. By my calculations the main body of the Viking army could only be a few days away, at most. Whatever I was going to do to escape had to be done quickly.

I didn't sleep well that night. A servant accompanied by two of Oscatel's warriors brought us a meal of sorts: stale bread, mouldy cheese and a flagon of water. After that we settled down and I listened to Godric's soft snores as I wracked my brains for some way out of my predicament, but without success.

Then, sometime after midnight when the hall was quiet, I heard a thud faintly emanating from the other side of the thick timber door. It was secured on the outside by a bar and two brackets which had been hastily affixed the previous evening. I pressed my ear to the door and thought I could hear someone carefully putting down a lump of wood, possibly the securing bar. They were being so stealthy that I began to hope that it might be someone coming to rescue us.

'What's going on?' Godric murmured sleepily from his straw palliasse at the foot of my bed.

I motioned for him to be quiet and he came to stand beside me, adopting an aggressive stance. He looked faintly ridiculous as he was barefoot and clad in just a linen undershirt. However, I was in the same state and would be at a serious disadvantage in a fight.

The door creaked open and I got ready to sell my life dearly, then relaxed in relief when I saw Æðelred peer cautiously around the edge of the door. He slipped inside the room and whispered for us to get dressed.

'There are horses waiting for us on the other side of the postern gate. The rest of the heathens are

41

camped five miles away so we need to get out of here tonight,' he told me as Godric and I clambered into our clothes.

'You're coming with us?'

'Yes, I'm not staying here to become some sort of Danish puppet. Eastern and northern Mercia are lost, but I plan to raise the south and west to resist them. Will Ælfred help?'

'I'm sure of it. If only to keep the devils away from Wessex.'

In fact I was far from certain. Wessex would support the might of Mercia led by its king, but a disparate and divided country led by an ealdorman without the authority to command others was a completely different matter. Nonetheless I would do everything in my power to persuade Ælfred that it was in Wessex's best interest to support Æðelred.

As we left the room I noticed two dead Danes against the far wall and two of Æðelred's gesith waiting to escort us. Godric began to pack my spare clothes and my armour but I hissed at him to desist. Much as I hated to leave the latter, time was of the essence. I did, however, pick up a sword and a dagger from one of the dead Danes. I passed the dagger to Godric.

I cautiously followed the Mercians down the passage into the main hall with Godric bringing up the rear. The only exit was through the doors at the far end of the hall. That meant making our way through sleeping warriors and servants. Thankfully Oscatel and his men slept in a separate hut but I didn't trust one of Burghred's Mercians not to raise the alarm if they were woken. As far as they were concerned I was his prisoner.

I had nearly reached the double doors at the far end when I heard a muffled sound behind me. I whirled around to see that one of the Mercians had risen to his feet, sword in hand, and would have thrust it into my back had Godric not stuck his borrowed dagger into the man's neck.

My would-be assailant fell to the ground as his lifeblood gushed out but, in doing so, he woke several others nearby.

'Quick, we need to make a run for it,' Æðelred cried from the doorway.

Men were getting to their feet groggily and, by the time that they had realised that one of their number had been killed, Godric and I were out of the door and following the Mercian ealdorman across the compound towards the postern as fast as our legs could carry us.

Æðelred's men had already opened the gate and we tumbled through it just as the hue and cry started behind us. Four mounted warriors waited on the other side, each holding the reins of another horse. Æðelred and the two members of his gesith clambered into the saddle but then I realised that there was only one horse left. Presumably my rescuers hadn't bothered to bring a mount for my servant.

'You'll have to leave your slave,' Æðelred snapped.

'No,' I replied stubbornly, 'we'll have to ride double.'

'That'll slow us down,' he hissed at me. 'Leave him; it's you they want.'

'My men are loyal to me because I'm loyal to them,' I replied, mounting up and holding out my hand to pull Godric up behind me.

'No, lord,' he said stubbornly shaking his head. 'Lord Æðelred is right; I'll only slow you down.'

Just at that moment the first of the Mercians from the hall burst through the postern. Godric was standing between me and the first of our pursuers and, before I could do anything, one of them had thrust a spear into Godric's back.

So savage was the blow that the spearhead stuck fast between the boy's ribs. I knew that Godric was either dead or dying and there was no point now in hesitating. Nevertheless I swung my borrowed sword at his killer's neck with all my might and had the satisfaction of seeing his head fly off his shoulders. That caused the rest of Burghred's men to hesitate; enough time for me to yank my horse's head around and gallop off in the direction taken by the others.

As I disappeared into the darkness I glanced behind me and saw the main gates being pulled open and the first of several horsemen emerge in pursuit. Then I entered the maze of streets and alleys of the settlement and I lost sight of them. Unfortunately I had also lost contact with Æðelred and his warriors. I was on my own in the midst of what was now enemy territory.

# Chapter Three

## MERCIA

## March/April 874

I found being on my own a strange experience. Ever since the age of thirteen, when I left home in search of my brother Alric, I had always had at least one companion by my side. Oh, I had always been the leader, and that in itself can be a lonely place, but I always had someone to watch my back. Now, as I cantered away from Hreopandune with only the weak light of a new moon to show me the way I felt vulnerable; not something I was used to. The death of Godric, to whom I owed my life, had shaken me too. I needed to find somewhere safe to recover and decide what to do.

As I rode along the road towards the wood that lay to the south of the settlement I heard a shout behind me. I'd been spotted. Now was no time to be maudlin. I kicked my heels into the flanks of my horse, urging into a gallop. I felt better once the trees closed around me but I needed to get off the road and find somewhere to hide.

The area under the tree canopy, even devoid of leaves as it was now, was darker than the open countryside had been and I was forced to slow to a trot or risk the mare I was riding breaking a leg.

I could hear the sound of pursuit getting louder behind me so I dismounted and led the mare into the trees on the right hand side. Holly and other shrubs grew thickly at the edge of the trees and they tore at my clothes as I forced my way into them. The horse neighed and jerked backwards against the leading reins when her flanks were pricked but I rubbed her nose to calm her and got her to follow me.

Once under the canopy the shrubs didn't grow so densely and we made good progress. I stopped and put my hand over the mare's nose again when I heard my pursuers pass by. I heard one call out to another in Danish. That was bad news; the Danes were better trackers, and better fighters, than the Mercians. They would also be more dogged in their pursuit of me. If Halfdan and Guðrum knew that Oscatel had let me slip through his fingers, they would be less than pleased with him.

I waited for the sounds of their horses to fade into the distance and led my mare back towards the road. I gambled that it would be sometime before they realised that their quarry had given them the slip and by then I hoped to have found a proper track leading away from the road.

It wasn't easy in the dark and I had just heard the sound of horses' hooves faintly in the distance when I found what I was looking for. It was more than a footpath, it looked as if it had been used infrequently by a cart and so I guessed that it led to a farmstead, but the turn-off wasn't obvious unless you were looking for it. As the sound of the returning Danes got louder I decided that I didn't have much option. I trotted along the track, the sound of the mare's hooves deadened by the soft mud of the track.

However, it didn't lead to a farmstead, as I'd supposed, but to a clearing containing a mound in which wood was being turned into charcoal as well as a hut. There was also a second mound under construction. I dismounted and drew my borrowed sword from my belt. It was a good place to hide, but I had no idea if the inhabitants would prove friendly. Most charcoal burners didn't like strangers, and conversely people avoided them as much as possible.

The pale light of dawn was filtering down through the trees and, as I sat on my horse at the edge of the clearing, the first rays illuminated the grass in front of the hut. I could just make out bluish white smoke emanating from the hole in the top of the completed mound. On the other mound logs had been piled into a conical shape and the bottom half had been covered in soil and turfs.

I knew little about the making of charcoal, although it was in great demand by blacksmiths, armourers and iron smelters because charcoal burned at a much higher temperature than wood itself.

Just at that moment the door opened and a man who I took to be in his late thirties stepped out with an iron spike in his hand. He was followed by a youth who looked to be about sixteen or seventeen who was carrying a metal rake.

'It looks to be about ready,' the man called out.

It was only then that I noticed a boy of about twelve or thirteen sitting on a peculiar one-legged wooden stool not far from the smouldering mound.

'Yes, father,' the boy called back in a voice that was on the verge of breaking. 'No flames at all last night.'

The man nodded and thrust the long metal rod into the pile of earth. More thin smoke came out of the hole he'd made. He then repeated the process all around the mound.

'We'll leave it until this afternoon,' he decided. 'Let's get the other one completed.'

All three went back into the hut and emerged with wooden shovels. I deduced that the expensive metal tools were necessary when dealing with the hot charcoal but normal wooden ones sufficed when building a mound.

The three still hadn't noticed me when the mare whinnied. They spun around and regarded me warily, holding their shovels like weapons.

'Peace, my friends,' I called out. 'I mean you no harm. I merely seek somewhere to break my fast and rest for a while.'

They continued to regard me warily and the youth whispered something to his father.

'Leave your sword and get down off the horse,' the man said. 'Can you pay?'

I cursed. I'd left my purse behind in my chamber in the rush to escape.

'No, but I'll willingly give you a day's labour in exchange for food and a bed.'

The man continued to study me. My expensive clothes, marred by dirt and a few tears in my cloak where it had snagged on thorn bushes, must have looked incongruous.

'It's hard work,' he warned.

'I'm not some lord who's frightened of manual labour.'

I was a lord, of course, but the less this family knew about me the better – for my sake and theirs.

'Very well. Put the horse in the stable with our pony. Eomær will go with you and show you where the feed is. Then come back here and help us cover the log pile with earth. We don't eat until that's done.'

The younger of his two sons dropped his shovel and led me around the back of the hut. The so-called stable was a lean-to with open sides in which a pony stood beside a small cart. Evidently this was how the family took their charcoal to sell. The cart was half full and I assumed that it was the produce from one burning. There was less than I had thought. No doubt that was why charcoal was so expensive.

The boy looked at me with a mixture of anxiety and admiration as I unsaddled the mare and rubbed her down with a rag. He said nothing as he fetched some oats from a bin and put them into the feeder in front of her.

'Is it just you, you father and your brother here?'

'No, lord,' Eomær stuttered. 'My mother, sisters and the baby are in the hut.'

'Don't be afraid of me, Eomær, I don't bite,' I said with a smile.

'Oh, I'm not afraid of you. If you meant us harm you would have attacked before we knew you were there,' he replied, grinning. 'I'm somewhat in awe of you and perhaps a little jealous,' he confessed. 'You aren't much older than my brother, Wuffa, but you have fine clothes, a horse and a sword. On the other hand, we work hard just to survive and are detested by our fellow men.'

'Why is that?'

'I suppose because our clothes and our faces are always black from the charcoal, however often we wash, and of course we live apart from them,' he replied with a shrug. 'Come, we must get back or father will get angry.'

✝✝✝

I stayed with the charcoal burners for several days. I had never worked so hard in my life, but I enjoyed the physical exercise nearly as much as I did their company. They were simple folk with an uncomplicated outlook on life; a refreshing change from the intrigue and jockeying for power amongst the nobility of Wessex.

The two girls, aged fourteen and eleven, simpered and giggled in a corner, giving me bold glances now and then, much to the annoyance of their mother. I never did discover what the names of the parents;

they were always called *father* or *mother*, even between themselves.

On the third night I was trusted enough to keep an eye on the newly constructed mound. Thick grey smoke emerged from the top and what I had to watch for was any sign of flames. If the wood burned too quickly the result would be ash, not charcoal.

I discovered why they used a one-legged stool that night. If you fell asleep the stool would deposit you onto the ground with a thump. By dawn I was shattered but I was still expected to do my fair share of work the following day. We finished piling the charcoal from the first mound in the cart ready for sale and then headed off into the wood to cut more logs, leaving Eomær to watch the fire. I wondered why the girls didn't do it but it appeared that charcoal burning was exclusively men's work.

I had intended to leave the next morning but it was the day that the charcoal would be taken into Hreopandune for sale and I couldn't resist the temptation to find out what was happening in the wider world.

Unlike the previous few days, which had been fine and sunny, the sky was overcast and rain threatened as we harnessed the pony to the cart and set off. Wuffa was left to watch the mound in which new charcoal was being burned whilst his brother, being the lightest, drove the pony and cart. His father and I walked behind. Much as I would have loved to ride my mare, it would look strange for a charcoal burner to be mounted, especially on such a fine horse.

I had discarded my own clothes on that first day, wearing a pair of Wuffa's homespun trousers and his father's spare tunic instead. The mother and her daughters were busy weaving new clothes for the coming summer and set about mending the tears and rents in mine at the same time.

We did the rounds of the blacksmiths, silversmiths and armourers in the settlement without incident. I learned several interesting things whilst we were unloading the sacks at each workshop. Burghred and his family, with a handful of nobles and a few servants had departed for Rome the previous day. None had been armed and they were escorted to the coast by Danes.

I was more interested in the latter. I knew that Ívarr the Boneless, Halfdan's brother, had died in Ireland two years ago. He had made himself king of Dyflin and, so the rumour had it, his brother Halfdan was determined to oust the man who had taken his brother's throne and take it for himself as Ívarr's heir.

Guðrum had tried to dissuade him. He was no relation to Ívarr and his brothers and was intent on conquering the rest of Mercia and then Wessex. My ears pricked up at this bit of news. If Halfdan and Guðrum split their forces, that made Wessex all the safer. I prayed that the rumours were correct.

We had finished selling the last of the charcoal and were about to head back when Eomær's father took me to one side and pressed something into my hand.

'You've earned this and more. I bought it for you at the armourer's; I hope you like it.'

He had given me a dagger. It wasn't an expensive one by any means, but it had a good blade and a plain handle carved from oak and sanded until it was as smooth as a pebble.

I thanked him and told him it wasn't necessary to give me anything, but he insisted.

'It was chosen by Eomær; I think he rather hero-worships you,' he said with a wry smile.

I tucked the dagger into my rope belt and we headed back along the road out of the settlement. On our way in we'd seen a few drunken Danes sitting outside taverns and raucous songs in Danish coming from within. Twice we'd seen a group of the heathens confront a young girl before hauling her into an alley. I could guess only too well what was going on and the screams confirmed it. I seethed inside and itched to do something but that would just be signing my own death warrant.

I was walking beside Eomær, who was sitting on the seat of the cart urging the pony to walk faster. He must have sensed my mood.

'Ignore them, please Jørren,' he said anxiously. 'There's nothing we can do.'

Just at that moment a Dane staggered out of one of the taverns and collided with the far side of the cart from me. He swore volubly in Danish then noticed the boy driving the cart. We had started the day clean but unloading the sacks of charcoal had covered out clothes, hand and faces with black dust once again.

Nevertheless, he oaf must have seen what a good looking boy Eomær was. It was just our bad luck that he was one of those rare men who preferred boys to girls.

'What have we here?' he asked in slurred Danish, grinning wolfishly at the cowering boy.

He was a big man and he effortlessly lifted the boy off the seat and dumped him in a nearby horse trough. Eomær's father protested and tried to pull the big Dane off his son. Without even looking up, the giant backhanded him and he reeled away with a smashed nose and broken cheekbone. The Dane ripped off the boy's tunic and scrubbed his face with it.

'Ah, I thought so; aren't you the pretty one,' he mumbled to himself as he lifted the dripping boy out of the trough. 'At last someone I'll enjoy having in my bed in this dump of a place.'

He said no more. I had crept up behind him as he held Eomær in the air with both hands under his arms. I put my new dagger to good use, sawing across the Danes' thick neck. Thankfully the blade was extremely sharp and it cut through skin, flesh, windpipe and both carotid arteries with ease. The man collapsed, blood jetting out of his severed neck and soaking Eomær's face and chest in the process.

The Dane let go of him as he fell and the boy fell back into the horse trough. He emerged a second later spluttering and with most of the blood washed off. I threw his tunic at him, telling him to put it on, whilst I glanced up and down the street.

Several of the inhabitants had witnessed the incident but they hastily disappeared as soon as I looked up. I could hear Danes singing and shouting inside the tavern but none emerged, thankfully.

It was all the three of us could do to pick up the dead Dane and dump him in the horse trough. He sank below the surface and, unless you stood right by the trough, he wouldn't be visible. We breathed a collective sigh of relief and I motioned for us to get going again. However, instead of getting back into the driving seat, Eomær threw his arms around my waist and thanked me profusely for saving him from a fate worse than death.

'Stop that, Eomær,' his father shouted, looking shocked. 'It's not seemly and you're attracting attention.'

How the boy hugging me would draw more attention than killing a Viking in the street I didn't know, but the boy's father wasn't one to show affection, even to his wife and daughters, so I suppose that he was embarrassed that his son had done so.

'Thank you,' the man muttered once we were clear of the settlement. 'I owe you a debt for saving my son that I can never repay.'

'You paid any debt, as you put it, when you gave me the wherewithal to kill that brute,' I replied, taking out the blood encrusted dagger and cleaning it on my borrowed tunic.

He nodded but said no more. He was a taciturn man by nature, usually speaking only when it was necessary to give instructions or berate one of his family. However, his wife and children seemed to love him for all that.

That evening was to be my last in the charcoal burners' hut. The atmosphere was one of sadness and Eomær sulked throughout the meal of vegetable broth and somewhat stale bread. Afterwards his father took me to one side.

'The boy wants to go with you,' he said succinctly.

I was astounded. It had never occurred to me that he'd become so attached that he would want to accompany me.

'It's just because I saved him from that Dane,' I started to say, but the man shook his head.

'He asked me last night and I said that I would speak to you. He doesn't want the life we have here. It suits me and Wuffa well enough, but I've known for some time that Eomær wanted more. You're the means for him to escape. What you did today only reinforced his determination to go with you.'

'Does he realise that, if I agree, he'd be my servant, not a warrior?'

Of course, I could have easily arranged for him to train as a warrior, but I needed a replacement for Godric. Even if Eomær couldn't cook I knew I could trust him with my life.

And so, when I left the clearing and set off back to Wessex, my new body servant came with me, clinging on for dear life as he rode behind me. He may have driven a pony and cart but he'd never been on horse before and he was terrified. However, he soon overcame his fear of being so far off the ground and whooped for joy. I smiled but told him to be quiet; we needed to listen out for danger. Then I began to educate him in the ways of a scout.

†††

It took us over two weeks to reach the River Temes, which formed the border between Mercia and Wessex. I hoped that the hue and cry for me had died down by now, but I wasn't taking any chances. We had stuck to little used tracks and pathways, hunting and gathering what we needed to eat on the way. I discovered that the boy was a quick learner and soon he could set traps on his own and even learned to cook a passable meal.

I had to be careful not to exhaust the mare and so we took it in turns to ride, the other walking. At first Eomær rode like a sack of flour but by the third day he had mastered the rudiments of gripping with his knees and moving his body in time with the horse. We progressed from walk to trot to a gentle canter without him falling off, even if I did get exhausted trying to keep up.

I tried to teach him how to fight in the evenings, using cut and shaped branches as swords, but he showed less aptitude for that. He was thirteen and well-muscled for his age so he should have been able to carry out the basic moves, but he didn't have the guile to anticipate even the simplest of attacks and I gave up after a while. He seemed rather relieved and so I decided that he would never be a warrior. However, he had broad shoulders and strong arms for a boy his age, and he had good eyesight. I had hopes that he might make an archer in due course.

I had to decide where to cross the Temes. We struck the river just to the east of Stanes, some twenty odd miles from Ludenwic. There were two bridges, one about twenty feet wide over the Temes itself, and a much smaller one over a tributary which joined the main river from the north. We would have to cross the smaller one to continue along the north bank of the river, but ideally we wanted to cross both to enter Wessex.

I remembered the place well from the confrontation with the Great Heathen Army some five years previously. On that occasion they had given us the slip and had marched along the north bank to seize my present home at Readingum. It all seemed such a long time ago now. I'd been sixteen at the time and already a seasoned warrior.

Ludenwic was held by the Danes and it seemed that they had extended their territory as far as Stanes already as there was a small guard on the two bridges. I counted six sentries standing around looking bored. There was a hut nearby out of which a man came to piss into the river. Allowing for a three watch system, there were probably twenty Danes in total; far too many for me to tackle on my own.

I had been concentrating on the bridges and so I didn't hear the horsemen until they were a couple of hundred yards away. Six mounted Danes were patrolling along the river bank and they were bound to see us in a moment. I grabbed Eomær's arm and pulled him back further into the trees. The mare had been grazing and as I yanked her reins to lead her out of sight, she whinnied in protest.

My heart sank. The leading riders had heard her and broke into a canter, heading straight for us. I mounted the horse and held out my hand to Eomær, but he shook his head.

'They're bound to catch us riding double.'

He smacked the mare's hindquarter and she bounded off into the wood, nearly unseating me. However, I was a good rider and I quickly regained control. I stopped to look for the boy but he'd disappeared. Then I heard the Danes crashing through the wood behind me and set off again. Once again I was a fugitive and alone.

†††

An hour later I was confident that I had lost my pursuers and I stopped to drink from a stream and allow my horse to do the same, as well as continuing her interrupted meal of grass. If I had had any sense, I would have continued along the north bank of the Temes until I reached the bridge north of my hall at Readingum. However, I'd grown fond of Eomær and I

59

wasn't about to desert him. I therefore retraced my steps until I was once again in the treeline near the two bridges.

My heart sank. Eomær was tied hand and foot to the wheel of a cart and the Danes were using him for axe throwing practice. Not that they had wounded him yet. Their sport was to hurl a throwing axe to land as close as possible to him without actually maiming him. I could tell that the boy was frightened to death by the brown stains down the inside of his trousers. One of the axes landed a little too close and cut off some of his long brown hair as well as slicing off the tip of his ear. Blood started to flow down the side of his face as he wept in shame and humiliation.

The Danes laughed and poured scorn on the axe thrower. Another man was poised to throw when a man came out of the hut and shouted something. The Danes broke off their sport and went inside, presumably to eat. It was only then that I realised I hadn't eaten since first thing in the morning and my stomach growled in protest.

I wanted to rescue Eomær there and then but I curbed my impatience and sat down to wait for the sun to set.

Once it was dark I tied the mare securely to a tree and edged cautiously towards the first of the bridges. The two Danes on duty there weren't their finest warriors. They were evidently poor because they had no armour or helmet, not even a leather over-tunic, and they were armed only with spear and dagger.

They were so busy talking that they didn't hear me until it was too late. I slashed my sword across the throat of one, cutting off any sound as he bled out and slumped to the ground. By the time that the other one had realised what was happening and went to lower his spear I had brought my sword around and thrust it into his chest, piercing his heart. He too dropped without a sound.

The second bridge was a hundred yards away. The hut, with the cart beside it, lay centrally between the two bridges and I hoped to be able to free Eomær without alerting the men who guarded it.

'Who's there?' a frightened voice asked as I reached the cart.

'Shh! It's me, Jørren.'

'You came back for me, lord?' the boy whispered in disbelief.

'Of course. Loyalty works both ways, Eomær,' I whispered as I sawed through the ropes that bound him to the wheel.

Just as I cut the last of his bonds the door to the hut opened and a man stood silhouetted against the candle-light inside the room. He had a waterskin and a loaf in his hands and was evidently coming to feed the captive.

'Stand as if you're still bound,' I hissed at him as I melted into the darkness.

The Viking came and stood in front of Eomær. Putting the loaf under his sweaty armpit, he pulled the stopper from the waterskin.

'Our leader says you're to be fed and watered, though Odin knows why when we plan to skin you alive tomorrow,' he slurred in Danish.

He chuckled as he poured a stream of water just out of reach of Eomær's mouth. Then he stiffened. Even in his drunken state he must have realised that the boy's hands were no longer tied to the top of the wheel. He dropped the waterskin and the loaf and fumbled to draw his dagger.

I emerged from the darkness and thrust my sword through his neck just as he tugged the blade free of its scabbard. He gurgled, blood spurting over both of us, and clawed at his neck before collapsing.

'Ugh!' Eomær cried, wiping blood out of his eyes.

'Come on, we can wash later,' I said grabbing his arm and pulling him after me.

We ran half-crouching for the smaller bridge and a minute later we were washing as much of the blood off us as we could. I hadn't seen any horses near the hut and so I felt safe in riding back across the bridge and heading west. Cries from the sentries on the other bridge followed us but I planned to be well clear by the time they could organise any pursuit.

Eomær whooped for joy as we reached the path along the north bank of the Temes.

I smiled at his exuberance but cautioned him to silence as I still didn't know how far along the Mercian side of the river was now controlled by the Vikings.

After half an hour I believed that we were safe and we stopped to wash ourselves and our tunics. We drank our fill but my stomach was growling with hunger. Imagine my surprise therefore when Eomær pulled the loaf of bread that the Dane had been carrying from inside his tunic. He had had the presence of mind to scoop it up as we made our escape. Some of it was covered in blood but most of it was fine, if rather stale. We chewed it ravenously and felt much better as we continued onwards.

We reached the bridge over the Temes north of Readingum late the following afternoon. It was protected on the south bank by a small fort that I had built but the northern side was unguarded. I rode over the bridge with the boy riding behind me only to be stopped by my own men. I suppose that it was unsurprising that I wasn't recognised, given my wild and unkempt appearance, coupled with the incipient beard that now covered my normally clean shaven face.

'I'm Ealdorman Jørren, you idiot,' I said to the two men barring my way. 'Don't you recognise me?'

'No, lord. Sorry lord. It's just that Lady Leofflæd told us that you were dead.'

'Well, you can see that I'm not. Now let me pass and tell her that I'm home.'

'She's not here, lord,' the other sentry said uncomfortably.

'Not here? Where is she?'

'She left for Basingestoches as soon as the new ealdorman arrived.'

'What new ealdorman?' I asked with a sinking feeling in my stomach.

'Ealdorman Cissa, lord. He was appointed as soon as the king learned that you were dead.'

# Chapter Four

## WESSEX

## Summer 874

Cissa provided me with fresh clothes and a horse for Eomær so that we could continue on our way to Basingestoches, but he couldn't help but gloat over his own elevation and my reduced circumstances. I intended to see King Ælfred as soon as possible, of course, but I didn't expect him to reverse his decision and make me the Ealdorman of Berrocscīr once more.

Most of the vills which had provided us with a significant income belonged to whoever was the current ealdorman and so I was reduced to the two I owned personally: Basingestoches and Silcestre. I learned that all my hearth warriors had accompanied my wife and children, but I wondered how on earth we were going to afford to keep a warband of twenty men with just what I earned from the two vills.

My friend Redwald was reeve of Silcestre and the income from that vill just about paid for the five warriors stationed there, but Basingestoches couldn't fund the rest, not to mention our household expenses, provisions and other necessities of life. I realised with a jolt that I would have to buy new armour and weapons as well, and they didn't come cheap. My old armour and sword had been left behind at Hreopandune, of course. It was therefore with something of a heavy heart that I set off for Basingestoches.

We hadn't travelled far before I realised that Leofflæd thought me dead. I couldn't just turn up alive and well without giving her advance warning. I therefore changed my mind and headed for Silcestre first. It wasn't far out of my way and I could get Redwald to send a messenger to tell Leofflæd about my survival.

Silcestre had been a Roman fort guarding the intersection of several roads. As such it had been a major trading centre,or so I had been told, before it was abandoned several hundred years ago. A small settlement had grown up on the site since then, but the stone walls had fallen into disrepair. When I bought it and became its thegn I rebuilt the defences, but with a much smaller perimeter than the old fort. Redwald had been instrumental in improving and expanding the area under cultivation and now it had a population of twenty seven ceorls and their families, as well as nearly forty slaves.

I enjoyed being reunited with Redwald and the five members of my warband stationed there, but I was eager to see my wife and family again and so I set out two hours after the messenger had left to give her the glad tidings of my return from the dead.

When I reached the hall at Basingestoches, not only was there a tearful reunion with Leofflæd and the children, but my warband gave me such an enthusiastic welcome that I thought that they were going to crush me to death and save the Danes the trouble.

'But where's Godric,' Leofflæd asked after everyone had calmed down, 'and who is this?' she asked, pointing at Eomær.

'Godric saved my life during my escape but, much to my sorrow, he was killed just as we were fighting our way clear. I was separated from my rescuers and stayed with a family in the forest whilst the hue and cry died down. When I left Eomær asked to come with me and so he's now my body servant.'

I saw no reason to reveal to everyone that the family I stayed with were charcoal burners. Most people were prejudiced against them and such knowledge would only serve to make Eomær unpopular. I intended to tell Leofflæd all about my adventures later when we were alone.

'Lord Jørren saved my life twice, lady; he has my allegiance and my devotion until the day I die,' the boy said earnestly.

'He's been my loyal companion whilst we fled through Mercia and I'm not sure how I would have survived without him,' I added.

'Then you are doubly welcome, Eomær, and I'm more grateful than I can say for bringing my husband safely back to me,' she replied with a broad smile.

The boy was about to open his mouth again - one of his few faults was that he didn't know when to stop talking - but I shook my head at him and he shut it again.

Once inside our bedchamber I was able to greet my children properly. Æscwin was now three and Cuthfleda six. They ran and hugged me and I threw them in the air and caught them in turn, producing squeals of delight. Eomær came in with our baggage, such as it was, and Leofflæd showed him where to stow everything. Then she grabbed his hands and examined them.

'Worker's hands,' she commented, 'and ingrained with black. Not a farm's son then? Let me guess. Your family are charcoal burners?'

I showed her my hands which still bore traces of soot, despite all the washing.

'I too worked as a charcoal burner whilst I hid from the Danes,' I said.

'Some regard charcoal burners as being in league with the Devil. I'm not one of them and, if you aided my husband's escape, I couldn't care less about your family's occupation. However, it might be best if others were kept in the dark. I think it would be better if everyone believed that your father was a ceorl with a small-holding, much the same situation as Redwald, the reeve at Silcestre.'

'Then I hope that I am never asked about it, although we did grow some vegetables at home, farming is not something I know much about,' Eomær said anxiously.

'Then tomorrow we'll ride around the vill and I'll teach you as much as you need to know,' I replied. 'But then I really must go to Wintanceaster and see King Ælfred.'

†††

As luck would have it, he wasn't there. He was at Hamwic on the River Ytene where it joined an inlet of the Sūð-sǣ to the north of Whitlond, a large island which protected the inlet. I had no idea what the king was doing visiting a port and trading centre but I climbed wearily back into the saddle and, followed by Eomær and an escort of six of my warband, I set off down the Ytene valley to Hamwic.

Leofflæd had, of course, wanted to come with me but, as she had just discovered that she was once more with child, I managed to persuade her to stay at home. The wise woman, who acted as midwife as well as producing herbal remedies, thought she must be about three months into her pregnancy and so I looked forward to the birth of our third child sometime in October. I think my wife was less than delighted with the news. She loved the children we already had but she resented not being able to ride, hunt and use her bow when she was expecting.

Hamwic was a two hour ride from Wintanceaster and we arrived in the middle of the afternoon to find the king deep in discussion with a master shipbuilder. The sky was overcast and a chill wind blew up the inlet from the south. Men were busy at work on three new craft in the nearby shipyard. None looked like the typical merchant knarrs used for trading with the nearby Continent; they looked more like smaller versions of the longships so beloved of Viking raiders.

'Cyning,' I called as two of the king's warriors barred my path.

Ælfred looked round, evidently annoyed at being interrupted. At first he looked puzzled and then he smiled with pleasure.

'Jørren, you're alive! Your wife told me that the Danes had killed you.'

'They tried, cyning, but I managed to escape with the help of Ealdorman Æðelred.'

'Come, you must tell me all about it.'

'This Æðelred sounds a resourceful fellow,' the king said after I had finished giving him a brief outline of my escape and return to Wessex.

I said nothing of my sojourn with the charcoal burners; nor of my amazement and anger at being replaced as ealdorman by Cissa. There was no need. Ælfred must already know how I was feeling.

'I wish now that I had waited before appointing a new ealdorman, but Berrocscīr borders Mercia and I needed someone to take charge of its defence. And, of course, I had every reason to think you had been killed.'

He chewed his lip. I had half a mind to point out that my shire had been left without a governor when he sent me on a fool's errand to see Burghred, but I bit my tongue. Besides, to be fair, he had thought my absence was permanent, not temporary.

'Well,' he said eventually, 'what's done is done. At least you still have Silcestre and Basingestoches.'

'That's true, but their income won't allow me to keep my warband intact; I doubt if I'll be able to afford more than four or five warriors now.'

It was an exaggeration; I intended to keep at least eight if I could, but I would have to let the rest go, much as I would hate doing it.

'But I need your men! They are amongst the most experienced fighters I have in all of Wessex,' Ælfred exclaimed.

I shrugged my shoulders, watching the king's face carefully. He was obviously wracked with indecision. He wanted to keep my warband intact but he accepted that a thegn with two vills couldn't be expected to bankrupt himself as a result.

'Can you at least keep them for now?' he asked, 'to give me time to find a solution.'

'Of course, cyning. Shall we say a month?'

'Make it three,' he snapped. 'I know you still have some of the plunder you gathered before you came to Wessex.'

I nodded. I certainly didn't want to lose the warriors who I had a special bond with. We had been through a lot together and I knew how distressed they would be if I released them from their oaths to me. On the other hand I didn't see why I should impoverish myself just because the king found himself in a difficult position.

'Now,' he said with a broad smile, 'let me show you my new navy.'

Viking longships varied in size from big dreki, some of which had a crew of eighty warriors, down to the smaller snekkjur with a crew half that number. Ælfred's new warships had from ten to fifteen oars a side and so wouldn't be able to match the longships for size. However, they were designed to be sleeker and faster, especially under sail.

'I'm building a dozen of them initially,' he told me. 'They will patrol the Sūð-sæ in groups of six. I know that they are no match for the Vikings at close quarters, but each will have half a dozen archers on board. Whilst the enemy's tactic is always to come alongside and board their prey, ours will be to circle them and reduce their numbers with arrows until they submit or are weakened enough to board.'

I examined the craft which had already been completed and made a few comments from my limited experience of longships.

'You seem to know something about warfare at sea,' the king said thoughtfully.

'Only a superficial knowledge, cyning,' I said hastily. 'I have a few men who served aboard longships when they were boys.'

As soon as I had uttered the words I realised that I had made an error. I'd been too eager to disassociate myself from the king's new venture and I hadn't thought it through.

'Send them to my master shipbuilder then, their knowledge will be useful.'

I had gone to see the king in the hope of obtaining some recompense for the loss of Berrocscīr and my home at Readingum.  Instead I had undertaken to keep all my warriors on and to meet the cost for the next three months; worse, I would lose the services of those of my men who had some previous experience of the sea.  To add insult to injury I would undoubtedly have to meet their expenses whilst they were at Hamwic.

†††

I read the letter from Æðelred out aloud to Leofflæd.  It was now late August, long past the three months I had promised the king I would keep my warband complete.  I had written to him to protest that my money chests were now nearly empty of silver, but all I got in reply was a peremptory demand that I remain at my present strength whilst Wessex was still threatened by Guðrum and his Danes.  Furthermore, my four former ships' boys were still training his embryonic navy at Hamwic.

However, Æðelred seemed to be offering a way to replenish my coffers.

*To my dearly beloved Ealdorman Jørren*, he began.  Perhaps he hadn't heard of my demotion; more likely he was trying to butter me up.

*As you may have heard, we have had some success in keeping the Danes out of South West Mercia. Although Ceolwulf is meant to my king, he does nothing to defend Mercia from Danish raids and that task has fallen onto the shoulders of my fellow ealdormen and me.*

*Of course, the heathens were severely weakened by the defection of Halfdan. No doubt you will be aware that he has left Northumbria for Irlond and now seems to be embroiled in the incessant struggles for power in that unfortunate land.*

*Guðrum has left this part of Mercia alone for the past few months whilst he confiscated Mercian land to give to his followers. I had hoped that the Danes - and they are now mostly Danes, the Norsemen having gone with Halfdan – would settle down as farmers.*

*However, I fear that is far from the case. More and more Vikings from all over Scandinavia have crossed the seas attracted by land to be had for the taking in Northumbria and in Guðrum's newly created kingdom of East Anglia and north-east Mercia. Consequently he is facing pressure to expand once more. Ultimately I fear he has his eyes on the rich lands of Wessex but I have good reason to believe that he intends to conquer the rest of Mercia this autumn.*

*I need every warrior I can muster to defeat him. I implore you in the name of friendship to ask King Ælfred for his support and to come yourself with as many men as you can muster to aid us in our time of need.*

*I am confident that, with the help of Wessex, we can defeat the Danes once and for all.*

*Your friend in Christ,*

*Æðelred*

He hadn't said it in so many words but he was calling in the favour he did me by rescuing me five months before. I looked at my wife after I had finished reading. The baby was now getting quite big and she was finding this pregnancy much harder than the previous two.

'You must take this to Ælfred, of course,' she said.

'I don't like leaving you,' I said frowning.

'Why, you haven't minded deserting me when I was carrying your other children?' she said bitterly.

Normally I would have taken the bait and we'd have had a blazing row, but I was growing older and perhaps wiser. I understood how uncomfortable she must be and how frustrated at being unable to do more that waddle around the hall for exercise.

'This time is different, and you know it,' I said with a smile.

'The wise woman thinks there may be two of the little bastards in there this time,' she muttered.

'One thing I'm sure of is that they aren't bastards; not unless there is something you're not telling me?'

She laughed and I grinned back, pleased at having succeeded in lifting her spirits, at least for now.

The next day I said goodbye to her and to my children before taking the now familiar road to Wintanceaster. I knew that the king had returned from his summer progress around Wessex, visiting each of his ealdormen in turn. I just prayed that he hadn't gone down to Hamwic again.

He hadn't, but it didn't mean that it was easy to gain an audience with him. When I was an ealdorman

I had found access relatively easy, except when one of his bouts of sickness had laid him low; but now I was a mere thegn, one of nearly a hundred in Wessex, I was told to wait my turn.

I waited a day and a half with everyone else who wanted an audience after the king's long absence touring the kingdom. The hall where we waited was full of merchants, artisans and others all wanting to present their petition to the king, not to mention a dozen thegns like myself. I grew increasingly impatient and I was on the point of leaving when a page came and summoned me. However, it wasn't Ælfred who waited to see me, but Eadda, the hereræswa.

'I understand that you have asked to see the king about the situation in Mercia,' he began without having the courtesy to greet me properly.

'Good afternoon to you too, Eadda. Yes, it was Ælfred I asked to see, not you.'

'The king is far too busy to see every thegn with an overdeveloped sense of his own importance.'

'Is the loss of what's left of Mercia to the Danes of no import then?' I asked. 'Do you wish to see the Danes facing us across the Temes all the way along its length?'

'Rubbish! Guðrum is content with what he has managed to conquer so far. His men are intent on becoming farmers not the Viking raiders they once were,' he replied scathingly. 'There is no threat to Wessex anymore.'

'That isn't what Ealdorman Æðelred says in this letter,' I said, struggling to keep a hold on my temper.

'What letter?  Give it me,' he ordered.

'No, it is for the king's eyes only,' I said stubbornly.

Perhaps in retrospect I should have let him read it. If I had, perhaps the outcome might have been very different.  He wasn't a clever man, and he loathed me for some reason, but he did have the wellbeing of Wessex at heart.  Perhaps he would have shown it to the king and urged him to cross the Temes to join with the Mercians against Guðrum.  As it was, it would take years and we would sustain many serious reverses before that happened.

'Then you are wasting my time,' he replied.  'You may leave.'

And that, it seemed, was that.  I returned to Basingestoches in a foul mood and told my warriors to prepare for a campaign against the Danes.

# Chapter Five

## MERCIA

## Autumn 874

We crossed the Temes at Pegingaburnan where there was a timber bridge guarded by two men from the settlement. They took one look at two dozen well-armed mounted warriors and wisely decided not to challenge us. As our hooves clattered over the wooden planks that formed the roadway over the river, the first droplets of rain hit my face. It looked as if we were going to have a wet ride to join Lord Æðelred at Oxenaforda, just over twenty miles from Pegingaburnan.

I hadn't parted from my wife on the best of terms. Leofflæd thought I was a fool for crossing into Mercia without Ælfred's approval, although she did accept that, by doing so, I stood a good chance of filling our coffers again. If I'd known then what was to happen I would never have left her. It was something I would regret to my dying day.

Thankfully the rain ceased as we neared Oxenforda but we were still soaked to the skin when we reached the settlement. An army of perhaps one and a half thousand was encamped between the settlement and the confluence of two rivers. I sent Erik with my men to find a suitable spot to erect our tents and continued up to the hall in the centre of

Oxenforda accompanied by Cei, who had holding my banner aloft, and Eomær, leading a packhorse.

Strictly speaking, as a thegn I wasn't permitted a banner, but I had retained the one I had flown as an ealdorman: a red stag's head on a blue background with the branch of an oak tree lying underneath it. I knew that Cissa had adopted one similar to it, but his was on a yellow field and it featured an oak tree, rather than just a branch.

Æðelred greeted me warmly but asked when the rest of the army of Wessex would arrive.

'I fear that Eadda, Ælfred's hereræswa, took the view that Guðrum no longer posed a threat as his men had now settled down and would be content to farm instead of going a-viking.'

Æðelred swore profusely and glared at me as if somehow it was my fault.

'Doesn't the idiot know that Danes are used to leaving their women and children to sow, reap and look after livestock whilst they go in search of plunder to supplement what they can scratch from the land?'

'Perhaps he thinks that will change as the land in England is fertile and not so densely populated as Danmǫrk,' I replied, shrugging my shoulders. 'I'm certain the reason why so many have left there to settle here is because there is much more land for each family.'

'It would certainly explain why so many keep crossing the seas and are now bringing their families with them,' he muttered with a scowl.

'I suspect that my own people, the Jutes, left northern Danmǫrk several centuries ago in search of new lands across the Norþ-sǣ for the same reason: not enough land and too many people.'

He nodded absently and paced up and down the hall, deep in thought.

I'm told that Guðrum can muster some two or three thousand warriors, including those who have joined him recently.  The most I can call on is less than two thousand and most of those are the fyrd - farmers and artisans who have only rudimentary knowledge of fighting.'

'My men are skilled trackers, archers and warriors, lord.  I suggest we use half of them to keep an eye on Guðrum.  The rest can help train those of your men who are hunters how to use a bow against the Danes, and the rest can make themselves useful in other ways.  How many experienced warriors do you have?'

'Including the few nobles I have, perhaps four hundred.'

'And how many in the fyrd?'

'Around two thousand.'

'So, not only are we almost certainly outnumbered by Guðrum, but the quality of his warriors is far superior to most of ours.'

'It doesn't look good does it?'

'Not if we fight them in open battle, no.  However, if we use unconventional tactics we may be able to wear his army down and convince them to leave this part of Mercia alone.'

✝✝✝

I gave Erik ten of my warband and instructions to find Guðrum's camp whilst Æðelred and I set about dividing his men into three groups – hunters and others who could use a bow; warriors and experienced members of the fyrd who I could use to harass the Danes and attack their lines of supply; and the rest, who were tasked to move all the grain which had just been harvested and the livestock deeper into south-west Mercia. The idea was to deny the Danish forage parties any provisions. Coupled with raids on any supplies coming from Danish Mercia, we hoped to starve them into retreating.

My ideas weren't accepted by the other ealdormen and thegns without argument, of course. They were Mercians and I was a Saxon from Wessex. When I argued that I was a Jute not a Saxon that made it even worse. They associated Jutes with Danes. I countered this by pointing out that most Mercians had originally come from Anglia in southern Danmǫrk.

'This is getting us nowhere,' Æðelred interjected. 'Jørren has an excellent reputation for fighting the Danes and we need his expertise if we are to defeat Guðrum. If we draw up our men to fight the Danes shield to shield we'll be slaughtered. I believe that Lord Jørren's ideas will enable us to wear him down, rob him of food for his men, and cost him casualties for little reward. I say we give it a try.

'It's now the beginning of September so I would hope that the onset of the cold weather will mean that the enemy will withdraw to winter quarters. Therefore, we have to keep the enemy from getting a foothold in our land for three months.'

There were a few objections after that but Æðelred countered them well. By the time we dispersed as night fell there was a general consensus.

At dawn I set out with Eomær and Cei to join Erik, leaving Wealhmær in charge of the training.

It was almost like old times. Cei had been my original companion when I set out aged thirteen to find my brother. Redwald was the first to join us and together we had killed a party of marauding Danes, capturing Erik, Ulf and Tove in the process.

They had been the same age as Cei and myself and, having lost their fathers and uncles in the ambush, would have become outcasts without a man to look after them had they returned to the Danish camp. After some persuasion they had joined us. Sadly both Tove and Ulf had been killed subsequently, but Erik was now the captain of my warband and a more loyal follower it would be hard to find.

Now, once again, just three of us were heading into Danish territory. We would need all our wits about us if we were to avoid being captured.

Guðrum was reported to be mustering his army at Hamtun but I had no idea how accurate this information was. However, that was where Erik had been heading yesterday and so that was where we hoped to find him.

I had been told that the settlement lay to the north of the River Neen and that there was a bridge over the river there. I hoped to find Erik somewhere on the south bank of the river and so we aimed to strike the river a few miles west of the bridge and scour the woods for Erik and his men as we cautiously headed eastwards.

Cei rode two hundred yards ahead of us and he was the first to spot the Danes. He rode back and gestured for Eomær and me to get into the trees at the side of the track. We did so but the packhorse proved obdurate and we had to dismount and smack his hindquarters to get him to follow the other two into cover.

Cei and I grabbed our bows and a quiver each and climbed a nearby oak tree, leaving my servant to hold our four horses. We had just settled into our respective positions when nine Danes came into view. Two were riding somewhat nondescript beasts and the rest were on foot. As I studied them I realised that only six were warriors. The other three were boys between thirteen and fifteen.

They were carrying waterskins, tents and sacks of what was probably food. They stumbled along, near exhaustion and I came to the conclusion that they were most probably Mercian thralls. Occasionally one of the warriors on foot would drop back and use the point of their spear to prod the boys to greater efforts.

I looked at Cei and he nodded. We might be outnumbered by three to one but we had the advantage of surprise. I had decided to attack but, even if I hadn't, the decision have been made for us when our pig-headed packhorse decided to whinny a protest.

The Danes reached for their weapons just as our first arrows struck the two horsemen. Both tumbled from the saddle, one dead and the other wounded in the shoulder. Their horses milled around in panic, causing confusion amongst the other four Danes. The thralls dropped their burdens and, when one of the Danes came within reach, they jumped on him, biting, punching and tearing at him.

Two more arrows reduced the number of our opponents to one and he turned to flee. He didn't get far. A well-aimed arrow from Cei took him in the middle of his back, penetrating his leather over-tunic and breaking his spine.

Cei and I dropped to the ground and I marched over to where the three young thralls were still mauling the hapless Dane. Whilst Cei slit the throats of the two wounded Danes I hauled the boys off what remained of their companion. He wasn't a pretty sight. Someone had bitten his ear off and his face was smashed to pulp. Judging by the peculiar angle of one of his legs and both arms, they were all broken. He was writhing and screaming and I did the only thing I could do. I leant down and put him out of his misery.

'That was too easy a death for the swine, you should have left him to us,' the eldest of the three shouted at me resentfully.

I hit him in the face with the back of my hand and he looked at me incredulously before wiping the blood from his nose off on his sleeve.

'I understand that you wanted revenge on these men for the way they treated you, but you were behaving like animals. You should be ashamed of yourselves,' I berated them.

The boy who had spoken raised his fists and took a step towards me.

'Go on try it,' I urged him, 'if you think that's the way to behave to your rescuers.'

'Don't be such a prick, Cerdic,' one of the other boys told him. 'Thank you for saving us from these bastards,' he continued. 'I'm Hrodulf and he's Oscgar. Cerdic you've already met.'

'Who are you?' Cerdic asked, his manner still as surly as before. 'You don't sound like a Mercian.'

'That's because I'm a Jute from Wessex. My name is Jørren; this is Cei and my servant is called Eomær.'

Cei and Eomær exchanged friendly grins with the other two boys but Cerdic continued to scowl at us.

'Come, it's dangerous to stand in the middle of the track like this. There could be more Danes about.'

Just at that moment five men emerged from the trees with bows at the ready. For a moment I stiffened and my hand went to my sword, but then I relaxed and gripped the leader by the shoulders.

'Erik! Just when I was wondering if I'd ever find you.'

'It's good to see you too, lord. But we need to get into cover.'

85

I nodded and we followed him and the others deep into the forest until we came to a clearing where my men were camped. Acwel, a fifteen year old scout, together with a warrior called Bjarne, originally hailing from Swéoland, brought up the rear.

That evening we shared out the plunder, such as it was, that we'd looted from the dead Danes whilst we feasted on pheasant and a small boar. The men had welcomed Hrodulf and Oscgar and they ate ravenously. Evidently the Danes hadn't fed them all that well. After the meal I offered to train them as scouts. I didn't make the same offer to Cerdic; something told me that wouldn't be a good idea.

The other two accepted eagerly, but Cerdic continued to sulk and kept himself apart. He would have starved if Oscgar hadn't taken him a plate of meat, which had accepted, albeit grudgingly.

'What's the matter with him?' I asked Hrodulf when I got him on his own.

'His father was a thegn and his parents were burned to death in their hall, together with his brother, two sisters and their servants. Now all he wants is to avenge himself on the Danes.'

'But why be so sullen and antagonistic towards us? After all, we rescued you and killed the Danes who held you captive.'

'He wanted to torture Agnarr to death and you robbed him of that opportunity, lord.'

I shuddered. I'd killed many men, and a few boys, in my time but always in the heat of battle or in an ambush like today. The thought of torturing a man was repugnant and I decided in that moment not to accept Cerdic into my warband. However, I had no clue what do with him. He was fifteen and had no family to return to. A Dane now owned the vill he would have inherited and he had nowhere else to go. I could have just abandoned him, but that wasn't in my nature.

However, I had more important things to think about. Erik told me that more and more Danes were arriving at Hamtun all the time. His estimate of their present strength was well over two thousand. About half were seasoned warriors, well-armed and with byrnies and helmets. The rest were young men and youths seeking to make a name for themselves and to make their fortunes.

Most had no armour, though some had a leather over-tunic or gambeson, and many had a helmet of some sort. Most were armed with dagger, spear and shield and a few had a sword of some kind. There were very few bowmen and those that there were only had hunting bows. My hopes grew. It sounded as if the quality of many of Guðrum's men was little better than our fyrd.

Swiðhun was watching from the edge of the forest at dawn and he returned just as we'd finished washing and breaking our fast. He'd seen a forage party leaving the Danes' camp via the bridge, and heading south-east.

'In what strength?' I asked.

'Twenty or so warriors, lord,' he replied. Five mounted and the rest on foot. There were five thralls with them and one of them was driving a cart.'

I nodded and thanked them before ordering Erik to get the men mounted.

'The three we rescued yesterday will have to stay here,' I added.

'I want to go with you. You can't leave me behind,' Cerdic blurted out.

'You'll do as I say, and you'll address me with respect and call me lord.'

'No, my father was a thegn, not the leader of some ragtag bunch or brigands,' he retorted defiantly.

'Your father may well have been a thegn, but so am I; and I used to be an ealdorman. You'll stay here, not just because I said so, although that is reason enough, but because you'd be a liability. Before you can join us you need to learn how to track, use a bow effectively and be able to fight with sword, seax and spear. But most importantly of all, you need to learn to obey orders and to respect others.'

I mounted my horse and, leaving the boy open mouthed, I led the warband out of the clearing at a swift trot.

†††

Swiðhun came riding back along the track to report that the Danes were three hundred yards behind him. Uurad, Lyndon and Ædwulf had remained further up the track, hidden in the trees, to prevent any escape back the way they had come. Two more of my men were stationed further along to kill any who tried to escape that way. The rest of us took up our positions in the woods on the north side. Five of my best archers had climbed trees in order to get a better shot down at the Danes whilst the remainder would release two arrows from the side of the track to kill as many as we could, then charge into the disorganised enemy. It was a tactic I had used many times before and it had always worked well; not this time though.

Just as the first of the Danes entered the killing zone, Cerdic erupted from the trees on the far side of the road and attacked the leading rider. He had managed to procure a dagger from somewhere and he stabbed it repeatedly into the Dane's leg and into the flank of his horse. It reared up in pain and deposited its wounded rider on the ground, whereby Cerdic recommenced his frenzied stabbing.

We had been caught unprepared and most of the Danes hadn't yet entered the ambush area. Nevertheless I gave the order to commence shooting. The saddles of the other horses were swiftly emptied and several of the leading Danes on foot were killed or wounded. The rest were out of range of our bows and they turned and fled up the way they had come, leaving the five thralls cowering under the cart.

I calculated that a dozen had managed to avoid the ambush; too many for Uurad and the other two to deal with. Whilst three of my men dispatched the wounded and collected the horses, the rest chased after the retreating Danes. I marched across to where Cerdic was still stabbing the long-dead Dane, albeit half-heartedly now and weeping as he did so.

I grabbed him by his hair and hauled him yelling and spitting with rage to his feet. He tried to stab me so I brought my sword down on his forearm, cutting into it , which caused him to howl in agony as his dagger fell to the ground.

'You bloody idiot. You warned the Danes of the ambush and put the lives of my men in danger,' I hissed at him furiously. 'Instead of killing them all, many may have escaped. Was that what you intended?'

'I just wanted to kill Danes and you wouldn't let me,' he shouted back, holding his injured arm to his chest.

'Bjarne, watch he doesn't escape. Eomær, make yourself useful and bind up his wound. You don't need to be too careful about hurting him as you do so.'

I stomped off to find my horse, wondering what on earth I was going to do with Cerdic. I was tempted to string him up by the neck and leave his corpse for the birds to feed on; God knows he deserved it. However, I couldn't bring myself to kill the young Mercian just because he had been driven to an unthinking hatred of all Danes by the murder of his family.

My inclination to spare the boy lasted until Ædwulf came back to report.

'We weren't expecting so many of the heathen swine to escape the ambush,' he said. 'We managed to hit half a dozen, but then the rest charged into us. I managed to kill another but we were outnumbered two to one and we were hard pressed. They had killed Uurad and wounded Lyndon before the others arrived. None of the Danes escaped and Lyndon should recover, in time. That's small consolation for the loss of Uurad though.'

Uurad had been with me for eight years, ever since we had rescued him and his brother, Cináed, from some Norse Vikings in Northumbria. They were Picts who had been captured and pressed into serving as ship's boys on a longship. Cináed took the news of his brother's death surprisingly calmly. He wandered away to be on his own whilst we stripped the Danes of anything valuable.

The five thralls turned out to be Mercians; three were young men and the other two boys of twelve and fourteen. All five had lost their families and wanted to join my warband, but I was unwilling to let them. They needed training from scratch and I was already hard pressed to keep the men I already had. In the end I decided to take them and the other two boys we had rescued with the wretched Cerdic back to Æðelred's camp. I would make a decision about their future then.

There remained the problem of Cerdic himself. I wasn't about to let him escape unpunished but I was still loathe to kill him. In the end I went to find Cináed. He was sitting morosely staring into a small stream. When he heard me he got up and put his arms around me. I hugged him as he sobbed into my shoulder. Then he pulled away and apologised for displaying such weakness.

'Nonsense; you musn't apologise. I know how close you and your brother were. It's good to release your emotions; then you can grieve properly.'

'What about that little bugger who sprang the ambush early, what's his name? Cerdic?'

'Yes. I had half a mind to kill him, but I thought that I should leave his fate up to you. You're the one who has suffered most because of his foolish actions.'

He shook his head.

'I don't want his death on my conscience. I'll take him deep into the forest and abandon him with nothing except his clothes. If he survives, then God will have spared him. If not...'

He shrugged again.

I agreed. It was a good solution. However, it turned out to be a serious mistake to spare him, but I wasn't to find that out for years to come.

# Chapter Six

## MERCIA

## Autumn 874

As September turned into October Guðrum advanced further into south-west Mercia but we harassed him all the way. My warband, and other groups trained by us, ambushed his forage parties and his patrols. By the middle of October the Danes had reached Berncestre, a sizeable settlement which stood on the site of an old Roman fort at the junction of several major roads. It was here that Æðelred had decided to make his stand.

The Danes' numbers had been reduced by our attacks and by desertions and, whilst we also lost men who decided to return home, our strength was more than maintained by those flocking to join us from elsewhere in Mercia, and even from Wealas. The latter were not natural allies of the Mercians, except when one faction fought another and needed outside help. However, they detested the Vikings, both Norse and Danish, even more than the Mercians.

The land around Berncestre was flat and featureless. However, there were two sizable woods to the south-east and Æðelred drew up his shieldwall between the north eastern tip of one and the north western corner of the other. The Danes would therefore have to advance between the two woods in order to attack him.

Guðrum must have suspected a trap. He halted his army four hundred yards from the Mercian shieldwall and sent mounted scouts into both the woods.

I had stationed my men, together with the best of the Mercian bowmen, inside the woods but several paces back from the edge. All those who wore armour and helmets had covered them with mud to stop the sun glinting off the metal. They were therefore almost invisible to the enemy, but we could still see them through the foliage.

I hadn't expected the Danes to check the woods for an ambush but I reacted quickly to the threat. I only hoped that Erik, who had command of the archers in the other wood, had moved to counter the danger as well. I whispered orders for the Mercian archers to withdraw further into the wood, whilst the men of my warband drew their daggers and hid behind the trees.

The enemy scouts dismounted just inside the wood and advanced cautiously. I estimated their numbers at some twenty or so and, as I only had a dozen of my own men with me, the odds were against us. However, the Danes had not trained as woodsmen and hunters, as my men had done since they were boys. The scouts were spread out in a long line and, as a Dane came to the spot where one of us was hidden, he rose up quietly behind his back and cut his throat.

The remaining Danes started to call to one another and they began to panic when half their number didn't respond. They began to withdraw in a panic, but we were quicker. Only half a dozen were left by the time they reached the spot where they'd left their horses and they made the mistake of thinking that would allow them a speedier retreat.

Their panic communicated itself to the horses and they milled about, making it difficult for them to mount. Seconds later my men reached the spot and killed the last of them. We didn't escape without casualties ourselves. Both Bjarne and Ædwulf had been wounded, but thankfully neither had been seriously injured. I only hoped that Erik had had similar success but, of course, there was no way of knowing.

I went back to the edge of the wood to see what the Danes were doing and to look across at the other wood. To my alarm I saw Erik emerge and wave at the main body of Danes. For a moment I wondered what on earth he was up to, but then I noticed that he had shed his byrnie and changed his trousers for the baggy type worn by most Scandinavians. He now looked like one of their scouts. The ruse worked and the Danes started to advance.

I sent Acwel to fetch the Mercian bowmen and we took up our positions at the edge of the trees once more. Whilst we waited I prayed to God for help. For the ambush to work we needed to wait until the Danes' blood was up and they were committed. If we started to send our arrows into them too early they would withdraw and the ploy would have failed. On the other hand, if we left it too late we wouldn't be able to damage them sufficiently before the two shieldwalls met. Unless we could whittle their numbers down, the Danes would overcome our main body.

✝✝✝

The day had started fine and sunny but as the morning wore on it began to cloud over. When the Danes started their advance the cloud cover intensified and what had been a gentle breeze stiffened into a strong wind. That would make it more difficult to hit individual targets, such as the jarls and hersirs leading the attack. Of course, the Danes were densely packed and even the most inexperienced bowman couldn't help but hit something.

I waited until the advancing mass was three hundred yards from Æðelred's line and then gave Cei the signal. He blew three blasts on a hunting horn and, almost as one, over a hundred Mercian arrows climbed towards the darkening sky before plummeting down into the midst of the enemy.

At the same time, my own men, who I had stationed at the northern end of the wood, from where they had a clear view of the Danish front rank, loosed their first volley. Unlike the Mercians, they aimed at low trajectory, targeting those with the most expensive byrnies and helmets. They would be the jarls and hersirs.

Unlike the broad-bladed arrows used by the other archers, my men were using those with thin, tapering points. Normal arrows were best against those who wore little or no protection as the barbed points made a wide cut and were difficult to remove without causing further damage. However, they were of little use against chainmail as the points couldn't break through the metal links. Conversely, the narrow points could penetrate the target by finding the gaps between the individual links. They could even puncture a metal helmet if they struck it at the right angle.

We had more success than Erik's archers because we were facing the enemy warriors' left hand side; the side unprotected by shields. Our first three volleys killed and wounded swathes of the Danes' flank. Then shooting became more ragged as the different speeds at which men could draw and loose affected the rate of fire.

At a rough estimate I calculated that perhaps three hundred Danes now lay on the grass; more were wounded than dead but that didn't matter. They were out of the fight. Moreover, the Danish line had been disrupted as they bunched towards the centre to get away from the storm of arrows.

I had lost sight of the front rank as the Danes moved past my position, but I was confident that at least a dozen of their leaders had been hit. Then something I'd been expecting happened. The left flank of the Danes, maddened by their losses, turned and broke away from the centre. Yelling their fury, they charged towards our wood.

We had time to send off two more volleys before it was time to withdraw. Perhaps another forty more Danes fell, but some of my Mercian archers panicked and their arrows were not well aimed. Cei blew his horn again and we melted back into the trees.

By now the first spots of rain had started to fall, not that many penetrated under the tree canopy, but the noise of heavy droplets of water hitting leaves helped to deaden sound. The Danes hunted us through the wood, but largely without success. The men we did lose were a small price to pay for breaking up the Danish attack.

The Danes became dispersed in the dense woodland and, having lost several men in individual fights with my warriors, quite a few turned back. When we reached the far side of the wood my warband and the Mercian bowmen kept running until we were a couple of hundred yards out into the open meadow that lay beyond. When I signalled for Cei to blow his hunting horn again, most of us stopped and turned about to face our pursuers.

Some of the bowmen from the fyrd kept running, which I suppose was inevitable, but perhaps eighty or ninety of us remained; enough for what I intended at any rate. We took in great lungfuls of air, trying to get our breathing under control as quickly as possible.

We each nocked an arrow to our bowstrings and waited. The Danes who had pursued us now hesitated. We stared at each other as the rain beat down. They had come to respect the damage that an archer could do but, what they didn't know was that a wet bowstring lacks power. Not only would the range be less, but arrows would be far less powerful when they struck their targets.

The Danes stared at us and then a heated discussion broke out amongst them. Evidently the majority decided that they had had enough and most turned and trudged back into the wood to rejoin their comrades in the shieldwall. They left behind a score of young hotheads who were still bent on revenge. I decided the time had come to persuade them otherwise and I gave the order to charge.

They beat a hasty retreat and we returned to the wood - not to resume our assault on the enemy flank; that time had passed – but to tend to the wounded, gather our dead and kill any wounded Danes we found. I left my men and the Mercians to loot the Danish corpses whilst Cei and I walked to the edge of the wood to see what was happening.

The enemy strength had been significantly reduced, both by our arrows and by the loss of those in the right flank who had charged into the wood. This had evidently allowed the Mercian shieldwall to gradually envelop the enemy centre and their left flank, forcing them toward the other wood. Erik's men had then been able to pepper the the Danes from the shelter of the trees until rear ranks had turned to attack the archers.

Erik's archers hadn't been so successful in evading their pursuers and they lost over two score as a consequence, but it had enabled Æðelred to break the enemy shieldwall and Guðrum had fled the battlefield, his men streaming after him.

The rain was now coming down even harder, but it didn't matter. The Mercians were euphoric. They had defeated a Danish army when, in theory, they had absolutely no chance of doing so. However, I didn't feel like celebrating and my men felt the same. We were exhausted and we had lost two good men. Øwli and Swiðhun had both been with Erik and had died in the final moments of the battle.

Øwli was Jerrik's younger brother; both were Jutes from Cantwareburh who had been thralls enslaved by the Danes. We had liberated them at the same time as we had rescued my brother Alric. Swiðhun had also joined me in Northumbria. I felt that a part of my past had died that day.

I wanted to do nothing more than mourn them and drink until I lost consciousness. However, Æðelred asked me to pursue the Danes and make sure that they kept on retreating. It made sense. I wouldn't put it past Guðrum to gather his men, or at least some of them, and return to attack our camp whilst most of the Mercians were too drunk to resist.

My warband and I climbed wearily into the saddle and set off. The path taken by the retreating Danes was littered with discarded weapons, shields and helmets. We came across a number of them who had either died by the wayside or had been too injured to continue. We sent the latter to Valhalla and collected all the plunder we could manage. My share of the loot would suffice to pay for my warband for some time to come, but that was scant recompense for the loss of two of my best warriors.

†††

It was the beginning of November before we crossed the Temes and re-entered Wessex. We had the satisfaction of knowing that we had been an important part of Æðelred success, but the loss of two of my oldest companions was a high price to pay. Worse was to come.

A sombre mood hung over Basingestoches as we rode through the settlement and up to the hall. I was puzzled; normally when we returned from a campaign there was great rejoicing and we were given a heroes' welcome; not so today.

When I saw that Leofflæd wasn't standing on the steps of my hall to welcome me a sense of foreboding crept over me. I knew what had happened before the reeve told me.

If I had mourned the deaths of Øwli and Swiðhun that was nothing compared to the anguish I felt when I learned that my wife had died. Her labour ten day's previously had been protracted. The wise woman and her maids had managed to save the two babies, but they had been unable to staunch Leofflæd's bleeding. It had taken some time, and she had fought until the last, but the life had slowly gone out of her. She had lapsed into unconsciousness and had died the night before we had fought the battle of Berncestre.

I asked about the funeral and I was told that in my absence my wife's brother, Ecgberht, had been sent for and he had made the decision that they couldn't wait for my return any longer. She had been buried two days previously and so I wasn't even able to say goodbye.

I was devastated, but it wasn't the end of my troubles. I had noticed two of King Ælfred's gesith standing behind the reeve but, in my misery I gave then no more than a passing thought. Perhaps they had come to offer the king's condolences? It turned out that that was far from the case. They had arrived three days before our return. They waited until we were alone in the hall and then they told me that I was to accompany them to Wintanceaster. When I asked why the elder one told me it was to answer various charges that had been lodged against me.

# Chapter Seven

## WESSEX

## Winter 874 to Summer 875

This wasn't to be a private meeting. Ælfred was sitting on his throne in the great hall of his palace when I was marched in accompanied by my two guards. The only person from my own household who'd been allowed to accompany me was my body servant, Eomær. Perhaps I should be grateful that I wasn't in chains? If I had been I wouldn't have cared. The loss of Leofflæd had completely numbed me and I was scarcely even aware of my surroundings.

When I'd left Erik had asked who I wanted to leave in charge: him as the captain of my warband or the reeve. I couldn't have cared less but I told him he should take over. He'd gone on to suggest that he should train the four Mercian boys we'd freed as scouts and I merely shrugged my shoulders. Evidently Erik had more faith in the fact that I had a future than I did at that point.

The men we'd rescued had returned to their villages but the boys were orphans and they'd stayed with us. Fatherless children were all too common in Mercia now and no-one else would have given them a home.

I had even failed to take in the news that I now had another son and daughter. If I had bothered to think about them at all, I think that I would have probably hated them for robbing me of their mother.

When I entered the king's hall I didn't bother to look around me. Had I done so I would have seen the looks of satisfaction on many faces, especially on those of Lady Ealhswith and Eadda, the Hereræswa. However, I was told later that many admired what I had done and thought that I should have been praised for my part in the defeat of Guðrum, not chastised.

'Jørren, Thegn of Basingestoches and Silcestre, you have been brought before the Witenaġemot to answer a charge of imperilling the kingdom,' Ealdorman Tunbehrt of Hamtunscīr intoned in a dreary voice. 'Who accuses this man?'

'I do,' Eadda replied with a note of triumph in his voice.

Of course, the king would be the chief judge and couldn't therefore bring charges against me. However, by the baleful way he was looking at me my guilt had already been established in his eyes. I think it was that glare that roused me out of my lethargy and self-pity. At that moment I decided that I was going to fight, and I was determined to win.

'How have I imperilled the kingdom, pray,' I demanded glaring at Eadda. 'If it wasn't for me and my warband the whole of Mercia would now be under Guðrum's heel and he would be preparing to invade Wessex.'

'Be silent!' Eadda roared. 'You will have your chance to defend yourself once the Witan have heard all the evidence against you.'

I bit back the retort that I was tempted to make, but I took some comfort in the fact that several of the ealdormen had responded to my words by nodding their heads and muttering to each other.

'What is this evidence?' I asked quietly.

'Did the king sanction your incursion into Mercia?' Eadda asked.

'No, Ealdorman Æðelred sent me a letter pleading for my help. Guðrum was about to invade south-western Mercia and there was no time. To delay would have been fatal.'

'So you, a mere thegn, admit that you involved Wessex in a war between Mercia and the Danes without bothering to consult your king, or even your ealdorman or me as hereræswa?

'What would be the point in consulting you? You are not known for your military ability, or even using the common sense God gave you.'

Several of those present laughed at my retort and Eadda went an interesting shade of purple. I was goading him and he was about to reveal the malice he bore me to all those present, but unfortunately Ælfred intervened. He got to his feet and shouted for silence.

'This is a serious matter and I will not have it deteriorate into a slanging match.'

The hubbub died down and, when silence was restored, he nodded for Eadda to continue.

'So you acknowledge that you crossed into Mercia to fight the Danes without the king's permission and by doing so endangered the kingdom.'

'I agree that I did not have King Ælfred's agreement to my actions, but I contend that I was acting to save Wessex from a Danish invasion. Surely even you can see that it is better to fight Guðrum's heathens on Mercian territory than here in Wessex?'

'That is not the issue,' he declared furiously. 'You acted like a rebel, with complete disregard for the king's position and authority.'

'You are saying that the means does not justify the ends, are you? Let me ask you, what has been the end result of my actions? No? Then I'll tell you; Guðrum has lost nearly a third of his army and he has retreated back into eastern Mercia with his tail between his legs. By acting as I did I have bought Wessex time to further prepare for the war that will inevitably descend on this land.'

'Do you maintain that you single-handedly defeat Guðrum? Your arrogance knows no bounds!'

'Of course not! But it was my plan that Æðelred adopted and it was my warband who led the Mercian archers when we ambushed the Danes and so weakened their advance that the Mercian shieldwall was able to overcome them.'

'So you say. It all sounds like a fantasy to me,' he sneered.

'If you don't believe me, then send to Lord Æðelred and ask him.'

'You are saying that Ealdorman Æðelred will attribute the victory to you, are you?' Ælfred asked quietly, holding his hand up to forestall Eadda's reply.

'I am, cyning.'

'Very well. I will write to him and ask him for the truth of the matter, not that it would excuse you for acting without my sanction, but it would be a mitigating factor.'

'Very well, cyning. I look forward to his reply. I have every confidence that he will support what I have said.'

'Then you are a fool,' the Lady Ealhswith snapped. 'No leader would admit that they had won a great victory thanks to the intellect of an underling.'

†††

I was kept a prisoner, albeit one in fairly luxurious surroundings. I had my own chamber with Eomær to look after me. The food was the same as the king ate, although it was served to me in my room. Servants even brought me a wooden tub and buckets of lukewarm water so that I could bathe once a week.

I was bored and, with time on my hands, I brooded over the loss of my wife and the ingratitude of the king. My only distraction was being allowed out to walk around the palisade accompanied by two guards once a day and playing nine men's morris with Eomær.

It was not a game that he knew prior to my captivity. It was played on a board consisting of a grid with twenty-four intersections or points. We each started with nine men, coloured black and white. The aim was to form mills: that is three of your men in line horizontally or vertically. This allowed you to remove one of your opponent's men from the game. You won by reducing the opponent to two pieces or by leaving him unable to move. It took me some time to teach him how to play but, as the long days wore on, he improved until he was able to give me a decent game.

It was the end of November before I was summoned to see Ælfred again. The ealdormen had dispersed to their own halls to prepare for the celebration of Christmas and so I was brought before a much smaller gathering. This time we met in the king's scriptorium.

It was still a large space but it was filled with shelves holding numerous scrolls and tables for the monks and priests to work at: copying the scriptures and other notable documents. Although Ælfred had a separate office, the scriptorium was where he preferred to work. Today there was only one monk present. He sat at one of the desks poised to record the meeting.

The king sat at another with his wife beside him. The other people present were Eadda, Ealdorman Tunbehrt of Hamtunscīr, Bishop Asser and the king's nephews: Æthelhelm and his brother, Æthelwold. I presumed that they were present as, being æthelings, they were the only other nobles available to give the hearing some degree of legitimacy.

Ælfred studied me for a time before he spoke.

'I have now had a reply from Ealdorman Æðelred,' he said, giving nothing away.

I glanced at the others in the room. Lady Ealhswith, Bishop Asser and Eadda all looked upset, which I took as a good sign. Æthelhelm looked bored; no doubt he would rather have been out hunting or gambling with his friends in a tavern. The only one who gave me a friendly smile was the thirteen-year old Æthelwold.

Ealhswith was now heavily pregnant with their second child. The first, their daughter Æthelflaed, had been born four years previously and now they were hoping for a son. Her state was a grim reminder of Leofflæd's death in childbirth but, much as I disliked the woman, I couldn't wish that on her.

The king nodded at Tunbehrt, who then read from a document that he held in his hand.

'The Ealdorman of Mercia confirms that he wrote directly to you to ask for your help. However, he says that he asked you to approach the king on his behalf to ask for the aid of Wessex. He agrees that he also asked you to come yourself with your warband, which he now regrets as he should not have done so without obtaining King Ælfred's permission. He also acknowledges the vital role you played in securing his victory.'

'Why did you go?' the king hissed at me.

'Three reasons, cyning,' I replied staring him in the eye. 'Firstly I owed Æðelred my life. Had he not rescued me from the Danes at Hreopandune they would undoubtedly have put me to death, probably quite painfully. Secondly, I realised that Guðrum would pose a significant threat to Wessex if he was allowed to conquer the rest of Mercia, and thirdly it was to enable me to discharge the duty you laid upon me.'

'Duty? What duty?' he asked, looking puzzled.

'You charged me to keep my warband intact when we met at Hamwic. I pointed out that, now I was no more than a mere thegn, I didn't have the resources to keep so many warriors. You said that you would find a solution to the problem, cyning, but I heard nothing further. By the time that Æðelred's letter came, my coffers were nearly empty. Fighting the Danes in Mercia enabled me to gain enough plunder to keep my men for a while yet.'

'Pah,' Eadda sneered. 'That's hardly an excuse for crossing into Mercia without permission. You could have turned to piracy on the sea and made that excuse.'

'Had I done so and confined my attacks to Viking longships, would you have then hauled me before the Witenaġemot?' I asked. 'I think not.'

'He makes a fair point, uncle,' Æthelwold interjected in a voice that was on the verge of breaking. 'As far as I can see, he did Wessex a great service by helping to defeat the heathen horde. I think he should be praised, not blamed.'

'What do you know about anything, puppy? Hold your tongue if you don't have anything sensible to say,' Ealhswith hissed at him.

Ælfred gave his wife a pained look. It was well known that she detested both of the æthelings, thinking them a threat to her husband's throne. Had

110

they been older when their father, Ælfred's elder brother had died, then the Witenaġemot would have probably chosen one of them to succeed. I didn't think that Æthelhelm posed much of a threat, but I'd heard rumours that his younger brother was trying to gather support for his own claim to the crown.

However, the king seemed to have a blind spot as far as the brothers were concerned. Perhaps he felt guilty that they had been passed over? Whatever the reason, he indulged them and forgave them trespasses that would not have been tolerated in others.

'Leave me, all of you,' Ælfred said after a pause. 'I need time to think.'

We all trooped out and the others dispersed to their own quarters. I was left with my two guards to kick my heels in the deserted audience chamber. Half an hour later a page came to summon me back into the scriptorium.

'I confess that I am torn, Jørren,' he began. 'There is no doubt in my mind that you saved the rest of Mercia from being overrun, on the other hand Guðrum will have known of the presence of you and your men. What you don't know is that I had an agreement with Guðrum that Wessex wouldn't interfere, and in return he would leave my kingdom alone. You have made me an oath-breaker.'

'No, cyning. I didn't know of your agreement with the Danes nor, I suspect, did the Witenaġemot. I would never have gone north had I known.'

'No, it was a secret agreement,' he said uncomfortably.

'Because your nobles would have opposed any more pacts with the faithless heathens?' I guessed.

'They don't trust them, but Guðrum is different,' he said stubbornly.

I thought he was wrong, but I didn't say so. Instead I waited to learn my fate.

'You should have consulted me before acting, in that you are guilty. However, I can see that I should have done something to help you keep your warband together, so I am inclined to be lenient. I was going to fine you, but that wouldn't be in Wessex's best interests. You need to be able to pay for your warriors. Instead you can help me to build up my fleet of warships.'

'But I'm no sailor, cyning,' I started to protest.

'No, but some of your men were in the past, and they are all good archers. That's what I need if my tactics are to work. You're a quick learner and a good leader; I'm sure you'll soon pick up the art of fighting at sea. You will serve me next year by taking command of my fleet and patrolling the south coast from Dyfneintscīr to Cent.'

✝✝✝

I couldn't face spending Yuletide at Basingestoches; there were too many memories of Leofflæd there. Instead I went to Silcestre and sent for my children. Cuthfleda was now six and she did her best to comfort me. Æscwin, at three, was bewildered and didn't understand why his mother wasn't there. As for the twins, I did my best to ignore them at first but Redwald and the priest kept insisting that they needed to be baptised.

In the end, I gave in and we held the christening just before the Christmas festivities started. I wasn't in the mood for feasting but I was happy enough to get drunk. At least I was sober enough on the day to decide on names: Ywer for the boy and Kjestin for the girl. Both were good Jutish names. Perhaps it would have been kinder to have given them Saxon names, rather than names which were similar to Danish ones, but I wasn't feeling well disposed towards them at the time.

That winter was harsh. The first snow came at the start of January and lasted until late March. Redwald was a good reeve and had laid in enough food to last us, even with the extra mouths I had brought with me. However, being confined to the vill was not good for me. It had been bad enough the previous winter when I had Leofflæd's company, even if we did bicker and argue. Now, without that outlet for my frustration, I became morose and depressed.

It wasn't until early February, when Jerrik came to me and asked if I would like to learn something about sailing and life at sea, that my spirits rose. Like me, he was in mourning; in his case for his brother Øwli. I think it did us both good to have something to concentrate on.

In my naivety I had imagined that sailing was just a matter of putting up the sail and letting the wind take you where you wanted to go or else, if there was no wind or it came from the wrong direction, of rowing towards your destination. Jerrik disabused me of the notion that it was a simple business.

He taught me about tides and currents, about the wind and how to use it to the best advantage, navigation, hazards such as rocks and sandbanks, how design affected the maximum speed a ship could go and, perhaps most importantly of all, what an unstable fighting platform a deck was.

Of course, he was far from a master mariner himself. He'd been a mere ship's boy when he'd sailed with Norsemen but he and the other boys were responsible for the mainsail and he'd picked up the rest by keeping his ears open. When he couldn't answer a question he brought Bjarne into our little group. The man was a Dane who'd been both a ship's boy and a warrior manning a Danish longship. He was able to fill in some of the gaps in Jerrik's knowledge but I still had a lot of questions that they couldn't answer.

By now my initial antipathy to the idea of commanding Ælfred's small fleet had faded and I had become quite keen on the idea. I couldn't wait for spring when I could travel to Hamwic and get one of the master mariners there to complete my theoretical education. I was even more eager to get to sea and start to put some of my new found knowledge to the test.

I wasn't the only one being educated that winter. The four young Mercians we'd rescued started to learn how to use a sword, dagger and a bow. Lessons in tracking, scouting and hunting would have to wait for the spring but they began to learn to ride within the vill. It would take time but, when they were trained it would bring my warband up to nearly thirty.

It wouldn't be prudent to take all of them with me to Hamwic. The fyrd could guard my two vills but I wanted to bolster them with a few warriors. Unlike Bjarne, the wound that Ædwulf had sustained at Berncestre had taken a long time to heal and he still wasn't fully fit. I therefore left him behind to train the four new recruits. I also left Lyndon behind. He'd just got married and it seemed a kindness not to drag him away from his pretty young bride, however much he protested that he wanted to come. I also left two of the married men who were based at Basingestoches there to help defend it.

When I rode out of Silcestre at the end of March I was accompanied by twenty warriors under Erik's command, Eomær and five boys from the settlement to serve the warband as servants and cooks. They would also learn to become ship's boys when we reached Hamwic.

The thaw had been slow this year, with several false starts when the ground had frozen again and then more snow had fallen. The morning was cold with clear blue skies. The road underfoot was still slippery and so we had to keep the pace slow to avoid broken legs amongst the horses. We travelled light, without wagons to slow us down, so Eomær and the other boys each led a packhorse. We carried little food; just oats for when the horses couldn't find grass and root vegetables and barley to supplement what we could find out hunting in order to make a pottage.

It took us three days to reach Hamwic. During that time the weather changed from cold and dry to cold with rain and even hail. We were soaked by the time we arrived and my first priority was to get the horses under cover and cared for. However, Hamwic was a fishing and trading port and it had little in the way of stabling; certainly not enough for nearly thirty animals.

One of the wooden warehouses was nearly empty and I decided to commandeer it, despite the protests of the merchant who owned it. He threatened to complain to the port reeve and I told him to go ahead. The king had appointed me as commander of his navy and, as far as I was concerned, that made me the most important man in Hamwic.

He bustled off muttering threats whilst my men started to rub down their mounts. I went in search of the master shipbuilder, a man called Eadwig, which meant fortunate in war, when the port reeve found me.

'Lord Jørren, my name is Stithulf. I'm the port reeve. You really can't go around taking the property of one of our most important merchants without even asking,' he protested.

'Yes, I'm sorry about that but there is nowhere else to stable our horses and this is not the weather to leave them out in the open. If there is alternative stabling I'll gladly use that instead.'

I looked at him questioningly.

'No, there is nowhere else suitable. Of course, there are small stables attached to some of the dwellings and for the horses who pull the merchant's carts, but not enough for yours as well.'

'Look, I'm here on the king's orders to produce a fleet capable of protecting the Sūð-sǣ. Surely this merchant can see that this is in his interest. Our patrols will make crossing to the Continent so much safer for his knarrs.'

'Yes, I can see that. I'll have another word with him. However, it would help if you offered to rent his warehouse; at least pay him something.'

'And will King Ælfred reimburse me? No, I thought not. I'm already maintaining my warband at my own expense to please the king. I'm not paying for anything else.'

Most of the merchants, tradesmen and sailors at Hamwic were pleased to see us. It meant that the king had meant what he said about sweeping the Sūð-sǣ clear of Viking raiders. Of course, we would never be a match for a large fleet of longships, but they were all moored at Lundenwic, or else busy conveying men and supplies along the waterways of Mercia.

There was no lord's hall at Hamwic and so, for the moment, we would have to live with the horses in the warehouse. I decided my first priority would be constructing a warriors' hall. Erik suggested building a separate hall for me, but I rejected the idea. Left on my own I would start to brood again. I had always

117

enjoyed my men's company and it would be good for me to live amongst them once more.

✝✝✝

Ten of the first dozen ships planned by Ælfred were ready by the time the weather improved in early April and we set out to put what we had learned into practice. My men were split amongst the various ships as archers and Stithulf found the crews from somewhere. Some were young fishermen but others were the sons of ceorls more used to the plough than a boat. Some were even bondsmen. They were the happiest of the lot. Life on board was tough, but it was better than working the land as a slave.

By the end of May we had all had gained some practical experience of seamanship and naval warfare. Eadwig was not only a master shipbuilder, but he was an experienced master mariner as well. As my longship was the largest and would serve as the command ship, he decided to captain her himself.

Our mock battles, pitching half the fleet against the other half, commanded by Bjarne, had taught us what was likely to work, and what wasn't. I came to the conclusion that Ælfred's idea of keeping one's distance from the enemy whilst picking off his steersman and rowers might well work and I was eager to try it out for real.

My chance came on the first of June. We had left Hamwic as usual and rowed down the inlet leading to the sea. Once we reached the end of it I decided to turn to the east along the north coast of Whitlond as we could use the wind and give the rowers a rest.

As we emerged into the open waters at the eastern end of the island I could hardly believe my eyes. Coming towards us was a small fleet of Viking longships. I did a quick count. There were three snekkjur and two of the larger drekars. That meant their crews added up to somewhere around two hundred and fifty to three hundred, if they were fully manned. Against that I had twenty experienced warriors who could also use a bow, fifty other bowmen and crews totalling two hundred and fifty men, few of whom would be any good in a fight against experienced Vikings.

If we fled, the enemy would follow us and land at Hamwic. We would be at even more of a disadvantage on land. Our best chance would be to fight them at sea. I gave the order for the fleet to spread out and we dropped the sails as the rowers began to put their backs into it. The gap between the enemy and us was closing rapidly. I had wanted to test Ælfred's new naval strategy for real, but I hadn't expected to have to do so quite so soon.

# Chapter Eight

## THE SOUTH COAST OF WESSEX

## September to November 875

We had practiced the manoeuvre many times. Two of our ships passed each Viking longship, one on either side, peppering them with arrows as they went. The initial volley was disappointing: some striking hulls, sails and the shields arrayed along each gunwale; the rest falling into the sea. As far as I could see none had hit anyone on board. Perhaps this wasn't surprising; a ship is a notably unstable platform and we had only aimed at static targets before.

The longships turned to grapple one of my ships, but we kept a good distance from them and sent another volley their way. This time we had more success. My archers had aimed at a higher trajectory so that the arrows fell into the body of the longships, striking down oarsmen and, in one case, a steersman. As he fell, his longship veered to larboard until it was broadside onto the waves, where it rocked helplessly whilst the oarsmen struggled to bring her back on course. The man who had been standing next to the dead steersman, presumably the captain, grabbed the steering oar, but he too was killed by the next volley.

When the next volley arrived many more Vikings were hit, but I saw that one of the drekars had managed to get dangerously close to one of our ships. I gave the order to alter course and urged my rowers on to greater efforts in order to reach the threatened ship in time.

Vikings were pouring out of their drekar onto the Wessex longship. It wouldn't take long before the Saxon crew were overwhelmed. Shooting at those Vikings still waiting on the drekar for their turn to board my ship was dangerous as we might hit our own men, but it was a risk I had to take.

One thing that surprised me was that none of the Viking wore chainmail, or even helmets. I learned later that they feared death by drowning and no one, however good a swimmer, could avoid that fate if they fell overboard wearing armour. They believed that to enter Valhalla a man had to die with his sword in his hand. Those who drowned went to Helheim, the land of intense cold and darkness in the afterlife.

The volley struck those still on the drekar in the back and ten of them were killed or badly wounded. That caused the others to turn around in alarm, just as our next volley ploughed into them. I told my oarsmen to back water on one side so that we could heave to sideways on near the drekar. Yet another volley struck down more of the Vikings and they panicked.

The attention of those fighting on board the Saxon ship had now been drawn to what was happening and they tumbled back aboard their own ship. A giant of a man lifted a large two-handed axe in the air, intending to cut the drekar loose, but a second later an arrow struck him in the neck and he toppled over the side.

I estimated that there were now less than thirty Vikings left who weren't severely wounded or dead, so I gave the order to close with her and board her. There were only nine of the crew of my other ship left alive but, together with my thirty five warriors, I was confident that we could defeat the remaining Vikings and capture the drekar.

As we came close, two of my men threw grappling irons into the enemy ship and hauled us alongside. I didn't wait for them to finish tying us alongside but grabbed the higher gunwale of the Viking ship and hauled myself over the side. One of the Vikings raised an axe over his head to cut me down but an arrow shot over my head and stuck in his shoulder. I thrust my sword up under the hem of his tunic and hot blood gushed over my arm. The man fell away mortally wounded to be replaced by a boy no more than twelve years old. He tried to stab me with a dagger, but I knocked it away before using the hilt of my sword to stun him.

I stepped over him to engage another warrior, but another of my crew ran him through with a spear before I could attack him. We didn't carry spears on board so he must have picked up one of those the Vikings had thrown at us earlier. I nodded my thanks and looked around for another adversary, but it was all over.

Only eight of the enemy remained and they had surrendered. We tied up the prisoners, including the ship's boy who I'd knocked out, and, with our own two ships in tow behind us, we raised the sail and headed back to the main battle.

However, it was all over. One of my ships had been taken but in return we had captured a drekar and two snekkjur. The other drekar and the remaining snekkja had fled, taking my ship with them. We had lost over forty men with the same number wounded, but the Viking raiders had lost three of their five ships and over half their men. It was a splendid victory and I felt immensely proud of my men. However, it had taken all of Ælfred's small navy to defeat a small party of raiders. They weren't even Danes; they were Norsemen from Orkneyjar.

Even with the two ships still under construction, we would be too puny a force to patrol the coast of Wessex, let alone take on more than a handful of Viking longships. Furthermore, there was a dire shortage of bowmen and oarsmen, not to mention sailors who were capable of captaining or steering a longship. The king's strategy needed a complete re-think.

†††

We replaced the dragon's head on the forepeak of the drekar with a carving of Saint Cuthbert holding a bible and a cross. It now became my flagship. It seemed inappropriate to keep calling it a drekar, which meant dragon ship, and so we used the other Viking term for a large longship – skeid - instead. The other change I made was to deck over the front and stern to give my archers a better platform from which to fire. The snekkja had to make do with a plain cross instead of the snake's head that had adorned it's prow until now.

The king was in a jovial mood when he arrived at Hamwic two weeks later to view the captured longships for himself. No doubt our victory had something to do with his good humour, but the fact that his wife had recently given birth to a son, who they had named Eadward, was another cause for considerable celebration. The succession now seemed assured.

'The problem is manning them, cyning,' I explained as I showed him over the skeid. 'After our losses against the Norse Vikings I don't have enough men to man every ship we already have, let alone those still under construction.'

'How will you use these two larger longships?' he asked, ignoring what I had said.

'If I had enough oarsmen, experienced sailors and warriors I would use our smaller ships with archers aboard, as we do now, but use these longships packed with warriors to board the enemy vessels after we have weakened them using the smaller craft.'

'So you advocate using larger longships to close with the enemy?'

'Yes, it's not a job for the present fleet. They can weaken and harass the Vikings, but they cannot realistically close in for the kill; they are too small and they cannot carry archers as well as enough warriors trained to fight at sea.'

'The rowers aren't a problem but I need my experienced fighting men on land in case Guðrum invades across the Temes.'

'Is that likely in the near future?'

The king sighed. 'I don't think so, but he grows stronger every day. More and more Danes are crossing the Norþ-sǣ to join him, and quite a few Norsemen from Irlond too.'

'They're crossing in small groups?'

Ælfred nodded. 'So I'm led to believe.'

'Then this is where we need to deploy your ships,' I said. 'If we can intercept small groups of longships and eliminate them, then we cut off Guðrum's supply of fresh warriors.'

'You're suggesting moving your base to Cent and operating against longships crossing to Lundenwic and Ēast Seaxna Rīce?'

'Yes. I'd like to patrol the whole of the East Anglian coast but we'd never have enough ships for that; besides it would make us vulnerable if Guðrum sends his whole fleet to hunt us down. If we operate from the port of Dofras, where the harbour is protected by the old Roman fortress, we could shelter there if the enemy proves too strong for us.'

'Yes, I think you may have something,' Ælfred exclaimed, his eyes glistening with excitement.

'The problem remains manpower and, of course, enough ships,' I pointed out, but it didn't dampen the king's enthusiasm.

'I can re-introduce the skypfyrd,' he replied.

'Skypfyrd?' I queried.

125

'It's a system which operated in the distant past when we were more of a seafaring nation. Each ealdorman of a coastal shire has to produce sailors and sea-borne warriors to serve for forty days a year in time of need.'

'They will need training,' I said dubiously, 'and that's if all the ealdormen of the coastal shires comply.'

'Well, I can make certain that the Ealdorman of Cent does for a start.'

I looked at him enquiringly.

'Ealdorman Glædwine had a riding accident. His horse threw him and he broke his neck.'

'Oh, I'm sorry. I hadn't heard.'

I knew of Glædwine from my eldest brother, Æscwin, Thegn of Cilleham in Cent, but I had never met him.

'I need to find a replacement as his only son is three years old. It's an ill wind, as they say. Making you the new ealdorman seems a sensible solution. You're a Jute from Cent, after all, and that way I can ensure that you have the means to establish a strong skypfyrd in the shire.'

✝✝✝

I didn't have much time to reflect on this sudden change in my fortunes. Ælfred decided that he wanted to experience a short voyage on the skeid for himself. The Saint Cuthbert needed a crew of eighty rowers plus twenty additional warriors. As half of the fleet were away patrolling the coast to the east of Whitlond at the time, I could only man three of the smaller Saxon ships to escort us. I prayed fervently that we wouldn't encounter any Viking longships. If I was responsible for the loss of the king, my new found good fortune would be very short-lived indeed.

Of course the king had brought eight of his gesith as his escort and they accompanied us, but they would probably be more of a hindrance than a help if we ran into trouble. They got in everyone's way and eventually I banished them to the bows.

We turned westward after emerging from the inlet as I thought that there was far less chance of running into any Viking longships coming from that direction. Unfortunately, as I was soon to find out, I was wrong.

The wind was coming from the south so the ship's boys hoisted the yardarm and then hauled in the sheets until the flapping sail was taught. As soon as they had sheeted it home the heavy oiled woollen sail billowed out, filled by the wind, we began to speed through the water with the wind on our beam.

Eomær scrambled up the steps nailed to the mast. He nimbly climbed above the yardarm and then swung his legs over it so that he was sitting astride it with one leg either side of the mast. He quickly wrapped an arm around the top of the mast to steady his precarious seat as the ship's motion pitched him one way and then another. He proceeded to scan the horizon ahead of us, occasionally twisting his neck around, one way and then the other, to check that there was no other ships on our rear quarters or behind us.

The king was relishing the experience but several of his gesith were seasick as soon as we entered the rougher waters to the west of Whitlond. I was busy watching them, not without amusement, when Eomær yelled down to attract my attention.

'Two sail on the horizon, lord; no there's more. I can see four now. They're too far away to be certain but they look like Viking longships.'

'Take her back into to Hamwic, quickly now,' I told the captain and he nodded, but the king stopped him.

'Why aren't we engaging the pirates,' he asked. 'I didn't go to the expense of building a navy to run away as soon as the enemy appears.'

'We only have one skeid, cyning,' I explained. 'Our other three ships are much smaller than the longships coming towards us. I would be remiss in my duty if I put your life or liberty in peril.'

'Nonsense! You yourself agreed that our own ships can keep the Vikings at a distance whilst our archers reduce their numbers.'

I tried to persuade him that the sensible course of action was to turn about and sail back to Hamwic but the king was adamant; he wanted to experience a sea engagement. I had no option but to obey and so I told Cei to blow the call which meant *prepare for battle*.

As the longships got closer they spread out into a long line and dropped their sails. A few moment later we did the same and the rowers unshipped their oars whilst the ship's boys secured the yardarm to the cradle on the deck.

'Cyning I suggest you and your gesith go aft and use your shields to protect the steersman. None of you are trained to fight on board a ship and it is quite different to fighting in a shieldwall.'

Thankfully he didn't demur. It was somewhat crowded on the aft deck but at least all those bodies should keep the king – and my steersman – safe from enemy spears. I told the captain to slacken the pace so that the three smaller craft could enter the fray first. Their task was to close within range and then the archers on board would try and kill the enemy steersmen and as many rowers as possible on the three smaller longships. Meanwhile we headed straight for the largest of the Viking ships.

It was a drekar, but it was smaller than my longship. Whilst we carried eighty oarsmen, all of whom could also fight, as well as twenty warriors, the enemy only had thirty oars a side. I hoped that meant it had some eighty fighting men compared to our one hundred and twenty, not including the king's gesith.

I saw our other three ships close with their prey and then, when the range had lessened to sixty yards, they began sending volley after volley into the enemy craft. I forgot about them and concentrated on our opponent. The usual tactic was to row until they were nearly alongside, whilst keeping two oars length away. Then the strongest men would throw grappling irons on board their opponent and pull the two ships together. Whilst this was happening the rowers would ship their oars and grab their weapons ready to board.

I wasn't about to follow the conventional method of fighting at sea. Instead of slowing down and keeping our distance whilst the grappling irons were thrown, I yelled 'now!' and the rowers pulled for all they were worth whilst the steersman turned our skeid towards the enemy. We caught the enemy by surprise; they still had their oars in the water whilst our rowers on that side had shipped their oars at the last moment, just as our steersman leaned hard on his oar. Our bows swung around and we scraped down the side of the enemy drekar, splintering every oar on that side like a sickle slicing through a field of barley.

Not only did we break asunder the oars, we also crippled most of the rowers on that side of the ship. The impact crushed chests, broke arms and cracked skulls like eggshells. The Vikings had never suffered from this tactic before; I only knew of it because I had read a little Roman naval warfare as soon as I'd been told about my new role. It was a favourite way of disabling an enemy galley; the other was to ram their opponent at full speed, but our ships weren't designed to do that. The Romans had a prow with a protruding ram just under the water.

With nearly half their crew incapacitated, we grappled the two ships together and, before they could sort out any sort of defence, I led my warriors aboard her. Unlike the heathens, we didn't fear drowning and we all wore byrnies and helmets. No one carried a spear or a shield; they were too unwieldy aboard the narrow confines of a ship.

Instead we used seaxes, hand axes, maces and daggers.

I didn't wait until the two hulls crashed together, but jumped down onto the enemy deck when the two ships were still two feet apart. Consequently I stumbled and that probably saved my life. I landed in front of a large Viking brandishing a two-handed battleaxe. It might have been fine for fighting on shore but it was too unwieldy here.

He swung it at my head but, because of my stumble upon landing, it whistled over the top of me. Before he could recover, I thrust my seax into his belly as I regained my feet and then brought my mace down on his right forearm, smashing the bone. He howled in agony but still had enough spirit to draw a dagger and try to spit at me. I had thought him done for and I was caught by surprise. However, the dagger slid off the chainmail protecting my chest and this time I chopped my seax into his neck.

My next opponent was easier to deal with. He was probably the same age as I was, but he lacked experience. He aimed his sword at my head and it glanced off my helmet. It left him exposed and I smashed my mace into his face. He dropped his sword and clutched at his ruined nose and broken jaw. It was then an easy matter for me to slice through his neck.

'Lord Jørren!' I heard someone shout and I whirled around to see who had called. 'One of the snekkjur have grappled us on the other side.'

The speaker was the king. With a sinking feeling I realised that few of my men would have remained on my ship and now Vikings were climbing up over the far gunwale onto its deck. Ælfred, his gesith and the remainder of my crew would be heavily outnumbered and fighting for their lives in a few moment's time.

'Back!' I yelled. 'Back to the Saint Cuthbert!'

Thankfully several of my men heard me over the din of battle and we climbed up from the smaller drekar back on board our ship. The king's gesith had formed a short shieldwall two ranks deep to hold off the attackers and I breathed a sigh of relief. But then I saw that Ælfred had taken his place in the centre of the front rank.

The Vikings clambering aboard from the snekkja had waited until there were enough of them before attacking. Perhaps a score of my men had remained on board and they now formed up in front of the aft deck, adding another layer of defence. To my consternation I saw that the ship's boys, including Eomær had joined them, although they only had daggers to fight with.

I acted without thinking and charged into the Vikings, laying about me with my seax and mace. It was foolhardy and I deserved to die, but somehow I cleared a gap around me and then more of my men from the other skeid joined me. For a moment the advantage was with us, and then it swung in the Vikings' favour as more and more of them swarmed aboard.

Suddenly the pressure on us slackened and I saw that more Saxons were attacking the Vikings in the rear. One of my other ships must have come alongside the snekkja, taken it, and then climbed aboard the Saint Cuthbert.

Five minutes later it was all over. We had captured the enemy's drekar and a snekkje. The other two longships got away, but only having suffered at the hands of our archers. They withdrew hurriedly to the west, pursued by my other three ships, but after an hour they gave up the chase and returned to join us.

We cut the throats of the enemy wounded and then tipped their dead over the side into the cold waters of the Sūð-sǣ. We hadn't escaped unscathed, of course. We had fifteen dead to take back for burial at Hamwic and another nineteen had suffered serious wounds. It wasn't until Eomær came and told me that I realised that I had several flesh wounds myself, both to my arms and my legs, which he proceeded to wash clean and sew up.

Whilst he was doing so Ælfred came over and congratulated me on a tremendous victory. The Vikings were apparently Norsemen from Dyflin in Irlond who had raided all along the coast of Dyfneintscīr and Dornsaete and would have carried on to plunder the shores of Hamtunscīr, Suth-Seaxe and Cent had we not stopped them. It was a vindication of the expense of establishing Ælfred's navy, something that many of his nobles had criticised him for.

# Chapter Nine

## CENT / DORNSÆTE

## Winter 875 to Spring 876

I hadn't forgotten Loefflæd, far from it, but the excitement of two sea battles and the work needed to train crews had dulled the pain somewhat during the day. It was a different story at night. I missed sharing my bed with her more than I can say. It wasn't just the passionate sex we had enjoyed, it was her companionship and having someone I could share my deepest thoughts with.

If I had wanted to, I'm sure there were a number of girls in my hall who would have been more than happy to oblige, but I couldn't bring myself to take anyone else to my bed just to satisfy my carnal lusts. However, things changed when I arrived at Cantwareburh at the beginning of October.

The ealdorman's hall stood high above the burh on top of Saint Thomas' Hill. It was a good defensive position, if a somewhat windswept one. I had already decided to base myself in the old Roman fortress at Dofras but I needed to pay my respects to Archbishop Ethelred, whose hall lay within the monastery at Cantwareburh, and to visit my predecessor's widow.

The Ealdorman of Cent at the time that I'd left the shire nearly ten years previously had died at Salteode, the first of many battles against the Great Heathen Army. It seemed a lifetime ago now. He had been succeeded by a wealthy thegn named Glædwine.

I knew that when he'd become the ealdorman Glædwine had been married. However, he'd soon put his wife aside because, so it was said, she was unable to give him children. It was not that uncommon where the wife of a noble was thought to be barren and Glædwine's first wife had become a nun. He'd then married a girl much younger than him. According to rumour she was very pretty and she'd given birth to a son ten months after their wedding day. The boy had been christened Oswine and he was now four, the same age as my son Æscwin.

I had decided that it would be inappropriate to arrive with a large escort and so I had only taken Eomær, Cei and Erik with me. The gate into the palisade around the hall and its associated buildings was in a good state of repair and the two sentries looked alert. Before we climbed the hill I told Cei to unfurl my banner. The gates had been closed but they hastened to open them as soon as they saw it fluttering in the wind. Evidently I was expected.

Glædwine's widow was called Hilda. She was standing outside the hall holding the hand of a little boy. Two men stood with her. Both wore tunics cut from good quality wool, but unadorned. One had a sword and a dagger at his waist but the other was unarmed. I thought that they were probably the captain of the late ealdorman's warband and his steward. However, I wasn't paying much attention to the two men. I was captivated by the girl.

Hilda can't have been more than seventeen, which meant that she was probably twelve when her elderly husband had married her and got her pregnant. I was outraged by the thought of it. I had never met Glædwine so I suppose it was wrong of me to judge him, especially as he was now dead, but was unable to overcome a feeling of loathing for the man. My thoughts were interrupted by Hilda.

'Lord, welcome to Cantwareburh. I'm Hilda and this is my son, Oswine.'

Her voice was mellifluous and I was charmed by it. I was captivated by this girl but I repressed the idea of any emotional involvement with her at first. I was now twenty four and I felt deep down that it was quite wrong to be sexually attracted to someone who was so much younger.

'Lady, thank you for your welcome. My condolences on the death of Ealdorman Glædwine,' I replied after gathering my wits.

Her face twisted in repugnance at the mention of my predecessor's name. No doubt his death was a merciful release. I was to learn later just how true that was.

The cold wind blowing from the north made her shiver and I suggested that we should go inside the hall. It was nothing special. It was built of timber but at least the walls inside had been lime washed to make the most of the little light that filtered in through the three small windows down each of the long walls.

There was the usual fire pit in the centre of the hall with tables and benches for her warriors and the others who ate in her hall. The high table was at the far end and beyond that I could see two curtained off chambers; presumably her bed chamber and another for important guests.

We sat at the high table and a nurse came to take the little boy away. Moments later an elderly man appeared with a platter of bread, cheese and cold meats. Another servant brought us two goblets and a pitcher of ale. He poured for both of us and then went to attend the captain and the steward, who had sat at a table a discreet distance away. I thought it a little strange that the two men hadn't been introduced to me, but I didn't think much about it at the time.

'Do you have family you can return to?' I asked, realising that I knew very little about her background.

'No,' she replied, looking down at the table top. 'I'm an orphan. My father was the Thegn of Ægelesthrep. As his only child I inherited it, but when Glædwine forced me to marry him, he took it from me.'

'So you have nowhere to go?'

'No, lord,' she replied, shaking her head. 'Glædwine didn't make a will and so his property reverts to the king. If it wasn't for Oswine I could retire to a monastery, but...'

Her voice trailed away and she gave me a piteous look. I felt a little guilty as Ælfred had handed Glædwine's property onto me. That meant that not only could I afford the upkeep of my warband, but I could also recruit men for the skypfyrd in Cent. The thought of this pretty young girl being forced to become a nun made my mind up for me.

'No, you must stay here. I insist; this is your home.'

'But you are the ealdorman now; it's your hall. It wouldn't be proper for me to stay with you living here.'

'Oh, I shall only use Cantwareburh occasionally. I intend to base myself in the fortress at Dofras. As well as being Ealdorman of Cent, King Ælfred has made me his sǣ hererǣswa.'

I didn't add that my appointment as his naval commander had infuriated Eadda.

'Oh, I see,' she said giving me a radiant smile. 'That is most generous of you, lord. Oswine and I are forever in your debt.'

We smiled at each other and then I remembered what she had said about being deprived of her father's vill.

'What happened to your vill? I don't recall Ægelesthrep being on the list of vills transferred to my ownership?'

She jerked her chin in the direction of the two men who had followed her into the hall and who were now silently watching us. I had an uncomfortable feeling that they were trying to hear what we were saying.

'Glædwine gave it to Pejr. He's the captain of my husband's warband who's sitting over there with his brother, Ajs. He's the steward.'

'Well, they will have to seek other employment now. I have my own captain and I will want to appoint a steward of my choosing.'

Hilda looked relieved and concerned at the same time.

'Be careful, lord. They are dangerous men.'

I regretted not having brought a larger escort. There was a danger that, notwithstanding my position as the new ealdorman, the warriors here might side with their captain. I would have to tread carefully but I gave her a reassuring smile.

'Well, that can wait for now. Of course, you will remain as lady of this hall.'

I left her and walked over to the steward and his brother, who got up warily as I approached.

'We haven't met before. You know who I am and Lady Hilda had told me who you are. She will be remaining as the lady of this hall for the immediate future as I intend to base myself at Dofras. You will continue to serve in your present roles for now. That will be all. You may leave us.'

They looked angry at being summarily dismissed without having had the chance to speak, but they had little option. They bowed perfunctorily and left. I watched them go and Pejr turned to look at me before going out of the door. The look he gave me was venomous and I wondered whether I should have been friendlier towards them. However, it wasn't in my nature to be duplicitous.

Hilda and I dined together that evening. Erik and Cei joined us at the top table but Pejr and Ajs ate with the others in the body of the hall. I spent the whole meal talking to Hilda. She seemed as fascinated by me as much as I was by her and it was only with great reluctance that we parted. I lay awake tossing and turning in the guest chamber that night, wishing I was with her instead. I knew then that I had fallen hopelessly in love, despite the shortness of our acquaintance.

However, she was in mourning and it would be most unseemly for me to even think about courting her until she had finished formally grieving for Glædwine. Furthermore, to prevent a scandal, I would have to shun her company for the next three months at least; something that I would find very difficult. However, I needed to solve the problem of Ajs, Pejr and his men before I did anything else.

✝✝✝

I had left Bjarne in command at Hamwic with orders to patrol the coasts of Hamtunscīr, Dornsæte and Dyfneintscīr. I had taken the large skeid, one of the snekkjur and six of the smaller Saxon longships to look after the coast of Cent and Suth-Seaxe plus the estuary of the River Temes. Over the winter I intended to get the shipwrights to build two more large longships and four smaller ones at both ports.

I was too busy agreeing the design and cost for the new ships as well as thinking how to recruit the skypfyrd to worry about Ajs and Pejr during those first few weeks. However, Hilda wasn't far from my thoughts and, after it had rained for three days without stopping in early November, I decided I had to act now before the roads became impassable.

I took twenty of my warband with me. I had managed to increase it in size to forty five over the past few months but, of course, I had to leave half with Bjarne in Hamwic. Not all of my escort were warriors; it included three young scouts and four who were still training with sword and bow. I had learned that Pejr had nearly thirty men and I wanted to avoid a violent confrontation at all costs. I only hoped that my plan would work.

We stopped at the monastery to make ourselves more presentable and to wash down our mud-splattered horses. I asked to see the archbishop but he was away consecrating the new Bishop of Scirburne. Instead I asked the abbot, Father Ælfnoð, to accompany me. I wasn't hiding behind him, but I thought that even the most rebellious man would hesitate to attack both the king's representative and a senior churchman. I wasn't being craven, just stacking the cards in my favour.

At first the gates remained closed when the sentries saw a cavalcade of heavily armed men approaching. Cei was holding my banner aloft but it was damp and there was little wind and so no one could see what device it displayed. However, when Erik demanded that they opened the gates in the name of the king and their ealdorman, they hastened to obey.

We rode into the area in front of the hall and dismounted. Stable boys and other servants came running to take our horses and several of my men mounted the steps leading to the walkway behind the palisade. Each carried a bow and a full quiver.

Pejr emerged from the warriors' hall, strapping on his sword belt as he approached. He was followed by a score of men, most were armed but many were rubbing sleep from their eyes. Ajs came out of the lord's hall followed by Hilda, who was looking fearful. However, she smiled tentatively when she saw me.

'Ah! Captain Pejr. Good! Assemble your men please; I wish to address them.'

He looked behind him.

'Looks like they are all here,' he said in a tone that implied that I was an idiot.

'You will call me lord!' I demanded.

'Yes,' he paused. 'Lord.'

'My lady I apologise if I have alarmed you but I need to make some changes here.'

'It's always a pleasure to see you, Lord Jørren,' she said with a broad smile that caused her cheeks to dimple.

I mounted the steps outside the hall so that I could stand beside her. Cei and Erik came to stand behind me, shouldering Ajs out of the way.

'My remarks are addressed to those of you who have followed Pejr as captain hitherto,' I began. 'My name is Jørren of Cilleham and I am your new ealdorman. I am also King Ælfred's Sǣ Hereræswa and these men with me are veterans of many battles with the Danes on sea and on land. I hope to recruit some of you to join us, but I warn you I will only take those I consider worthy. Those not chosen may be retained to guard my hall here or the fortress at Dofras; or you may choose to find a new master.'

'You're forgetting something,' Pejr exploded. 'I'm the captain of these men! They answer to me.'

'You were Glædwine's captain. He is no longer ealdorman, I am; and I choose who serves me. Just so we understand one another, I will not be choosing you to serve me in any capacity.'

Pejr put his hand on his sword hilt and half drew it from its scabbard before he became aware of the six archers aiming at him from the palisade. I waved my hand and the archers relaxed.

'Go ahead and draw your sword Pejr. If you attack me, then I will be justified in killing you. That might save a lengthy battle in the king's court before I can restore Ægelesthrep to its rightful owner, the Lady Hilda.'

He hesitated, then spat at me.

'Ægelesthrep was given to me by Ealdorman Glædwine and there's nothing you can do about it!'

'But it wasn't his to give,' I replied calmly. 'Father abbot?'

143

'Ealdorman Jørren is correct,' Ælfnoð said, coming to stand beside me. 'The vill was left to Lady Hilda for her lifetime. Her father's will specifically states that it may not become the property of any husband or descendants. After Lady Hilda's death, it passes to the Church.'

He turned to me with a smile.

'I don't think you need worry about a lengthy dispute, lord. I've rarely seen a will drawn up in such watertight terms.'

With a roar of rage Pejr drew his dagger and ran towards me. I had thought the matter settled and so I was totally unprepared for his reaction. There is little doubt in my mind that he would have reached me before anyone else could draw a weapon, least of all me.

Suddenly there was the twang of a released bowstring in the stunned silence and Pejr pitched forward with an arrow in the middle of his back. The dagger in his outstretched right hand thudded into the timber planking an inch from my boot. Whilst Erik knelt down to check that he was dead I scanned the parapet looking for the archer who had just saved my life, but I couldn't identify him. They all looked ready to use their bows but none stood out as the man who had fired the arrow. To this day I don't know who it was.

I looked at Hilda, expecting to see her terrified by the violence she had just witnessed, but she had a look of quiet satisfaction on her face and she mouthed the words 'good riddance' at me.

After that it was all a bit of anti-climax. All but six of the old garrison seemed trustworthy. Some I left, with a few of my own warband, to garrison the hall; others went to bolster the garrison at Dofras, but most joined my warband and would serve on board my ships.

Lady Hilda was still in mourning but I left her in no doubt how I felt towards her before I left the next day. She didn't say anything, quite properly, but she gave me every indication that my suit wouldn't be unwelcome. With that I had to be content. I made two other changes at Cantwareburh before I left. I made Cei my captain there and, pleased as he was by the promotion, he accepted it reluctantly.

He and I had been together even since I ran away from Cilleham as a boy and we had been close friends for nearly all that time. He was as loath to part from me as I was to leave him. However, I knew that he would give his life to look after Hilda for me.

The other change was to sack Ajs. Hilda was as certain as she could be that he and Pejr had been stealing from the estate. Instead I appointed a young cleric who Abbot Ælfnoð had recommended. Ajs left vowing revenge. Perhaps I should have charged him with embezzlement and sold him into slavery. Instead he joined the growing number of my sworn enemies. If I had a fault, it was being too lenient with those who had good cause to hate me.

That winter was another harsh one. Blizzard driven snow blanketed the land and fierce storms kept all shipping in harbour. It suited me because, if my fleet couldn't venture out, neither could the Danes and other Viking raiders from Irlond, Mann and Orkneyjar.

The weather finally broke in the middle of March and we recommenced our patrols of the coast. In early April six of my ships came scuttling back to Dofras to report sighting a vast fleet of longships leaving the estuary of the Temes and sailing along the coast of Cent. I sent six ships to shadow the Danes and a mounted messenger to warn Ælfred at Wintanceaster before riding on to inform Bjarne at Hamwic.

The messenger returned several days later with a letter from the king.

*To my trusted and well beloved Ealdorman and Sǣ Hererǽswa, Jørren,*

*It seems I owe you an apology. Guðrum was not to be trusted after all. He has landed at Werhām in Dornsǽte in some strength. The burh was taken unawares and was captured by the Danes, apparently with ease. I shall make for Werhām with all haste, raising the fyrd and collecting my nobles and their hearth warriors as I go.*

*No doubt we shall have to besiege the burh and starve the Danes out. However, they can re-supply*

*themselves by sea and I therefore want you to blockade*
*the harbour to prevent this.*

*I fully realise that, whilst the Danes have over a*
*hundred ships you can call upon a mere score, but I*
*leave it to your ingenuity to prevent them using the*
*harbour.*

*Your servant in Christ Our Lord,*

*Ælfredus Rex*

I groaned. The king had set me another
impossible task. The fact that I'd been right about
Guðrum all along didn't help. Furthermore, with the
better weather I was intending to go and ask Hilda to
marry me, but now that would have to wait.

I sent out orders to my captains to get the fleet
ready to sail and I quickly penned a message for
Bjarne to do the same. Meanwhile I wracked my
brains for a way of bottling up the harbour at
Werhām. I had concluded that it was an intractable
problem when Eomær interrupted my train of
thought to inform me that Archbishop Ethelred had
just arrived.

I was wary of the archbishop. I had kept my
meeting with him as short as possible when I had
paid my respects to him on arrival in Cent. He was in
dispute with the king over Ælfred's authority over the
clergy. Ethelred claimed that any crime committed
by a cleric could only be tried by an ecclesiastical
authority, usually the accused's bishop or abbot. This

even applied in serious cases like murder. The last thing I wanted to do was to get involved in the dispute. However, if someone was brought before me charged with a crime, I intended to give judgement whether the accused was laity or clergy.

'Lord archbishop, this is an unexpected pleasure,' I greeted the man as he was shown into my hall, together with his chaplain and a monk I didn't know. 'Please be seated. My servants will bring refreshments directly.'

'Thank you, Lord Jørren. I won't waste your time with pleasantries; I know that you must be busy preparing to go to the king's aid at Werhām.'

The surprise must have shown on my face. I had only learned of the Danes' landing a few hours ago myself. Ethelred smiled at my reaction.

'I think you will find that the clergy are the first to know when anything momentous happens; they are a fund of minor gossip as well.'

'Yes, of course. What can I do for you?'

'It's more what I can do for you. I have brought Brother Simeon with me. He's something of an expert on Roman naval warfare.'

'Indeed,' Simeon beamed at me. 'We have countless ancient manuscripts in the library at Cantwareburh, including many from the time of the Roman Empire. I was the son of a fisherman and so I've always been interested in the sea and in ships.'

'Yes, yes brother,' Ethelred butted in. 'The ealdorman doesn't want to know your life history. Tell him what you know about blockading ports.'

'Ah, yes,' Simeon continued, not in the least put out by the archbishop's irritable rebuke. 'Well, normally they would blockade ports, like that at Syracuse, by stationing a few ships at the harbour entrance and beaching or anchoring the fleet nearby. That would be enough to bottle up the enemy merchant shipping and if a relieving fleet arrived, the rest of the ships could put to sea to meet them in battle. The aim was, of course, to prevent supplies reaching the besieged and, in some case, as with Carthage, to cripple the economy.'

'But I have little more than a score of ships and the Danish fleet is four or five that size,' I protested. 'Besides, the enemy fleet is anchored in the natural harbour of Poole Hæfen. Werhām lies a couple of miles up the estuary of the River Freumh, which flows into the harbour.'

'Then your best tactic is to restrict the entrance to the harbour by using sunken ships and tying your longships across the gap.'

It was a good idea. Not mooring my longships across the gap, but if I could restrict the entrance enough, the enemy could only exit the harbour one or two ships at a time. They would then be vulnerable to attack by my fleet. It would also stop the Danish supply ships running the blockade and thus we could starve those in the burh into surrender.

However, it would only be feasible if the majority of the Danes' longships were already in the harbour. If sufficient numbers remained at Lundenwic, then they could attack our ships from the sea. I therefore sent a patrol along the south bank of the Temes to count the number of longships still moored at the Danish base. When they came back and said there were only twenty five longships there I knew we had a chance of making Simeon's idea work.

# Chapter Ten

## WESSEX

## Summer and Autumn 876

I had never considered myself a sailor but I realised with a start that I had grown to relish the lively movement of the deck underfoot as the Saint Cuthbert skimmed across the waves, pushed on by a brisk south easterly wind. The other eleven longships had fanned out behind me. For late May the weather was fine but the wind was chilly. Before we had sailed Hilda had sent me a present. It was a black cloak made of bearskin that had belonged to her late husband. At first I was reluctant to wear it, knowing who its last owner had been, but the fact that it was a gift from Hilda overcame my scruples.

I was glad of it now, but even more so later on when the weather got colder with the arrival of autumn. Just after noon the blue sky darkened to grey and then black rain-bearing clouds appeared further out to sea.

'We are in for a bit of a blow,' Wilfrið, the captain of the skeid, said pessimistically. 'You'd better find something to hang on to.'

He shouted orders and a few minutes of frenetic activity followed. The sail was swiftly lowered by the ship's boys and then stowed in the cradle on deck. Anything that could be washed overboard was tied down and the rowers turned Saint Cuthbert's bows into the wind, as if in defiance of the brewing storm.

I looked aft and was relieved to see that the other ships were lowering their sails and turning to face the wind.

'Ship oars and brace yourselves,' Wilfrið shouted above the howling wind.

He joined the steersman in grasping the steering oar so as to keep Saint Cuthbert facing the right way. I knew enough to realise that if we turned sideways on - what Wilfrið termed broaching - the waves would capsize us.

I took one look at the mountainous seas coming towards us with the wind whipping streams of foam away horizontally from the crest and I sat down hurriedly, bracing my back against the gunwale.

Suddenly the ship rose into the air as if some giant was picking up a toy. The bows pointed towards the heavens for a moment and then they dropped. The stern, where I was, rose into the air so fast that I left my stomach somewhere way below me and the bows dropped before heading for the bottom of the trough. I was convinced that they would carry on down into the depths and that we'd all drown, but suddenly they lifted, salt water cascading over every one, and we headed once more towards the heavens.

This continued for what seemed like forever, but I was later told that it was less than an hour. The front of my bearskin cloak was covered in vomit but I had no recollection of being sick. As suddenly as it had arrived the wind died, although the sea continued to toss us about.

'Just a little bit of a squall,' Wilfrið said cheerfully as he helped me to my feet. 'Nothing to worry about.'

'Really? You could have fooled me,' I replied, scanning the horizon for the rest of my ships.

They were scattered but thankfully they had all survived. I learned later that three men and one ship's boy had been swept overboard, but it could have been far worse.

We stayed at Hamwic for two days whilst minor repairs and a certain amount of re-caulking took place. The violent movement had opened some small gaps between the horizontal strakes that clad the hull. These had to be plugged using oakum or cotton fibres soaked in pine tar. When we sailed again the fleet had grown to twenty three ships with the addition of those stationed at Hamwic. However, only seven of them were longships such as the Vikings used. The other sixteen were the smaller type which we now called birlinns. The first to use the term was Erik who had anglicised the name from the Norse word byrðingr, meaning ship of boards.

We were also accompanied by five knarrs that I'd found at Hamwic. Their owners hadn't parted with them voluntarily, of course. It had taken a mixture of veiled threats and promises that the king would compensate them before the merchants had been persuaded, albeit reluctantly, to part with them. They would have been even less happy had they known that I proposed to sink their craft across the narrow entrance to Poole Hæfen.

Brother Simeon had described the entrance to me but I wasn't sure that I had completely believed him.

As we approached I could see a long sand spit to the east of the entrance and a wooded peninsula to the west. Beyond was a vast expanse of water with a sizeable island just to the north of the entrance. As Simeon had said, the entrance was a mere three hundred yards wide.

I didn't have much time to put my plan into action. I could already see activity aboard the thirty longships anchored either side of the nearby island. Then I relaxed. They only had an anchor watch on duty. The rest of the crew would probably be camping on the island. This blocked my view further into the harbour but I expected the bulk of the fleet to either be tied up at the quayside in Werhām or anchored near the mouth of the River Freumh. No doubt their crews would be garrisoning the burh itself.

The knarrs varied in length from between thirty five and sixty feet. End to end they would measure no more than one hundred yards; however, the sea at both ends of the gap would be shallow. Even so, a reduced entrance of maybe one hundred and sixty or seventy yards would too wide for us to contain the Danish fleet. However, I was prepared for this.

Just as the first of the Danish longships got underway, the last knarr was anchored in position. One of my smaller longships was moored alongside each one and their archers stood along the gunwale of each knarr. I gave the signal and my men commenced hacking at the planking below the water line.

As the first of the longships approached my archers rained arrows down on them, killing and wounding both rowers and the warriors standing in the bows, eager to get to grips with us. Then the first of the knarrs started to sink. The archers on her scrambled back aboard their own ship and it cast off. Slowly the same thing happened all along the line.

The knarrs had been anchored at even intervals across the entrance, leaving a gap of ten yards in the middle. Of course, there was also a gap of between twenty five and thirty yards between each sunken ship. Before leaving Hamwic I had replaced the ballast on board each knarr with chain. This was now tied between each ships' stern and the bows of the next one, forming an underwater boom.

The harbour was shallow but longships only drew between two and three feet. They could therefore pass over the booms at high tide. To prevent this I had also tied chain part way up each mast so that it was above the surface at most states of the tide but still less than a foot below it at the highest tide.

Given that the beam of a longship was more than two and half yards and oars added another four yards, only one longship could pass through the entrance at a time. Even if the wind was in the right direction and they could use their sails, no more than two could pass through at a time.

Wilfrið had asked why I didn't close off the entrance completely but I was loathe to do that. There might come a time when we would need to use the entrance ourselves.

✝✝✝

A few longships tried to leave the harbour but two had been dismasted when they ran into the booms and came to a sudden halt; the strain on the back stay proving too much and it parted. Another had been captured after passing through the narrow exit. The rest gave up and returned to their anchorage.

I fully expected them to make another attempt that night, when my archers were at a severe disadvantage, and sure enough we saw dark shadows creeping towards us in the early hours. The moon appeared sporadically from behind the clouds and the next time it did so we could see perhaps fifty longships heading our way. Ten of my ships packed with archers lay twenty yards beyond the gap. On each ship more men waited with torches. As the nearest longships neared the gap I said 'now' and a horn sounded a single blast.

Almost as one, the archers dipped their arrows into small urns of pine pitch and then held them for others to light. Half a minute later small dots of flaming light soared into the air and began to fall into the nearest ships. Some lodged in the furled sails and others in the woodwork; they were not the ones that did the damage though. The Danes quickly doused them using buckets of sea water, but those fire arrows which landed in spare tarred cordage or set alight the rigging were much more difficult to extinguish and before they had a chance to deal with them several more volleys hit them.

Shortly afterwards three of the approaching ships were seen to be well ablaze. One swung across the course of two others and they crashed into it. The fire spread to the rigging of the other two longships and the three drifted into the gap between my submerged knarrs, effectively blocking it.

There were no more attempts to escape Poole Hæfen that night. In the morning we towed the burnt out hulks clear and sunk them out at sea. After that I asked to be put ashore well to the east of the harbour. From there I made my way on foot to a nearby farmstead accompanied by a dozen of my warband. The place had been raided by the Danes, which rather dashed my hopes of being able to hire some horses. Nothing living was left.

However, one of the scouts accompanying me knelt down and studied the ground. With surprise I noticed that it was Hrodulf, one of the Mercian boys we'd rescued from the Danes the previous year. He hadn't been in training that long, but he had a natural talent for reading tracks and signs.

'The tracks are confused by the Danes' boots, lord, but I'm pretty certain that the farmer and his family went that way.'

He pointed towards a wood about a mile away.

'Did they have any animals with them?' I asked.

He rose and went further towards the trees before examining the ground again. He went backwards and forwards before he was satisfied.

'It looks as if there were three, maybe four cows, some sheep and five or six horses. One of the horses was pulling a cart.'

157

'Well done Hrodulf,' I told him, fishing in my purse. 'You've earned this,' I added, throwing him a mancus, a gold coin worth thirty silver pennies.

An hour later we came across the ceorl and his family hiding in a glade in the wood. I withdrew another mancus from my purse and he agreed to hire me his six horses. Leaving the rest of my men with the family, I rode off to find Ælfred's camp accompanied by Erik, Eomær, Hrodulf and three warriors.

As we rode past two smaller lakes, which were offshoots off the main harbour, I saw several longships moored in each. Their crews were camped nearby and they got to their feet as we cantered past. I made a mental note of the locations of the two camps; the less Danes who were free to roam, pillage and burn in the local area the better, but that was another's problem, not mine.

When I got to the camp I encountered a suspicious group of sentries and when I asked the way to the king's tent they started to get quite agitated. There were five of them and so I don't quite know what they thought they could achieve had we indeed been the enemy but, just as my impatience began to show I heard a friendly voice.

'Jørren, I haven't seen you for quite a while. How are you?'

I dismounted and my brother Alric threw his arms around me, thumping me hard on the back.

'Phew, where did you get that smelly bearskin. It makes you look like a Viking!'

'So these men evidently thought,' I said with a smile. 'Where are you camped? I need to see the king now, but we must catch up later.'

'My tent is just over there; these rascals are my men,' he said indicating the men who'd stopped me.

'You should know that you have impeded a man who is not only my brother, but the Ealdorman of Cent and the Sǣ Hererǣswa of Wessex,' he told them with mock severity.

The men shifted from one foot to the other and looked apprehensive.

'You weren't to know and I'm glad that you are keeping such a good watch,' I told them with a smile.

'Come, brother, I'll take you to the king,' Alric said, waving a dismissal at his warriors.

'I was really sorry to hear about Leofflæd,' Alric said as we made our way through the camp. 'I know how much you loved her.'

'Thank you. I was devastated at the time, but sadly death in childbirth happens all too often.'

He looked at me in surprise.

'I thought you would be inconsolable,' he said, sounding puzzled.

'I was, and for a time I lost all interest in life, but now I have little time to dwell on my loss, except at night, of course.'

Just then we arrived outside Ælfred's tent and I breathed a sigh of relief. I wondered what Alric would have thought of me had he known that I had fallen in love again and was planning to wed Hilda. I had no doubt that I would have gone down in his estimation. I handed the reins of my horse to Eomær as Alric told the sentry outside the tent who I was.

'I'll see you later,' he said as I was announced to Ælfred.

I nodded and entered the tent. To call it a tent was a misnomer. It was a miniature hall made of oil impregnated woollen cloth spread over a stout timber frame. There was a central space for meetings and several areas leading off it through curtains. I assumed that these were sleeping chambers for the king and his servants.

Ælfred was sitting at a table on which lay a map and several scrolls. Bishop Asser and Eadda the hereræswa sat beside him studying the map. One of his pages stood behind them, as did two sentries.

"Ah, Jørren, excellent timing,' the king said, rising and coming around the table to greet me by gripping both shoulders. 'Come, join us. We were just discussing how best to conduct the siege. Have you eaten?'

'Thank you cyning,' I said as I took the other seat at the table. 'I have eaten but something to drink would be welcome.'

I ignored the scowls on the faces of the other two men and gave them a beaming smile in return.

The page disappeared and moments later a slave appeared with a goblet brimming with mead. I took a large swallow and looked at the map.

'With Jørren's ships cutting off access from the sea and our army watching the three gates into the burh, the only way for the Danes to get supplies is along the

River Freumh from the west. I therefore intend to build two forts, one on each bank, here.'

He pointed to a spot where the river narrowed some two miles from the burh.

'But how will that prevent the Danes from sailing past them?' Asser asked, looking puzzled. 'And how will they get there if all their longships are bottled up in Poole Hæfen?'

'They will steal them, of course,' Eadda replied. 'We know that there are forage parties abroad who left Werhām before we arrived.'

'And the crews of more than twenty longships are camped on the shores of these two lakes,' I said pointing them out on the map.

'Thank you, Jørren, we'll deal with them this afternoon, you may rest assured.'

The king didn't say so, but it was evident from his tone that he thought that Eadda should have already discovered their presence.

'We will man these forts with what few archers we have,' Ælfred added. 'Hopefully they will be able to stop them getting past.'

'Not at night, cyning,' Eadda pointed out, still smarting from the king's implicit criticism.

'Then put a boom across the river,' I suggested.

'A boom?' Eadda queried, his tone implying that it was an idiotic idea.

'Yes, a boom. A chain or heavy rope stretched between the two forts to stop shipping going past.'

'But some of our own supplies come up by river,' he objected.

'Then you lower the boom to let them through,' I explained patiently, as if the hereræswa was a little child.

'An excellent idea, well done, Jørren,' Ælfred responded before the rage simmering inside Eadda could erupt.

'What about Halfdan and Ubba? We seem to have lost sight of those two in our discussions,' Asser put in.

The two were Norsemen, the sons of Ragnar Lodbrok, who, with their brother Ívarr the Boneless, had led the original invasion by the Great Heathen Army a decade before.

'What about them?' I queried. 'I thought that they were both in Irlond.'

'My sources tell me that they plan to sail to join Guðrum in a two pronged attack on Wessex.'

My heart sank. It was bad enough having to deal with Guðrum's army. He was reported to have over three thousand men against our four thousand; but his were all seasoned fighters whereas many of ours were farmers who had never killed a man before. If Halfdan and Ubba came to Guðrum's aid, their combined forces would outnumber ours quite significantly.

'What can we do?' I queried.

'Not a lot, except pray and ask you to use your fleet to patrol the western approaches,' Ælfred said glumly.

Leaving the rest of my fleet under Bjarne's command to blockade of the Danish fleet, I set sail in the Saint Cuthbert with five birlinns,

Any longships sailing from Dyflin in Irlond to the south coast of Wessex would have to round the southern tip of the peninsula known by the locals as Kernow, but which we called Dumnonia, the old Roman name for the province. It had been invaded and conquered by Wessex nearly forty years before, but it wasn't a true shire like the rest of the kingdom. It was ruled by a native sub-king who paid taxes to the King of Wessex and it was theoretically subject to Ælfred's laws, but in practice it was largely autonomous.

We didn't have the provisions to stay at sea permanently so I decided that a pair of ships would be enough to patrol the sea south west of the southern tip of Dumnonia. Those not at sea would base themselves at a small fishing village called Hæfen Kernow, which meant port of Dumnonia – a grand name for such a tiny place.

The harbour, if you could call it that, lay in a small bay sheltered from the prevailing winds. There was no wharf or quay so we beached our ships near the fishing boats on the golden sands under the cliffs. The village itself lay up a steep path beside a small stream. By the time we had got there the inhabitants had fled. I wasn't certain whether the local population would prove hostile or not, so we decided to camp on the beach rather than occupy the half a dozen mean hovels that constituted the fishing village. I stationed two sentries to keep watch for any danger and we returned to the beach.

The next morning I sent two of the birlinns to keep watch for the Viking fleet and set out to retrace my steps up to the village.

'Be careful, lord. We've seen movement up in the village,' one of the sentries warned me as we passed.

I had taken just Erik and Cináed with me. I hoped to persuade the locals that we meant them no harm and arriving with an armed guard would only panic them. We had shed our byrnies and helmets and wore just a dagger at our waists. Cináed was a Pict who spoke the Brythonic tongue, the common language of the Picts, Strathclyde Britons and the Wealas as well as the people of Dumnonia. I was hoping that, even if the version spoken here was different to that of Pictland, he could make himself understood to the local fisher folk.

As we approached he called out the Pictish words for friend and peace. Several men appeared, each brandishing some kind of weapon, mainly gutting knives and crudely made spears – sticks with a sharpened point that had been hardened in a fire.

'What do you want with us?'

The voice startled me. Whoever it was had spoken in English, and in the dialect of English spoken in Wessex at that. I scanned the men facing me and settled on a man with fair hair. He was taller that the rest, who were not only smaller but had black or dark brown hair.

'You're a Saxon?'

'Yes, I was a trader whose ship was wrecked on the rocks a year ago. These kind folk rescued me and nursed me back to health. There was nothing left in Wessex for me, except debts, so I decided to stay here.'

'My name is Jørren. I'm King Ælfred's Sǣ Hereræswa. We've heard reports that a large Viking fleet is heading this way and I've been sent to watch for it.'

'Sǣ Hereræswa? It's not a term I've heard before. Does that mean that Wessex now has a fleet? If that's it beached down below, I wish you the best of luck against the Vikings,' he jeered.

'Mind your tongue,' I snapped. 'The rest have Guðrum's fleet bottled up in Poole Hæfen.'

'My apologies, lord. I meant no offence. We're relatively cut off from the outside world here, but we hear tidings of events elsewhere through peddlars and the monks who occasionally come to make sure we remain good Christians. Brother Branock came only a week ago. He told us of a big battle in Irlond between Bárid, the Viking King of Dyflin, and his uncle, Halfdan Ragnarsson. He said that Halfdan had been killed and Bárid wounded; however Bárid's men won the battle.'

If true, this was excellent news. If Halfdan was dead, then perhaps the threat of invasion from Irlond had been removed. But then I remembered the last of the Ragnarssons.

'What about Ubba? Did Brother Branock have any news of him?'

My informant shook his head. 'Sorry, no.'

'Thank you. You've been most helpful.'

I moved on to discuss buying fish and vegetables from the locals and then returned to the beach to send one of the birlinns back to tell the king what I'd been told about Halfdan.

✝✝✝

It wasn't until early October that my two patrolling birlinns came racing back to Hæfen Kernow with the news that Ubba's fleet of over a hundred longships had been sighted. If my captains had estimated correctly, that probably meant a force of over three thousand warriors. My heart sank. It was far more than I had expected, but then, perhaps Halfdan's men had joined Ubba.

I sent one of the birlinns off post haste to warn Ælfred and I also sent two messengers on horseback to tell the ealdormen of Dornsæte and Dyfneintscīr, just in case the Vikings raided their coastline on their way to Werhām.

There was little I could do in direct conflict with such a huge fleet, but I determined to harass them as much as I could. What followed was a game of cat and mouse. We waited close inshore, hidden behind a rocky promontory, until the enemy fleet had passed us by, then we darted out to attack the stragglers.

The westerly wind enabled the Viking longships to sail at a good five knots, but having the wind directly aft wasn't a fast point of sailing. As soon as we emerged from behind the promontory we were able to sail on a broad reach, skimming through the water at a greater speed than the Vikings. It was one of the mysteries of the sea. The fasted point of sailing wasn't to have the wind directly aft of you; it was when you were on a beam reach; that is, the wind was coming at you sideways on and the mainsail was braced hard over. A broad reach – when the wind was coming from your rear quarter – lay between the two.

One of the boys threw a line with a piece of light wood over the bows and then ran along, yelling for the unoccupied rowers to get out of the way whilst counting the seconds until the marker bobbed past the stern. He hauled it in and shouted the time to Wilfrið.

'Not bad,' the captain grunted after making the necessary calculation. 'Near on eight knots.'

The enemy evidently didn't keep as good a watch as we did because we managed to get within a hundred yards of the rearmost longship before the alarm was sounded. I let the birlinns take the lead and, as they swept past the longship, still heading out to sea, their archers sent several volleys into the bewildered men on board. As the last of the birlinns left her in its wake I estimated that we had killed or wounded at least a third of those on board.

We did the same to the next four ships. By that time we were well to seaward of the Viking fleet. Some twenty ships broke away to attack us, but we changed tack to head back towards the main fleet, leaving them in our wake.

This time several ships turned to meet us but the wind was against them and they were forced to drop their sails and use their oars. We gave them a wide berth, pouring more arrows into them as we swept past. Now we were in the middle of their fleet but it was so spread out that we had little trouble in avoiding the longships, sending more volleys of arrows into individual ships whenever the opportunity presented itself.

Many of the longships attempted to come alongside so that they could board us, but we managed to elude their clutches; all except one birlinn who got trapped between three enemy snekkjur. Much to my frustration there was nothing I could do and I had to watch her being boarded and overwhelmed. It was a chastening moment but I consoled myself with the thought of the havoc we had managed to wreak. We may not have significantly weakened Ubba's force, but we must have killed or incapacitated some two hundred of his warriors.

We broke free of the enemy fleet and I was about to give the order to go about and resume our attack when Wilfrið gripped my arm.

'Storm coming, and it looks like a bad one.'

I looked towards where he was pointing and my heart sank. The clouds billowing up on the horizon were black and I could make out streaks of heavy rain even from here.

'How long before it reaches us?' I asked

'Not long. Perhaps a quarter of an hour if we're lucky. We need to run for it.'

He ordered the steersman to change course to due north and the ship's boys ran to the sheets to change the angle of the sail for the new heading. At the same time I waved at Wolnoth, who had taken over from Cei as my signaller, and he sounded his horn repeatedly to alert our other ships. We fled towards the coast with a dozen enemy longships on our tail.

'Where to?' I asked. 'Can we find shelter?'

'Suttun, at the mouth of the River Plym,' he replied, watching the approaching storm to gauge the moment we would need to drop the sail.

The rowers had already taken their places and had unshipped their oars. They knew what was at stake and put their backs into it, giving us another two or three knots through the water.

I had heard of Suttun. It was one of the major trading ports in Dyfneintscīr and, if I remembered correctly, the harbour was more of an inland system of interconnected lakes with a narrow access to the sea. Ten minutes later, just after we had sighted land ahead of us, the storm struck us. The wind had backed from the west to the south, which aided us. As the wind howled and the seas grew mountainous, we shipped oars and ran under bare poles.

By now the wind was lashing down with such great force that raindrops bounced back four or five inches into the air when they hit the deck. I wrapped my bearskin cloak around me and crammed my helmet on my head to protect me as the rain turned to hail. I pitied the ship's boys and other sailors who had no armour or shield to protect them. I saw

Eomær flinching as his head and exposed skin was bombarded by hailstones the size of small pebbles.

We all clung on for dear life to whatever was available. In my case it was the stern post. Wilfrið and the steersman were wrestling the steering oar to keep the skeid heading downwind and I prayed fervently that we were heading for the entrance to Suttun harbour and not the rocks at the base of the cliffs which surrounded it.

I risked a glance behind me and was greeted by a somewhat surreal sight: the bows of the nearest birlinn hung in the air just ahead of an enormous wave some forty feet above my head. I watched as the birlinn skidded down the wave no more than twenty feet behind us as we, in turn, rose high into the air. The next moment I was looking down onto the deck of the other ship far below me.

The hail ceased and changed to rain again, although this time it didn't seem quite so heavy. I prayed fervently that the Lord God would see us safely into the harbour, closing my eyes to do so. When I opened them again I could just make out land either side of us through the murk.

'We've done it,' Wilfrið yelled in relief although, as his words were whipped away by the wind, I doubt if anyone except for the steersman and I had heard him.

A little further on he called for the rowers to unship their oars but few heard him.

'We need to turn in a few minutes or we'll end up being dashed against the rocks,' he shouted at me.

Taking my life in my hands I let go of the sternpost and made my way, carefully and with lurching steps to the nearest oarsman.

'We need to row,' I yelled into his ear.

He nodded and got up from where he sat braced against the side of the ship and went to sit on his sea chest. The wind was easing a little now and the motion of the ship was less violent. Seeing the first oarsman getting ready to row, others copied him. I stayed where I was so that I could relay Wilfrið's instructions down the length of the ship.

'Port side back oars, he yelled, larboard side keep rowing.'

He and the steersmen leant on the steering oar and gradually we began to turn to the left. The wind was still blowing us towards the rocks though and for a moment I thought that we would still end up crashing into them sideways on.

'Forward all together,' he called and I repeated his instructions.

Slowly the ship began to gather speed in the new direction and I saw the rocks slipping passed us not forty feet away. The wind was still pushing us towards them and, as our shallow draft meant that we made a lot of leeway, there was still a danger that we would founder.

Then we were past them and we entered the calmer waters beyond before dropping anchor. I breathed a sigh of relief and dropped to my knees to thank God for our survival. However, we might be safe but I was worried about the rest of my little fleet. I counted each one in as they came to join us. After a

while I stopped counting.  Two were still missing and
I had to assume that they had been wrecked.  With
the birlinn which had been overwhelmed during our
attack, we had lost over a tenth of our number.

# Chapter Eleven

## WESSEX

## Spring 877

I learned later that most of the Viking fleet had been destroyed in the storm and those who had survived had returned to Irlond. The rest of the autumn and the following winter was spent enduring the tedium of siege warfare at Werhām. Occasionally the Danes would sally out and there would be a skirmish before they withdrew within their ramparts. Ælfred made no attempt to assault the burh; he had learned the lesson during the preceding years that it was a futile exercise that merely cost him men.

There were several attempts by the Danish ships to break out of the harbour, but they all failed and only resulted in many more losses amongst their crews. Similarly we managed to stop nearly all supplies reaching them. It was stalemate but time was on Ælfred's side. His only real worry was desertions amongst the fyrd.

More and more information about Ubba's fleet trickled in as Christmas passed and the New Year began. The wreckage of some seventy longships had been found along the coast near Suttun. Any survivors had been ruthlessly killed by the local populace. However, Ubba's corpse didn't appear to be amongst the dead washed up. Of course, he could have been lost at sea, but then reports reached us that he and some thirty of his longships had survived and were now overwintering at Sveinsey in Wealas.

In late March a delegation of Danes came to see Ælfred to sue for peace. He agreed to meet Guðrum and two others in a tent erected halfway between the main gates of Werhām and his own camp. He took Eadda and me with him whilst Guðrum brought along my old adversary, Oscatel, and another jarl called Anwend as his advisers.

As soon as the three Danes walked into the tent everyone could see what the ravages of winter and starvation had wreaked on our enemies. All three men looked gaunt, hollow cheeked and thin. Nevertheless, they stared defiantly at the king and remained standing, despite being offered a bench to sit on. That left them looming over the three of us as we sat on our chairs. If it was meant to intimidate us it didn't work.

None of us were armed, our weapons having been left with attendants outside the tent. It was a tense moment and for an instant I thought they were intending to attack us with their bare hands. However, after several minutes they gave in and sat on the bench.

'Good,' Ælfred said with a smile. 'Welcome. Do any of you speak English?'

'I do,' Guðrum replied, 'but it may help if you have an interpreter to avoid any misunderstandings.'

His English was good and I was certain that he didn't need anyone to translate; it was merely a ploy to gain him thinking time.

'I speak Danish, if that helps,' I volunteered.

Oscatel had taken one disdainful look around him when he had entered but then stared fixedly at Ælfred, perhaps hoping to disconcert him. Now he jerked around and hissed 'you!' at me.

'I promised I would kill you, now is as good a time as any,' he said, reaching for his sword which, of course, wasn't there.

'Behave Oscatel. The time will come, but now is not the moment,' Guðrum said with a sneer.

'You know this Dane?' Ælfred asked me in surprise.

'He was the one who held me captive when you sent me as an emissary to King Burghred, cyning. His word is not to be trusted.'

Clearly Oscatel understood what I had said and reacted angrily, but Guðrum put a restraining hand on his shoulder. He subsided, but continued to give me murderous looks.

The meeting dragged on for hours. The Danes clearly wanted supplies and to be allowed to leave the prison they had found themselves in, but they weren't prepared to go quietly. As Guðrum pointed out, he had to have something to give his men in return for their months of hardship. He wanted Wessex to give him enough silver to satisfy his men and to be allowed to sail away unimpeded.

Ælfred retorted that they should be satisfied with their lives. If they didn't like it, they could stay inside the fortifications of Werhām until they starved to death. It seemed an impasse, but of course it was merely the opening moves in a lengthy and frustrating game.

I grew impatient as the talks dragged on for a second and then a third day, but eventually a compromise was reached. Guðrum would be give provisions for two weeks and be allowed to march away north into Mercia but he would leave his fleet behind. In return, Wessex would pay him compensation for the loss of the ships. Each side would deliver up forty worthy men as hostages to ensure that each side kept its word.

Neither Eadda nor I were happy with the agreement, and I suspected most of the ealdormen would be furious. They had made their opposition to paying the heathens a hefty inducement to leave - Danegeld as it was termed – several times before. They felt, quite rightly, that it impoverished Wessex whilst only serving as a temptation for more Danes to come and be bribed to leave. But Ælfred was adamant.

He needed time to raise the Danegeld through taxation and so it was agreed that the Danes could stay in Werhām for now and limited supplies would be provided to ensure that they didn't starve in the meantime.

For my part the blockade continued. April passed into May whilst the king's tax collectors visited every part of Wessex to collect the silver needed to pay off Guðrum but eventually, in June, the day came for them to leave. The coffers of silver were handed over and loaded onto five ships which would be allowed to leave and return to Guðrum's base in Ludenwic. I watched them sail away then sent a birlinn to shadow them. I wasn't at all surprised when it returned to report that the five longships had sailed east until they were over the horizon and then they had turned and headed west. Guðrum was plainly up to something.

I told Ælfred of my suspicions but he waved them away. As far as he was concerned he had a truce which the Danish leaders had sworn to honour in a solemn ceremony and he trusted them to keep to its terms. The fact that the oaths had been sworn by both sides, Christian and pagan, on Holy relics which were sacred only to us was lost on him.

The hostages were exchanged that evening in a feast attended by the leaders of both sides. Guðrum and his three thousand men were due to be escorted north into Mercia the next day, but when dawn broke they had already left.

✝✝✝

A horrific sight greeted us when we entered Werhām the next morning. All forty of the hostages from Wessex, mostly thegns and members of the king's gesith, had been slaughtered. Not only had they been killed, but they had evidently been hacked down unarmed and then their corpses had been stripped bare and mutilated.

Most of us were incandescent with rage at the atrocity. Ælfred took a different stance; his reaction was more sorrow than anger - sorrow that Guðrum's sworn oath wasn't to be trusted.

Worse was to come. One of the stable boys who looked after the army's horses at a paddock two miles away from the main camp came looking for the king. He was covered in blood, but seemed unwounded. He told us that the Danes had taken the sentries guarding our horse herd by surprise during the night and had slaughtered all fifty of them. They had killed most of the grooms and stable boys as well. He had only managed to escape by feigning death.

The Danes now had five hundred horses and we would be unable to catch them on foot. The big question was where would they make for? Evidently it was somewhere in Wessex, otherwise they would have marched off into Mercia as planned.

Most of the ealdormen advocated killing all the Danish hostages in revenge but I suggested finding out who they were first. It turned out that they were all minor jarls or Hersir, many of whom owned one or more longships, or had done until their fleet was abandoned.

'They must die!' Eadda thundered. 'Giving them Danegeld was bad enough but then sparing the hostages would make them think we are gutless old women. What possible reason can there be for sparing them?'

His statement was greeted with acclaim by all the nobles gathered in the hall at Werhām.

'Because to defeat the Danes we need a powerful navy,' I replied calmly. 'The few ships we have of our own aren't enough to do more than patrol a few stretches of coastline. We now have all of Guðrum's longships at our disposal, but they're useless to us if we can't sail them. Oh, we can recruit and train men to crew them and to fight, but we need experienced seamen to command them. These men are nobles in their own country who have been betrayed by Guðrum just as much as he's betrayed us.

'A Viking's loyalty is a two way thing,' I continued, ignoring the hostile reception my words were receiving. 'They give their leader their oath to serve him faithfully and in return he swears to look after them and to ensure that they prosper. Leaving them to die is hardly looking after them, nor furthering their prosperity.'

That drew a few sniggers and nods of acknowledgement from those present and, thus encouraged, I ploughed on.

'Offer these men a choice: death, but without a sword in their hand so that they go to what they call Helheim, or become Christians and serve Wessex as captain of one of our longships.'

A long discussion ensued but eventually Ælfred brought matters to a close by agreeing to offer the hostages life if they would convert and serve him. All but a few did so and they were hung from the palisade around Werhām before the army left in pursuit of Guðrum.

Of the rest, twenty eight were longship captains I could make use of. I decided that I would give them the largest of the skeids and burn the rest of the ships to prevent the Danes getting their hands on them again.

179

Ælfred's men managed to find half a dozen horses, enough for his scouts to locate the Danes fairly quickly. Those on foot were moving along the south coast heading westwards. No doubt Guðrum and his mounted contingent had taken the same road.

'Where can they be making for?' Eadda asked as he and I poured over the map with the king.

'My guess would be to secure another base on the south coast,' I replied. 'No doubt Guðrum still hopes to link up with what remains of Ubba's army. To do that he will need a harbour. Perhaps he has also sent for reinforcements by sea from Ludenwic and East Anglia?'

'That makes sense,' Ælfred agreed. 'How soon will your fleet be ready to sail?'

'I hope to leave at dawn tomorrow, cyning.'

I now had fifty ships. Admittedly most of the crews of the twenty eight longships we had taken from the Danes were recruited from the fyrd; mainly young men who thought that sailing in a longship would be an easier life than eating the dust of others as they trudged in pursuit of the fleeing heathens. It might be easier on the legs and feet, but not on the shoulders, arms and hands, as they would soon find out.

Finding enough ship's boys had also been a problem. In the end we had used some of the urchins and orphans from Werhām. They were little more than skin and bone as they had existed on rats and what little they could steal and scavenge during the siege. Every one of them was eager to escape their current lives of grinding poverty, but I could only use the strongest of them. I found the rest of the boys I needed from the youngest of those serving in the fyrd. By spreading the experienced ship's boys amongst them, I managed to allocate four boys to each ship, divided more or less equally between experienced hands and novices.

Ælfred studied the map again. Suddenly he jabbed a finger at a place where the River Lim flowed into the sea.

'The Danes appear to be following the road along the coast and it comes down to the sea here. The estuary looks big enough for your fleet to enter and moor. Disembark your warriors and do what you can to delay and disrupt the enemy.'

I looked at the map for a minute or two longer to make sure it was imprinted in my mind before heading back to the fleet. I had a force of over fifteen thousand men at my disposal. It was far less than Guðrum's army and the fighting quality of most of the fyrd was inferior, as were their weapons, but I thought that I should still be able to inflict significant damage on them.

I had fully expected that keeping control over so many ships would be difficult, even with experienced captains, but I hadn't expected progress to be so slow or so chaotic. At first the ships from my original fleet were kept fully occupied herding the new ones together. It was a frustrating business, but at least the wind was steady and from the south east, so we didn't have to use the oars. God knows how we would have fared if my landsmen had had to learn to row in order to make progress.

Gradually the fleet settled down as the newcomers got used to their new environment. Within a couple of hours things had settled down and, after we had passed a long headland jutting out into the sea, we turned and headed downwind towards where I thought the mouth of the River Lim should be.

The Danes had a two day start on us and so Guðrum and his mounted warriors would have passed over the Lim already, but I thought it likely that the bulk of the army would take the best part of four days to reach the river. I calculated that, if the wind held, it would take us another six hours to get there, so we should reach our destination well before them.

Entering the estuary would mean rowing and so, shortly after passing the headland, I gave the order to unship oars. Slowly the message was passed around the fleet. As I had expected the result was chaos. Some oars clashed, others dug too deep and the offending rowers nearly lost their oars as a consequence. Yet more missed the water entirely and fell off the sea chests on which they were sitting. It would have been laughable had it not been so pathetic. It took an hour before nearly all the new crews were able to row with some semblance of coordination. I kept them at it for another hour and then gave the order to ship oars. By then the rowers were adding significantly to the speed of the ships through the water, but I wanted them rested before the final pull into the estuary.

Our arrival wasn't exactly a model display of seamanship. The lowering of the sails went well, but the novice rowers pulled unequally on each side of their ship. Consequently the former Danish longships see-sawed from side to side as one bank of oars proved stronger than the other. In time the captains would be able to move men around so that each side had the right mixture of strong and weak oarsmen, but for now the steersmen had great difficulty in maintaining a straight course into the estuary and up the river to the next available space along the bank. However, they all got there without serious mishap.

Once disembarked, I sent a dozen scouts led by Bjarne across to the east bank of the river with instructions to locate the enemy. Of course, it was entirely possible that we had guessed incorrectly and the Danes weren't coming along the coast, but had headed inland instead, but that seemed unlikely.

I left the ship's boys and a hundred men behind to guard the ships and led the rest north along the west bank in search of a crossing place. We hadn't gone far before we came across a timber bridge. It was only wide enough for a cart to pass over it in one direction at a time, which suited me well. The enemy would find it extremely difficult to force a passage over it.

Once I'd set men to work digging a rampart and building a palisade to defend the west side of the bridge, I went off to reconnoitre the east side. I also sent scouts north in search of any other crossing places. I had no intention of being outflanked.

I found what I sought quite quickly - a wood no more than forty yards from the coastal road. It was the best part of a mile from the river and it was just I'd been looking for.

I returned to brief my captains and we deployed our forces into position. That night there were no campfires and we had to make do with a meal of bread, cheese and water before settling down to grab what sleep we could.

†††

We got into position at dawn. Now it was just a matter of waiting. The day had started misty but slowly the sun dispersed it. At this time of year there was little warmth in it but a blue sky with fluffy white clouds raised the spirits. Many of the fyrd had never been in a battle before and their fear was almost palpable. I had interspersed their ranks with a leavening of my own warband and others from my original fleet, but I needed to keep some of them for two other important tasks.

In the middle of the morning the vanguard of the Danes appeared. A dozen scouts on foot preceded them but thankfully they didn't bother to check the woods. However, they soon went running back to report the fact that the bridge was defended. There was a lengthy discussion amongst the leaders, one of whom I noted was my sworn enemy, Oscatel. Then the scouts loped off northwards whilst the rest sat down to wait.

I was confident that they wouldn't find another crossing. The river was too wide and deep to cross for the first two miles upstream and then, when it did narrow, it ran through a marsh. Had there been a ford anywhere near I had no doubt that the coastal road would have headed north to it. The bridge wouldn't be there unless it was necessary.

The Danish column stretched for a long way but eventually the stragglers caught up with the main body. Shortly afterwards the scouts came back to report failure. There was another discussion and then the whole column formed up ready to attack the bridge. The enemy had two dozen archers and they moved ahead of the rest, presumably to try and weaken our guard at the bridge.

I climbed up an oak tree so that I could see what was going on. As soon as the Danes fired their first arrows over the palisade at the far side of the bridge, a roof of shields appeared so that the volley did little or no damage. Before they could knock a second arrow to their bowstrings, the thirty archers I had stationed there responded and a dozen enemy bowmen fell. This was repeated three times before the remnants of the Danish archers decided that enough was enough and they hastily withdrew. So far so good.

I had been in command for many an ambush and small scale skirmish, sometimes against much larger enemy forces, and I had fought in several battles, occasionally leading a sizable contingent of the army, but this was my first large scale battle where I was in sole charge. I therefore felt more than a little apprehensive. If I lost, then Wessex would lose half its field army and Ælfred would be at Guðrum's mercy. It was a heavy responsibility and I felt it keenly.

After another discussion amongst the enemy jarls, Oscatel, who was evidently the Danes' leader, sent in his most fearsome warriors, the berserkers. I had heard of them but I had never before seen them in action. They were Norse warriors who reputedly took drugs to work themselves up into a frenzy and who then fought with uncontrolled ferocity. They were impervious to pain and ignored even the most serious of wounds in an effort to kill their enemies.

They believed that they were favoured by their gods and, so I had been told by Erik, sought death in battle so that the Valkyries would carry them straight to Odin's side in Valhalla. That made them almost invincible.

I wondered where they had come from. Ubba's men were Norsemen from Irlond, but I hadn't heard of any Norsemen with Guðrum's army. They had all gone north with Halfdan, or so I believed. Perhaps they were with a contingent who had joined him recently? However, where they had come from was immaterial. I just prayed that we could defeat them.

There were a score, bare-chested and daubed with strange designs in blue. Each carried a sword, axe or spear, but no shield and their heads were bare. They cavorted like madmen, chanting in a language I'd not heard before. Then suddenly they set off at a sprint towards the bridge. They seemed to fly across it and then leaped high in the air. One even cleared the newly erected palisade but most either tried to claw their way up it or landed far enough up for them to grasp the top and haul themselves over it.

I couldn't see the far side of the palisade, but the sound of furious fighting reached me, although muted by distance. I saw one of my warriors lean over the parapet to stab down at one of the berserkers who was trying to clamber his way up the smooth tree trunks. The spear point entered the Norseman's shoulder but he ignored it. Instead he reached up and grabbed at the spear. Instead of letting go, my man tried to pull it back and was suddenly yanked from his perch on the walkway. He landed with a sickening crunch on the other side of the parapet and, before he could get to his feet, the berserker grabbed his helmeted head and gave it a savage twist. He let go and the warrior rolled down the sloping rampart like a rag doll. It was a terrifying sight, but I didn't have time to dwell on it. With a yell, Oscatel led his Danes forward in a charge across the bridge.

I saw with amazement that two of the berserkers had grabbed the tree trunks of which the palisade was constructed and were tearing them out of the ground. If they opened the gap much wider the Danes could storm through it and my plan would come to naught. As I watched anxiously I saw Wealhmær and another of my men stab one of the berserkers repeatedly with their swords. His wounds would have incapacitated any normal man but the berserker killed one man with an axe before Wealhmær chopped halfway through his neck. Even he couldn't survive that.

The sole surviving berserker tugged another tree trunk out of the ground before three arrows hit him at point blank range. One of them must have pierced his heart because he fell and rolled to the bottom of the rampart where he lay unmoving.

By now Oscatel and the leading Danes were pounding across the bridge. A score of arrows rained down on the leading Danes from the top of the rampart. Several of the leading Danes fell, but not Oscatel. He reached the bottom of the rampart and climbed up to the gap, where he was met by a wall of shields closing the hole in the defences.

A number of Danes had followed him up the slope but they were unable to breach the shieldwall. Several fell to the spears poking through the interlocked shields but Oscatel miraculously escaped.

Meanwhile, more and more arrows poured down on the Danes crowding the bridge. Eventually they realised that the situation was hopeless and started to withdraw. Even Oscatel gave up and, bleeding from cuts to his biceps and legs, he joined the retreat. This was the moment I'd been waiting for.

As the Danes moved back, twelve hundred Saxons emerged from the trees and charged towards the unprepared Danes. At the same time archers hidden in the tops of the trees fired volley after volley into the enemy.

We were outnumbered, but the Danes had been starved into submission at Werhām, had lost their fleet, had seen their berserkers wiped out, had been left behind by Guðrum and had now failed to capture the bridge. Their morale was at rock bottom and they were disorganised.

I wasn't sure how the fyrd would behave. They would be frightened and hyped up at the same time. Would they remember what they had to do? Thankfully most did. They halted a hundred yards from the Danes and formed a shieldwall. Not all did and some charged into the midst of the Danes where they were quickly cut down.

Oscatel's army were enveloped by my shieldwall on two sides and had the river and the unassailable bridge at their back. Although they still outnumbered us, they were crammed together and most were no more than spectators to what followed. The moment had come and I sprang my last surprise. Another sixty of my archers had hidden in the rushes growing along the river bank south of the battlefield. Now they emerged and lined up, sending volley after volley into the exposed left flank of the packed mass of Danes. They could hardly fail to miss. Although many arrows failed to penetrate the shields that most of the Danes carried on their left hand side, enough missiles managed to find exposed legs, necks and even the heads of those without helmets to cause numerous casualties.

The attack by the archers was the final straw. Several hundred Danes broke away and charged towards their tormentors. The archers sent two more volleys their way, cutting down perhaps another fifty or sixty of them before they turned and ran, heading for a wooded hill to the south east. Every so often they would stop and fire once more, cutting down the leading pursuers. This was enough to discourage the rest and they turned away to follow the river south instead.

It was the start of the rout. More and more Danes fled to the south, thus easing the pressure on my shieldwall, who made ground against the enemy as they pushed them back. About a hundred of the enemy were trapped against the river and were forced into it to drown. I estimated that only a third of the original army got away.

Eventually only about a hundred Danes were left. They were surrounded and I offered them the chance to surrender. All did so except one: Oscatel, who challenged me to single combat. He had sworn to kill me and he would do so, or die trying. I didn't think the contest was a fair one. He had been wounded on the arms and legs in several places and was losing quite a lot of blood. I, on the other hand, was unwounded; and I was much younger than him.

However, my men urged me to kill the swine, chanting my name over and over, and Oscatel kept calling me a coward and a woman for refusing to fight him. Eventually I agreed, but I insisted that his wounds were treated first. If I was going to fight him, I wanted it to be as fair a contest as possible.

✝✝✝

Eomær sewed up the worst of Oscatel's cuts whilst the Dane maintained a stoical silence, despite the pain he must have been in. My servant then bound them with clean white linen. I still thought that this was hardly going to be a fair fight. The jarl looked deathly pale and we were surrounded by my men, all shouting encouragement to me. The Danes who had surrendered had been taken down to the ships under guard. Ælfred could decide their fate when we reached Escanceaster, which is where one of the captives told me that Guðrum was headed.

I had given Oscatel the choice of weapons and he had opted for sword and shield. He insisted on retaining his own weapon, although the edges had been blunted in the fighting and had a number of notches. My own sword hadn't even been drawn from its scabbard since Eomær had sharpened it the previous evening.

I hefted the heavy shield on my left arm to test the weight and swung my sword through the air a few times to loosen the muscles of my right shoulder. Oscatel did the same but his movements were slow as if he was in great pain. Of course, he might well be, given his wounds, but I thought that it was more likely that he was trying to lull me into overconfidence.

His first attack was slow and deliberate and had I been less experienced I might have been fooled into a parry followed by a thrust in order to end this quickly. However, I didn't fall for it. He suddenly changed the clumsy swing at my head to a thrust towards my shoulder. His speed was unbelievable. However, instead of parrying his feint, I leant back out of the way and twisted to avoid the follow up, bringing my shield up a split second later to hit him on the chest. He backed away slightly winded.

I noticed with surprise that the failure of his ploy had made him angry. That was a good thing. To win a sword fight you needed a cool head. His next move was a series of blistering attacks, aiming for my head, legs and right arm in turn. He was fast and his blows were powerful but I managed to turn them all aside with my sword and shield.

He withdrew to get his breath back and now it was my turn to go on the offensive. However, instead of raining blows down on him, I thrust at his head and, when he drew back out of the way, he was off balance for a second. I used the moment to thrust the point of my sword into his right thigh just above the knee. That hurt and it showed. Before he could recover I brought my shield around and smashed the boss into his face.

His nose was protected by the nasal on his helmet, but I had put a lot of force behind it and the metal guard did nothing to stop me flattening his nose and knocking out several of his front teeth. For an instant he was blinded by pain and I used the opportunity presented to move sideways so that I could cut into the rear of his knee with my sword. It was still reasonably sharp and it sliced through flesh and tendons, crippling him.

He was done and he knew it. For a split-second I considered toying with him and inflicting a slow death upon him, but that wasn't in my nature. I knocked him flat on his back with my shield before pushing the point of my sword down through his neck. It was over. One of the leaders of the Danish host was dead, but Guðrum and Ubba were still at large.

# Chapter Twelve

## THE BATTLE OF CYNUIT

## Late Summer 877

When Guðrum had surrendered to King Ælfred at Escanceaster in July, he and his remaining warriors were escorted over the border and back into Mercia. I thought that at last peace had come to Wessex. It had, but it was destined to be of short duration.

Accompanied by the fleet, I sailed back to Hamwic, where I left Bjarne with half the ships before continuing on my way with the remainder to Dofras.

Of course, we couldn't continue to man every ship after the fyrd returned home, but I managed to keep half of them at sea. The rest were taken out of the water, had their hulls cleaned and re-caulked and were then laid up.

As soon as I could get away I set off for Cantwareburh for a reunion with my children, who had been taken there so that Hilda could care for them in my absence. Of course, much as I wanted to see the four of them and see how much they had grown in the past fifteen months, my heart raced at the thought of seeing Hilda again. Her period of mourning was now a distant memory and one of the first things I intended to do was to propose to her.

I was so eager to go that I only took Eomær and Wolnoth with me. The latter was an orphan who had joined me in Northumbria nine years previously. He was a quiet man who always kept himself to himself. He was a good tracker, hunter and pathfinder but he seemed to prefer his own company to that of others. At first I thought that something was bothering him but, as time went on, I came to the conclusion that he just enjoyed solitude.

Recently he seemed to have become more morose and the main reason I had chosen him to accompany me was in the hope of finding out if there really was something wrong. However, when I asked him about it he assured me that he was fine. I didn't believe him. Eventually I discovered that he had fallen in love with a girl but didn't know how to go about approaching her.

I was about to explain that he needed to act, not brood, when he held up his hand and we came to a halt in the middle of the muddy road.

'Stay here,' he whispered as he dismounted and led his horse into the trees.

I didn't know what Wolnoth had heard or sensed but I trusted his instincts completely. I loosened my sword in its scabbard and Eomær dismounted before stringing his bow.

Suddenly there was a crashing sound to our left and four men and a child emerged from the dense undergrowth. At first I didn't recognise their leader but something about him rang a bell. Then I realised who he was; it was Cerdic - the rescued thrall who'd caused me so much trouble in Mercia three years previously.

'I've been waiting for you, lord,' he said nastily. The way he pronounced lord conveyed utter contempt rather than respect. 'As soon as I heard you were back in Dofras I knew it wouldn't be long before you went to Cantwareburh to have your lustful way with the Lady Hilda.'

'Cerdic! I rather hoped I'd seen the last of you. Don't you dare let her name pass your foul lips. I should have killed you three years ago.'

'But you didn't; instead I intend to kill you, and slowly, to make up for the miserable years I've had to spend as an outlaw.'

'What, you and this ragtag bunch of misfits?'

I let my gaze wander over his companions. One was an ox of a man who hefted a heavy double-handed battleaxe as if it weighed nothing. He was probably the most dangerous of the lot. A thin youth held a bow with an arrow nocked ready but both were poorly made. I doubted that the bow was very powerful and the arrow didn't appear to be very straight. An elderly man held a rusty sword in his hand but he was plainly nervous and the fifth outlaw was a boy with a knife who looked to be about twelve. He might be young but he had a wild and feral look. It would be unwise to underestimate the threat he posed.

Cerdic had bridled at the insult but he managed to retain a hold on his temper.

'You, boy,' he said, pointing at Eomær, 'I have no quarrel with you. Drop your bow and you may go.'

My body servant didn't reply but he raised his bow and pointed the arrow at Cerdic, who licked his lips nervously.

'Kill them both,' he screeched jumping to the side as Eomær released his arrow.

I had expected it to be a wasted shot, which would leave us at a severe disadvantage, but he'd changed his aim when he saw Cerdic jump sideways. The arrow struck the big man with the axe in the neck. He'd been totally unprepared for it and he sank to his knees, dropping his axe and clawing at the arrow.

There was a stunned silence. The thin bowman let fly his own arrow aiming at Eomær, which was a stupid thing to do as, having released his arrow, Eomær wasn't a threat for the moment. As I'd expected, the outlaw's arrow didn't fly true. He had aimed at Eomær' chest; instead it struck him in the shoulder.

Furious that my servant had been wounded, I yanked back the reins of my horse and it reared up, his iron shod hooves flailing as he did so. The old man had summoned up the courage to rush forward just at that moment and so he was the one who was struck by the hooves. They crushed his skull like an eggshell and he dropped without a sound.

Cerdic launched himself at me screaming imprecations as he dragged me from my horse. We both crashed to muddy ground but I landed on top. I smashed my gloved fist into Cerdic's face and rolled away. The thin bowman stood above me with a dagger in his hand and I thought my time had come; but then he arched his back and dropped to the ground. I barely had time to register the fact that he had an arrow jutting from his back when Cerdic launched himself at me once more.

We had both lost our weapons and he bit and scratched at me whilst I tried to fend him off with my arms and hands. Out of the corner of my eye I saw the feral boy staring fixedly at me, waiting for an opening to gut me. Seconds later a second arrow struck Cerdic in the back and his limp body fell on top of me. I struggled to push him off me before the boy had a chance to attack me but, when I succeeded I found that he'd disappeared. It was only then that I noticed that he'd stabbed Eomær before he fled.

I rushed over to him and checked him over. He was still breathing but the boy had stabbed him in the side and I didn't know what damage had been done internally. I tore off strips of my white linen under-tunic and held it against the wound with one hand whilst I frantically searched in the pouch at his belt for catgut and a needle. I looked around for Wolnoth, for it must have been him who'd shot both Cerdic and the outlaw with the bow, but I couldn't see him.

I washed the wound clean with water from my leather bottle, then sewed the wound up before using more of my under-tunic to bind it. Then I looked at the arrow. It had penetrated the flesh but there was no barbed point and I pulled it out easily. Again I washed the wound and sewed it up before bandaging it.

Just as I'd finished Wolnoth appeared holding the struggling urchin. Evidently he'd tracked him down after the boy had fled.

'Is Eomær alright, lord?' Wolnoth asked, looking concerned.

'I hope so, but it depends what internal damage this spawn of Satan did with his dagger.'

I glared at the boy, who continued to struggle and utter foul-mouthed imprecations. I got up and hit him hard across the face to shut him up. He looked startled and then spat out a gob of blood before cursing me further.

'If he dies, you die. Do you understand?' I hissed at him menacingly.

He shut up and nodded sullenly.

'And if he lives, do I live?' he asked after a moment.

'I'll think about it, now do you know where we can get a cart?'

For a moment I thought the boy would refuse to help but a slap about the head from Wolnoth changed his mind.

'There's a farmstead a mile further on,' he muttered.

'I'll go and get the cart,' Wolnoth volunteered.

I nodded my thanks and he mounted and rode off.

'What's your name, boy?'

For a moment I thought he wasn't going to answer then he surprised me by saying that he couldn't remember. His story was a sad one. His father had killed his mother in a drunken argument and he'd grabbed a knife and killed his father in revenge. He'd fled into the woods and eked out a living, drinking from streams and eating wild berries and the flesh of dead animals like a carrion crow. He didn't know how long he lived like that but eventually Cerdic and his band had found him and he'd joined them after they offered him food. That was a month ago.

I'd been furious with the boy for wounding Eomær but, after hearing his story, I felt nothing but pity for him. Brought up being beaten by an abusive father and then living like an animal went a long way to explain his outlook on life. Nevertheless he was an outlaw and, by his own admission, a killer. Normally I would have hanged him from the nearest tree and that would have been that. But I'd more or less promised him his life if he looked after Eomær and nursed him back to health and I would keep my word.

✝✝✝

My arrival accompanied by an ox cart wasn't quite the way I had envisioned returning to Hilda. We had borrowed the cart from a ceorl and it was driven by his son. No doubt he didn't trust us to return it otherwise.

Eomær lay on a bed of straw in the cart, trying not to moan with pain whilst the feral boy tended to him: cleaning up when he was sick and feeding him sips of water. Now that he had someone to care for, the boy seemed transformed. As he had put his name, along with memories of his unhappy past, into the furthest recesses of his mind, I decided to call him Eafer, which meant wild boar. He seemed not only to like the name, but to be rather proud of it.

I had been looking forward to our reunion immensely, but now the moment had come I found myself feeling like a callow youth, anxious and shy. Hilda also seemed nervous. I suppose that it was really surprising; we hardly knew one another and it had been fifteen months since we'd last seen each other.

'Who's in the cart,' she asked as soon as we'd greeted each other.

'My servant, Eomær. We were attacked by outlaws on the way here. The boy attending to him is the one who wounded him.'

'Good gracious! Do you trust him?'

'Not in the least, but Wolnoth will keep an eye on him. The boy has had a hard life up to now but I think I can turn him around, with God's help.'

'That's one of the things I love about you, you're a warrior, but one with compassion.'

'What are the other things you love about me?' I murmured as we went inside the hall.

It was a good beginning and I allowed myself to hope for a successful outcome.

We didn't have much more chance to speak again until the evening. As soon as we entered the gloomy hall I was attacked. Cuthfleda threw her arms around my waist and hugged me hard. Æscwin did the same, although he was only big enough to grab my thigh.

The two twins - Ywer and Kjestin – toddled unsteadily towards me, watched carefully by their nurse – and then stood wide-eyed regarding me. Meanwhile Hilda's son stood looking at us uncertainly.

My elder son let go of me and took his friend by the hand, pulling him forward.

'Father, this is Oswine, he's a month younger than me and we do everything together,' Æscwin said confidently. 'I wish he was my brother,' he added wistfully, giving a disparaging look towards Ywer.

I laughed. 'Ywer will soon grow and I'm sure he'll make a fine playmate for you. In the meantime, I'll see what I can do about making Oswine your brother.'

I gave Hilda a mischievous look and she blushed. It was an oblique way to make a proposal but I knew from her reaction that she would say yes.

We were married two weeks later. The archbishop himself presided and my eldest brother, Æscwin, who I had just made the Shire Reeve of Cent, acted as groomsman. Hilda was attended by Cuthfleda with the younger Æscwin and Oswine supposedly helping her.

The day was hot, even for August, and I sweltered in my thick scarlet wool tunic and cloak of bright blue as I stood in the sunshine outside the monastery church waiting for my bride. Then she appeared and all thoughts of discomfort were forgotten. Hilda was eighteen and I'd never seen anyone look prettier than she did on her wedding day. She was dressed in virginal white, despite the fact that she'd had a son with her first husband, and her luxuriant hair, bound by a circlet of gold, framed her perfect oval face. Tomorrow her hair would be covered, but today she was showing it off.

The service itself and the feast that followed back up in my hall passed by in a blur. The next thing I knew I was in bed with my beloved. I thought that she would be a gentle lover but I was in for a surprise. From the start she was wild and passionate and the next morning I had a few scars on my back and bites on my neck to prove it. Not that I minded. I just hoped that I would have the stamina to keep up with her.

The next two months were the best of my life to date. I was loved by the woman I was infatuated with and I got to know my children properly for the first time. I even taught Æscwin and Oswine the basic principles of riding on two small ponies I had found for them. One of the happiest moments was when Oswine called me father for the first time.

Eomær made a full recovery in time, tended conscientiously by Eafer. After five weeks he was well enough to return to his duties as my body servant and I kept my word and rewarded Eafer with his freedom. To my surprise he elected to stay and became a servant in my hall. I suppose it wasn't surprising that he and Eomær became as close as brothers.

Of course, I couldn't spend all my time with my family and I occasionally rode over to Dofras to check that there were no problems that I needed to resolve.

Once Hilda came with me, but she found anything to do with warfare and maritime affairs quite boring. In that respect she couldn't have been more dissimilar to Leofflæd. I realised quite quickly that she resented the time I was away from her, but I was both the ealdorman and Ælfred's sǣ hereræswa and I wasn't about to neglect my duties.

We had our first row when I announced my intention of sailing to Hamwic to see Bjarne before winter set in. Despite the fact that I assured her that I shouldn't be away for more than a week, Hilda refused to acknowledge that my visit was necessary. We parted without making up and part of me wanted to punish my wife for being so unreasonable. I therefore tarried at Hamwic longer than was strictly necessary, so I was still there when Ælfred's messenger arrived.

†††

It was late in the year to be sailing the high seas, but I had little option if I was going to arrive in time. It had taken me a little time to put together all the pieces since the king's letter had arrived, but I concluded that Ubba had probably set sail from Sveinsey intending to join up with Guðrum, who had captured Glowecestre in Mercia. It seemed more than likely as Glowecestre was a settlement near the River Sæfern, not far upriver from the estuary.

It should have been a short and straightforward voyage along the south coast of Wealas and then up the river. However, Ubba's fleet must have got caught in yet another storm and were blown southwards across the sea to be wrecked on the north coast of Dyfneintscīr near a place called Cynuit.

Instead of moving inland straight away, Ubba spent time gathering together his scattered ships' crews and, by the time that he was ready to head for Glowecestre on foot, the nearby hill fort had been occupied by the local fyrd. Ubba had launched an attack but, by this time Odda, the Ealdorman of Dyfneintscīr had arrived with his personal warband.

The Norsemen had been repulsed but there was no water supply in the old fort and Ubba controlled access to the only source locally. The Norsemen therefore sat down to wait for Odda's surrender. Most of it was supposition on my part, but it fitted the known facts.

Whatever the truth was, Odda had sent a messenger to Wintanceaster to inform the king about Ubba and his own predicament and, as I was at Hamwic when Ælfred's order came for the fleet there to go to Lord Odda's aid. I took command of all the available ships and we put to sea.

My forty three ships with fourteen hundred men aboard arrived at the mouth of the River Lyn, some two miles from the hill fort, ten days later. The Viking longships which had survived the storm were moored or anchored near the mouth of the river and so our first task was to capture them and eliminate those left to guard them. It wasn't difficult and it was soon over. Some of the warriors put up a fight but the old men and the ships' boys quickly surrendered. I left them under guard, hoping that I could convert them to Christianity later and take them into my service.

I took twelve hundred men with me to Odda's relief, dispatching Hrodulf, Oscgar, Ædwulf and Acwel with Wolnoth to reconnoitre ahead of us. Acwel came back after an hour and I halted the column.

'The old hill fort is surrounded on three sides by a steep sided valley,' he reported. 'There is a steep slope which approaches it from the south west and that's where the Vikings have set up a fortified camp. There's a stream at the bottom of the valley and it meets another one just to the north of the hill. Wolnoth says that there's another camp there but it's not fortified.'

'Excellent, well done Acwel.'

The youth beamed with pleasure at my praise for the succinctness and usefulness of his report.

'Did you see any sign of movement on top of the hill?' I asked.

'Yes, there's a gap in the ramparts at the top of the slope and I could see four Saxons guarding it. There were several more patrolling to the top of the ramparts.'

I breathed a sigh of relief. I wasn't too late; Odda and his fyrd were still alive. I did wonder how they had lasted so long on what water they had with them, but perhaps they managed to sneak down the steep slopes under cover of darkness and fill up containers.

The obvious course of action was to deploy into line and attack up the normal approach. However, I was never one to do the obvious. A lot of the ships with me were birlinns and they each had a complement of between twenty and thirty archers. They were all adept at fighting at sea; how much more accurate would they be on land?

Ubba's Norsemen felt themselves secure in their tents of oiled wool behind their fortifications. My surprise attack would soon dispel their complacency. We always carried a small supply of pitch pine on board for repairs to the caulking. I hoped we weren't going to need it as I was about to put it to another use.

We moved into position an hour before dawn and my archers built small stone walls to hide our fires from the enemy, then they melted the pitch pine in small metal pots. Once it was soft enough, they dipped their arrow heads, which had rags tied near the points, in the sticky pitch pine. Some of my other men used slivers of wood, lit in the fire, to ignite the rags.

As soon as the ends were sufficiently alight, each archer sent his arrow arcing through the night sky to land inside the camp. Then they all did the same again, and they kept the fire arrows going at a steady pace.

Some landed in the earth and did no damage, others hit men and set their clothing alight; however, the best results were achieved by those which struck the tents. The fire spread rapidly through the oil impregnated wool and tents went up remarkably quickly.

Within a few minutes I could see whole sections of Ubba's encampment ablaze. The fires silhouetted the sentries on the ramparts and soon they became targets for my archers. This time fire arrows weren't necessary. The Vikings soon learned the lesson and they withdrew behind the earthen ramparts.

Dawn was just breaking when the enemy got themselves sufficiently organised to sally forth in strength. They had wasted time trying to put the fires out before giving up. As soon as they had managed to put one out, more fire arrows would arrive.

I tried to gauge Ubba's strength and I estimated that he had about seven to eight hundred warriors. As the early September light grew stronger I scanned the ranks of the enemy and breathed a sigh of relief when I couldn't see any berserkers. I wouldn't guarantee that my skypfyrd would stand firm against them in the open. The Norse made a lot of noise, shouting insults and banging their weapons against their shields. To counter it we sang the psalm, the Lord is my Shepherd.

Suddenly the whole line of Norsemen surged forward. Facing them were an equal number of Saxons; some experienced warriors, but mostly ordinary men who served on my ships as rowers and were only occasional fighters. The Vikings were charging downhill; they must have thought that they were in for an easy victory.

The hillside itself was open meadowland but the sides, where the tongue of land fell away to the stream below, was wooded. I had stationed my archers in two groups: one behind the shieldwall and one in the woods on the north side. The rest of my warriors – those not in the shieldwall – were hidden in the woods to the south. They waited down the hill, in dead ground from any stray arrows from the bowmen in the woods opposite.

When the leading Vikings were a hundred yards from my shieldwall three notes on a horn blared forth and arrows from behind the shieldwall and from the Vikings' right flank darkened the sky like a murmuration of starlings about to migrate. Perhaps a hundred of Ubba's men fell to that first volley. The rest came to a skidding halt, some falling over and bringing others down with them.

They had been unnerved by the number of casualties they had suffered, but a warrior with long fair hair who stood head and shoulders above the rest yelled at them to charge our shieldwall. I didn't need the gold circlet and the engraving of a raven on the sides of his helmet to tell me that this was Ubba himself.

A second volley tore into them and then I saw what I had been waiting for: Odda leading his men in a charge into the rear ranks of the demoralised Vikings. They erupted from the gap in the ramparts and hared down the slope towards their enemies. Ubba was now being assailed on all sides.

The problem with the fyrd is that they aren't as disciplined as seasoned warriors. Seeing the men of Dyfneintscīr coming to join them, most of the men in our shieldwall charged into the enemy. I groaned with dismay. The Norsemen would cut them down with ease and, worse, my archers couldn't shoot again for fear of hitting our own men.

My own warband had resisted the urge to join in the general melee and stood in their original place in what had been the front rank of the shieldwall.

'Close together,' I yelled at them and I rode over to join them, taking my standard bearer and my signaller with me.

We dismounted and I shouldered my way to a place in the centre of the line. The time had come to stop being the commander directing the battle and to lead by example. The fyrd were losing and I sensed that they were on the verge of fleeing the field. Many of Odda's men were already streaming back uphill to the safety of the hill fort. I formed my warband into a wedge and we charged.

We shouldered aside those of my skypfyrd who were in our way and started to kill the enemy as we forced our way into the centre of their packed ranks. We had practiced this tactic many times and because those in the outer rank on the right hand side carried their shields on the wrong arm, it was difficult for the Vikings to attack us. We, on the other hand, could use our spears to stab the enemy as we forced our way deeper into their midst.

When the men of Dyfneintscīr and my own skypfyrd saw our success they gained more confidence and renewed the fight. The Norsemen were now being assailed on all sides once more. By this stage the wedge had lost momentum and we were forced to form a circle to defend ourselves. I cut down an inexperienced youth who was standing in front of me but he was swiftly replaced by an elderly man wielding a two-handed battleaxe. He whirled it over his head and brought it down towards me. I managed to raise my shield in time but the axe split it at the top, numbing my left arm in the process.

I pulled my shield to one side and the axe stayed embedded in it. This left the chest of its owner exposed and I thrust with my sword. The point struck the old Viking in the centre of his ribcage and penetrated his byrnie, leather tunic and flesh before passing through his ribcage and puncturing his heart. He fell to the floor, dropping the axe, but my sword was trapped between his ribs and it was dragged out of my hand.

I scrabbled for my seax and had just managed to draw it when my next adversary appeared. I didn't notice the expensive helmet but I knew the man was Ubba just from his size. He towered over me and his face was twisted into a vicious snarl. Had I had the luxury of time to look at him I would have seen that he was covered in gore and blood, none of it his own.

He roared with rage and brought his sword around in a bid to chop straight through my neck. I managed to raise my shield in time but the heavy axe embedded in it made it next to useless. The power behind the blow forced me down on one knee and the shield fell apart leaving me completely vulnerable.

I raised my seax in a feeble effort to parry the next blow but it never landed. Eomær had followed me carrying my banner and had stayed close behind me so he hadn't been involved in any fighting. Perhaps he thought it his duty, but all he had succeeded in doing was to identify me as the Saxon commander. No doubt that was why Ubba had sought me out; kill me and he'd won the battle.

Eomær kept the standard upright but drew his knife with his other hand. He thrust it into Ubba's eye and into his brain. The Viking leader looked for a brief instant as if he couldn't believe that he'd been slain by a boy but then the light went out of the other eye and he fell to the ground. The last of the Ragnarssons was dead.

Word quickly spread through the ranks of his men and, surrounded as they were, most surrendered. About a hundred fought on and they died to a man. Guðrum would wait in vain for his reinforcements from Irlond.

# Chapter Thirteen

## CIPPENHAMME

## January 878

Not only had we beaten Ubba and either killed or taken prisoner his entire force, but Ealdorman Odda's son had captured the Hrefn, the Raven Banner. This had once belonged to King Ragnar Lodbrok and had been the rallying point for recruiting the original Great Heathen Army.

My men and I might have been instrumental in winning a great victory, and Eomær might have been the slayer of Ubba, but the glory went to Odda and his son Eadred for capturing the Hrefn. I'd like to say that I didn't mind the praise that was heaped on Odda and the men of Dyfneintscīr, but I'd be lying.

In return for his heroic action in saving my life, I made Eomær a member of my warband and Eafer became my body servant in his place. Up to then he'd been a ship's boy on board the Saint Cuthbert and he seemed genuinely pleased by the change in role.

I returned home expecting a frosty reception from Hilda, given the terms under which we'd parted, but I was given a welcome such as only the prodigal son had received. It was as if we'd never argued and I certainly wasn't going to bring the matter up.

Autumn passed peacefully and I was looking forward to spending Yuletide with Hilda and my children at Dofras. However, a messenger arrived with another letter from Ælfred. He was spending the Christmas season at his hunting lodge at Cippanhamme with his family and a few close companions. We were invited to join him.

'Do we have to go?' Hilda said sulkily. 'I was so looking forward to spending Christmas here with you and the children.'

'An invitation from the king is a command, my love. I fear we have to go. We'll still be together, but we can't take all the children. Ywer and Kjestin are too young.'

'So are Æscwin and Oswine!' she retorted. 'It's too long a journey for us in a carriage, especially at this time of year.'

'I agree; the roads will be difficult after all the rain we've had recently but it'll be quicker by sea,' I replied.

'By sea?' she said, horrified by the idea. 'At this time of year! Do you want to be lost in a storm?'

'We can always take shelter if the weather turns nasty,' I pointed out. 'I'm not suggesting going all the way there by ship; just as far as Hamwic. We'll travel by road from there.'

To me it seemed like a sensible compromise but Hilda was adamant that I wouldn't get her or her son on a ship in winter. We argued about it for what seemed like weeks but which was in reality a couple of days. In the end we parted on bad terms once again, but she did reluctantly agree that Oswine could go, mainly because both boys kept pleading with her not to be parted.

I took my leave of Hilda and the twins and set out with a leaden heart. However, I soon cheered up once I was at sea. I always experienced a sense of freedom once we'd cast off. My cares seemed to be left behind on land, although the sea had enough perils of its own. I suppose it was because I was my own master with neither king, nor wife nor legal disputes to bother about.

The voyage along the coast was uneventful, if rather cold. I was glad of my bearskin cloak and made sure that the children kept as warm and dry as possible. Cuthfleda was now nine and she reminded me increasingly of her mother. Of my two eldest children, she was the adventurous one. She loved being on board and told me she wanted to be a ship's boy when she was a little older. I hadn't the heart to tell her that it wasn't a role for girls, especially not ealdormen's daughters.

Æscwin, on the other hand, tended to huddle by himself in the stern and pray. I sighed. He would be my heir but he seemed more likely to end up as a cleric than a warrior. Still, I comforted myself, he wasn't yet seven. Perhaps he would change? However, in my heart I knew he wouldn't.

Our arrival at Hamwic caught Bjarne by surprise but he hastened to find accommodation for us all. The crew of my skeid was eighty strong, the minimum needed. I didn't think we'd encounter any Viking longships at this time of year and so I hadn't packed her with warriors or archers. However, I didn't need them all as escort for the second stage of the journey. Besides there were only a score of horses at Hamwic.

In the end I took a dozen men with me in addition to Eafer. I found a small mare for Cuthfleda but none were small enough for my son or for Oswine. Consequently I sat him in front of me and Erik took Oswine. It was seventy miles to Cippanhamme and normally it would have taken a couple of days, but with the children I decided to take it a little slower with frequent rest stops. Consequently we arrived at the king's hunting lodge four days later, muddy and wet.

Cippanhamme was not what I was expecting. It was enclosed by the River Afne on three sides. The other was protected by a ditch and rampart surmounted by a twelve foot high palisade. The ditch was filled with water from the river with no crossing point. The only entrance was via a wooden bridge to the north which was guarded by a gate and a tower. The timber bridge was just wide enough for a cart and was the only entrance.

For a settlement it was quite small, housing perhaps a score of ceorls, their families and slaves. The inhabitants supported the monastery as well as the hall, which the kings of Wessex used as a hunting lodge. There were quite a few empty huts for guests and a long stable block as well as dog kennels. We had seen a large forest to the north and east of the settlement and it was presumably the reason that Ælfred had chosen to spend Yuletide here. Even at the start of winter there should be deer, boar and perhaps wolves to hunt.

As we clattered over the narrow bridge we were stopped, not by members of the king's own warband, but by warriors serving Wulfhere, the Ealdorman of Wiltunscīr. I was later to discover that Ælfred had only brought twenty five of his gesith with him as escort for himself and his family. Apart from myself and my children, the only other guests were Wulfhere and Odda, who was a widower, and his eldest son. Wulfhere hadn't even brought his own wife and children, which I thought was odd. Hilda had an excuse for not coming - it was a long way from Cent – but this was Wulfhere's own shire.

I was shown to a small hut which had been set aside for our use. My men were taken to the warriors' hall as soon as they had taken care of their horses. Once I had made myself presentable I took Æscwin, Cuthfleda and Oswine to greet the king and his family. Ælfred was sitting with the Lady Ealhswith, Wulfhere, Odda, Eadred and his wife at the high table talking and drinking mead. The king's two children, Eadward and Æthelflaed, sat playing some game with their nurse. The girl was now seven and Eadward was two and a half.

The only other people in the hall were Bishop Asser and a man I took to be the Abbot of Cippanhamme. They were engaged in earnest conversation in one corner. I presented the children to the king and Ealhswith before sending them over to join the other children. Cuthfleda began a lively conversation with Æthelflaed and Oswine played with the king's son but Æscwin soon got bored and, to my alarm, he went over to speak to the two senior

217

churchmen. At first they gave every indication of being affronted at being interrupted by a small child but soon they were both engaged in earnest discussion with my son, who sat himself at their feet.

Odda and I were talking to the king about our success at Cynuit, each paying due regard to the part played by the other, when the door opened once more to admit two newcomers. To say that I was surprised to see the king's nephews would be an understatement. Æthelhelm was as amiable a young man as ever, even if he did seem somewhat dim witted. The younger, Æthelwold, was completely different.

He had recently turned sixteen and he appeared to be as affable as his brother on the surface. However, as soon as he thought that no one was looking at him, the looks he gave both Ælfred and the infant Eadward smouldered with hatred. His resentment at being passed over for the throne when his father, King Æðelred, had died was well known, of course. I wouldn't have thought much more about it if I hadn't caught a look which passed between him and Ealdorman Wulfhere. It could only be described as conspiratorial. I had a prickly sensation at the back of my neck; there was something going on here that didn't bode well for the king or his family.

I continued to remain alert for any further signs of danger but Christmas came and went without incident. By now the first snow had normally put in an appearance but the weather remained mild and damp. The first day of the year was traditionally one on which the largest hunt was staged. For a change the day dawned bright and cold. There had been a frost overnight and so the ground was good going for the horses, if a little slippery at first.

The huntsmen set off with the greyhounds to locate the quarry followed by more men with alaunts straining at the leash. The alaunt was a dog which had been bred as a fearless attack dog. It was used to bring down stags and boars once they had been found by the greyhounds. Even their handlers had to be careful around them and they had been known to kill men who they didn't know by ripping out their throats.

The king waited until the huntsmen were a quarter of a mile clear of the bridge before leading the rest of us out into the forest. Although parts of it were densely wooded most of it was open grassland interspersed with thickets of trees. It was ideal country for hunting on horseback. I kept as close as I could to the king and I set Erik and Wolnoth to watching Wulfhere and Æthelwold respectively.

We had just entered a wood when we heard the excited barking of dogs ahead of us. Ælfred kicked his horse into a canter and we streamed out of the wood in pursuit. Out of the corner of my eye I saw that Æthelwold was trying to edge closer to the king and so I spurred my horse into a gallop to place myself between them. I saw the king's nephew put his hand on his seax and for a moment I thought that he was about to try and kill me in order to get at Ælfred, then we entered more trees and he was forced to veer away.

A minute later we entered a clearing where the dogs had a stag at bay. The greyhounds had been leashed but the alaunts kept trying to attack it. One of the dogs had already been gored to death and another lay whimpering nearby with a deep gash in its side. One of the huntsmen cut its throat and the whining stopped.

The other two dogs kept prowling back and forth, trying to find an opening, but the stag kept sweeping its head with its gore tipped antlers to and fro. It was breathing heavily and it was obviously close to exhaustion.

The huntsmen called off the dogs and one seemed glad enough to obey, but the other hound refused. Suddenly it leapt in the air and sank its teeth into the deer's neck. The stag shook his head furiously but it failed to dislodge the alaunt. So the stag backed up and swung its head again, this time crushing the dog against a tree trunk. The dog howled in agony and dropped to the ground, its ribcage crushed.

The stag was tired and badly wounded. It was time to finish it. One of his gesith handed Ælfred a spear as he dismounted. Taking careful aim the king threw the spear so that it struck the animal in the centre of its chest. However, the heart of a deer lay deep within its chest cavity, immediately above its forelegs. The spear did no more than wound it further. Suddenly it bolted into the trees behind it.

It wouldn't go far but it was against convention to allow a wounded animal to suffer. The king was honour bound to follow it and kill it properly. He didn't wait to mount up, but grabbed another spear and ran after the stag. I was caught by surprise and before I could follow him I saw both Wulfhere and one of his warriors take off after Ælfred.

I followed immediately but Æthelwold tried to head me off.

'Get out of my way!' I yelled as I shoulder charged him.

He fell off his horse with a startled yelp and I plunged into the relative darkness of the wood. I could hear the chase ahead of me but I couldn't see anyone. There was no proper path, just a track made by animals and thin branches and brambles whipped my face and snagged my clothing as I cantered on. Then suddenly I emerged into another clearing. I arrived just in time to see Wulfhere draw back his arm and throw his spear at the king's back.

Something must have warned Ælfred because he ducked at the last moment and the spear whistled over his head to end up in the side of the stag. The animal's forelegs buckled and it rolled over onto its side.

'A thousand apologies, cyning. The kill should have been yours,' Wulfhere said smoothly, 'but I thought it was about to gore you.'

'If I hadn't ducked,' Ælfred said furiously, 'that spear would have ended my life instead of the stag's.'

'There was never any danger of that, cyning. Even if you hadn't moved the spear would have gone over your shoulder.'

I think that the king knew that Wulfhere was lying, but he chose to ignore it. Suddenly he smiled.

'In that case, I congratulate you on a clean kill. The stag is yours.'

†††

Nothing else untoward happened during the hunt and I breathed a sigh of relief. However, Erik came to me later to report that before the stag had been brought to bay Wulfhere had met two men in one of the thickets. He couldn't get close because four of the ealdorman's warband guarded the track that led into the trees but he had waited until after they had gone and he saw two Danes emerge and ride off to the north-west.

I wanted to warn Ælfred but he always seemed to be in the company of either Wulfhere or one of his nephews. After two days of waiting for the right moment I decided to go and talk to Odda instead.

The old man nodded sagely when I had finished telling him of my suspicions.

'I wouldn't be surprised if Wulfhere was plotting with the Danes. That man is only interested in two things: his own best interests and making more money,' he said when I'd finished. 'He bleeds his people dry with extra taxes, none of which ends up in the royal treasury. If he thinks Guðrum will win in the end, he wouldn't hesitate to betray Ælfred.'

'Then we must warn him.'

'We can't go to him without evidence,' Odda objected. 'What do we have? Wulfhere meeting two Danes? They could be his tenants; after all some have converted to Christianity and been allowed to settle here.'

'What about Wulfhere trying to kill him on the hunt?'

'But the king had already accepted Wulfhere's claim that he was merely killing a dangerously wounded animal.'

I could see that I was getting nowhere and so I dropped the matter – for now.

Twelfth Night was the next day; after that Ælfred would return to Wintanceaster and I would be free to return to Dofras. I didn't think I gained much by spending Yuletide with the king. Bishop Asser and the Lady Ealhswith clearly detested me as much as ever and now I'd made an enemy of Æthelwold as well, not that it bothered me all that much. Of course, it would prove to be a problem if he ever became king.

The one positive thing that had come out of the visit was the close friendship that had developed between Cuthfleda and Æthelflaed. I was less pleased about Æscwin's growing interest in religion and the Church. If my son couldn't be found it was usually because he was somewhere in the monastery. When Asser offered to enrol him as a novice as soon as he was old enough it was the last straw, although I think he only made the offer to annoy me.

I was looking forward to leaving the next morning when everything changed. Eafer was late coming to attend me that night and I was about to scold him when he told me what he'd overheard. My suspicions were well founded. Wulfhere had betrayed Ælfred to

223

the Danes. Guðrum had left Glowecestre with eight hundred men several days previously and was now encamped in the forest waiting for Wulfhere to leave the bridge unguarded.

I did a quick calculation. Even forewarned, we had far too few men between Odda, myself and the king to hope to defeat Guðrum and Wulfhere combined. Our only hope lay in flight.

✝✝✝

The sentries on the door of the hall stopped us when Odda and I tried to see Ælfred. They had strict orders not to admit anyone after the king had retired for the night. Thankfully one of those on duty was Odda's youngest son, Drefan, and he persuaded his fellow members of the king's gesith to let us pass. He came with us to ensure that the two sentries outside the king's chamber would also let us past. They agreed but insisted that he should be the one who announced us.

Ælfred was angry at being disturbed and started to berate Drefan but his father and I pushed past the two sentries and entered the chamber. The king stopped his diatribe and glared at us instead.

'What is the meaning of this?'

'Your life and that of your family is in danger, cyning. We must leave and leave now, before Guðrum gets here,' I told him.

'Guðrum?' he asked bewildered. 'He's in Glowecestre.'

'Not any more. He's camped a few miles from here ready to attack at dawn. Worse, Ealdorman Wulfhere has betrayed you and is league with him.'

'What? No! How do you know this?'

'Cyning, you have to trust me. There will be time for explanations later,' I said, getting a little desperate at the king's failure to believe me.

'You are trying to trick us,' Ealhswith said, appearing from the adjacent chamber where she'd been sleeping with her children.

'And am I also lying to you, lady?' Odda asked.

'Very well,' Ælfred said, getting up from the bed. 'Let's go and confront Wulfhere and see what he has to say.

I wasn't happy about it but I had no argument to put forward against it and so we waited outside whilst the king got dressed. Thankfully he told his wife to get herself and the children dressed as well, just as a precaution.

'You had better be right about this,' Ælfred said to me quietly as he led the way out of the hall and across to the hut occupied by Wulfhere.

At least the king had the sense to take six of his gesith with him. I had already alerted my own men and they, together with Odda's escort had already gone to the stables to quietly saddle the horses.

'Where is Wulfhere,' Ælfred asked the man's body servant, the only person in the hut when we entered.

'He's not here, cyning,' the frightened man replied.

'I can see that, you fool. Where is he?'

'I cannot tell you, cyning.'

'You will or you'll die here and now,' Ælfred promised him.

'He's gone to the forest,' the wide-eyed servant gabbled as I drew my seax to add weight to the king's threat.

'Why?'

'I overheard him say that he was to meet Guðrum there.'

'Thank you. Kill him,' Ælfred said, turning on his heel to leave the hut.

One of his gesith drew his dagger but I didn't stay. As we exited the hut I noticed activity in the compound.

'We have excited the interest of Wulfhere's men it seems,' I said quietly to Ælfred.

'Where are your men?' he asked Odda and me.

'In the stables getting ready to leave,' I replied.

'Drefan, go and alert the rest of my gesith; you know what to do?'

'Yes, cyning.'

After he had left, the three of us went to fetch our families after agreeing to meet at the stables five minutes later. I collected the children and, followed by Eafer and two of my men carrying our belongings, we headed for the stables. We were nearly there when the sound of fighting broke the silence of the night. I wasn't certain but I suspected that Wulfhere's men had realised what was happening and were trying to stop the king escaping.

'Get them to the stables and down to the river. You're going to have to swim across on horseback,' I told Eafer and my two warriors. Tell the rest of our men to come and find me.'

With that I sprinted off towards the sound of conflict. My supposition was correct. Ælfred and his family were surrounded by his gesith who were fighting off a superior number of Wulfhere's warriors. When I arrived I had no qualms about stabbing two of the treacherous ealdorman's men in the back. I needed to lessen the odds, and quickly, before they fought their way through to the king.

Others became aware of my presence and turned to meet this new threat. Suddenly I found myself desperately fighting off three men. One had just wounded my left arm when Erik and some of my warriors arrived to rescue us. Several of the king's gesith were down and I saw with dismay a few of my own men killed as we fought our way back to the stables.

When we got there Erik grabbed me by the arm.

'Get the king and his family to safety, lord. We'll hold these swine off so you can get away.'

'I'm not deserting you, Erik. Forget it!'

'We're not important, Ælfred and young Eadward are. Your duty is to get them away from here. Now!'

He was right, and there was my own children to think of.

'Very well. Where's Odda?'

'He was killed I think. I saw him fall. His son made it to the stables though.'

I quickly embraced him, telling him to follow us as soon as we were clear and make for Bowden Hill. We would wait for those who survived there.

My warriors and those of Odda and Ælfred formed a shieldwall so that the king, Eadred and I could escape with our families and ride down to the river. The water was bitterly cold and we emerged the far side chilled to the bone. I led the cavalcade to Bowden Hill, some four miles away where we halted and got a fire going so that we could get warm again and dry our clothes. It was a risk, of course, but we lit it in a clearing on the far side of the hill from Cippanhamme and smoke wouldn't be seen at night.

I looked around to see who else had got away. I wasn't surprised to see Asser and his chaplain there but, apart from Eafer, Ealhswith and the children, there was no one else. I prayed that Drefan and my own warband would make it away safely, but I knew in my heart that many of them wouldn't make it.

We had dried out and Eafer had dealt with the wound to my arm by the time that the first fingers of sunrise were illuminating the sky to the east. Asser was urging the king to leave and we were on the point of doing so when we heard horsemen coming through the trees to the north of us. Staying was a risk - they could have been Wulfhere's men or the Danes – but only Erik knew where we'd gone.

I breathed a sigh of relief when he appeared. However, I was dismayed when I realised that only half of my men had survived. Even less of the king's gesith had done so but I was pleased to see that Drefan was one of them. Ælfred's captain was one of those that had fallen and the king asked Drefan to take over that role pro tem. I saw that Æthelhelm was with them but not Æthelwold. My conviction that he was in on the plot hardened, however I had no evidence I could present to Ælfred.

With the dozen warriors from Dyfneintscīr who had made it, we could barely muster a score of fighting men. We had no chance against our enemies if we were found, but where to seek sanctuary was problematical. We were likely to be overtaken, encumbered as we were by women and children, if we tried to make it to Wintanceaster and to seek refuge in one of the smaller burh would only prolong the inevitable surrender to Guðrum.

Then Drefan came up with a solution.

'The marshes of Athelney in Somersaete are two day's ride away. The Danes won't find us there.'

# Chapter Fourteen

## ATHELNEY
## Early 878

With Wolnoth, Acwel and Lyndon, three of my
longest-serving hearth warriors, scouting ahead we
made it to Freumh on that first day. We were all tired
and nerves were frayed. The children were
exhausted and Ealhswith and her two maids were
very saddle sore as they weren't used to riding any
distance. Nevertheless, I felt that we had
outdistanced any pursuit and could risk staying for
the night. Ælfred had become very introspective and
seemed content for me to make the decisions for now.

Freumh was another settlement similar to
Cippanhamme, albeit smaller, in that it contained
both a monastery and a hall used by the king when he
went hunting in the nearby Selwood Forest. There
were no warriors stationed there but there were a
dozen families who could produce twenty men and
older boys for the fyrd in time of need.

We ate well that night and in the morning
everyone elected to join the king in his flight to safety.
Ælfred seemed especially pleased to add the abbot, a
man appropriately named Halig - which meant holy -
and his seventeen monks to his entourage. There
were also ten novices, most of whom eyed our
chainmail and weapons enviously. I expect that the

life we led as nobles and warriors seemed glamorous compared to their humdrum existence of prayer and scholarship. I only wished that Æscwin shared their views.

Over the meal Bishop Asser said how worried he was about the monks left behind at Cippanhamme but the king assured him that, traitor though he might be, Wulfhere was still a Christian and he wouldn't let any harm befall them. I wasn't so sure. Having been cheated of their quarry, I had a feeling that Goðrum and his men were highly likely to take it out on whoever was available.

From then on we travelled much more slowly, impeded as we were by carts carrying all the provisions the monks and people of Freumh had laid down for the winter. I could see that it made absolute sense to take as much with us as possible; after all, who knew what food we would find at this place called Athelney? However, the slow rate of progress was exasperating. Furthermore, many of the ceorls, their families and slaves travelled on foot so we were lucky to cover two miles each hour.

I sent four of my men to watch our back trail for pursuit in addition to the scouts up ahead of the column. That day we only managed to travel a dozen miles from Freumh but it brought us to another monastery at a place called Glestingaburg. The day had started fine but the sky clouded over and it got colder during the afternoon. Just before dusk snow started to fall but by then we could see the distinctive conical mound east of the monastery. It disappeared as the snowfall intensified but by then we were nearly level with it and five hundred yards later we reached shelter.

We were shown into a long timber building which I would have called the hall but which the abbot termed his refectory. Whatever its name, it was where the monks and their lay servants ate and slept. The monastery was quite small, with a mere ten monks and half a dozen novices. Most of the latter where only there to be educated and wouldn't stay on once they reached the age of fourteen.

There was only room for the king, the nobles, our families and the senior clerics in the refectory, so the rest had to find what shelter they could. There was a spare hut which the king's gesith and our other warriors commandeered, leaving the ceorls and the rest to share the stables with the horses.

The monastery had no defensive works of any kind, not even a thorn hedge to keep out animals. This worried me but the abbot assured me that they were quite safe.

'Glestingaburg lies at the edge of the Somersaete marshlands. If danger threatens we merely retreat into the marshes, as you plan to do tomorrow,' he told me.

'How far is Athelney from here?' I asked.

'It's not that far but it will take you all day to get there, and then only if you have a guide. Athelney is the largest settlement in the marshes but its thegn is not a pleasant man. He refuses to acknowledge the authority of our ealdorman, Nerian, or pay the taxes due. I doubt he will bend the knee to the king either.'

'What's the name of this thegn?'

'Brennus,' he replied tersely.

I wondered how apt the name was. It meant slayer.

†††

The marshes were a forbidding place. They extended for miles either side of a river called the Pedredan. The whole area was a maze of tributaries and small lakes filled with reed beds, in between which bogs topped with a bright green covering gave the impression of solid ground. It was anything but. If the unwary stepped on it they would sink into the mixture of mud, slime and filthy water underneath.

The place was dotted with islands, mostly quite small, on which grew a variety of trees, shrubs and rough grass. Over the years trees had fallen into the marsh at the edge of the islands and rotted, giving off a foul miasma. The snow had fallen over the area, coating the solid ground and the crust above the bog equally in patches of white which meant that it was impossible to tell which was which where it had settled. Without a guide we would have no doubt disappeared, never to be seen again.

The elderly monk who led us, Brother Galan, had been born in Athelney and knew the marshes like the back of his hand, or so the abbot assured us. Galan was taciturn to the point that I initially thought he was a mute. He wasn't; he just preferred to use gestures rather than speak.

Our journey began along a causeway made of logs lashed together and tied to posts sunk into the water. The going was uneven and we had to lead the horses. Even so they shied and fought against being taken along the rough pathway. In the end we returned them to the monastery and left them there, giving the abbot enough money to feed them until the spring, when they could be turned out onto the nearby pastures.

When the road of logs ended, Galan led us onto an island and then along hidden paths in the reeds that took us further and further into the marsh. I began to worry that we would never find our way out again. I discovered that it was fifteen miles from the monastery to the area where the Isle of Athelney lay but it seemed more like three or four times that distance. We had set out, after leaving the horses, an hour after dawn and it was twilight by the time that we reached one of the larger islands. Galan broke his silence to say that it was a mile to the isle of Athelney itself but we should make our camp there.

'Brennus will react badly if he discovers you are here,' he said ominously but he refused to say more.

The island was bounded to the north and east by the confluence of two rivers, the Pedredan and the Thon. To the south and west lay reed beds in shallow water and marshland. It was a good place to defend and there were enough trees to provide a palisade and the structure for huts. We could also reach the outside world by water without going back the way we had come. Galan told us that the Pedredan ran into the sea just to the south of the entrance to the River Sæfern.

He left the next morning and, after conferring with the king and the newly appointed Ealdorman Eadred, I sent Acwel and Lyndon back with him. They carried a message for Bjarne back at Hamwic. I prayed that they would make it safely through the Danes, who I now suspected were rampaging through the shires of Wiltunscīr and Somersaete.

Bishop Asser was, as ever, suspicious of what I was up to but he seemed mollified when Ælfred told him that he would have an important task for all the monks with us once winter was over.

The snow departed as swiftly as it had arrived but it was replaced by dank mist and drizzle. This made the depressive atmosphere that pervaded the island and its surroundings far worse. However, it didn't stop us building wattle and daub huts with roofs made from bundles of reeds laid over a wicker frame. We also erected a simple palisade. The problem was finding dry wood for our fires and most of the time they smoked and spat sparks rather than blazed.

Our provisions were running low as well. There was no game other than vermin on the island and so we resorted to fishing. Much to my surprise I found that this was an activity that Æscwin, Oswine and I could enjoy together and for the first time in my life I felt that I was getting to know my elder son.

We were fishing on the bank of the River Pedredan when a strange craft appeared out of the mist. It consisted of a flat bed with four short sides, the front one of which sloped at an angle at the prow. There were three men in it, one of whom was propelling the boat with a pole.

'Who are you and what are you doing here fishing in Brennus's river?' one of the men demanded belligerently. 'Do you have his permission?'

'I don't need your thegn's permission,' I replied, getting to my feet. 'I have the king's.'

'King? What king?'

'Ælfred of Wessex, of course.'

'Never heard of him. In any case Brennus doesn't recognise the authority of any king, nor ealdorman come to that. We don't bother them and they don't bother us. Now clear off.'

'Are you going to let him speak to you like that, father,' Æscwin asked, sounding outraged.

'No, but I don't want you or Oswine involved. You know your way back to the encampment?'

'Yes, but I want to see you thrash these insolent men,' he objected in a high treble voice that carried clearly to the men in the boat.

'Oh, you do, do you?' the man who was clearly their leader scoffed. 'When I've finished with your father, I'll give you the thrashing of your life to teach you some manners.'

'My father can kill you with one hand behind his back,' Oswine claimed, joining in the verbal exchange.

The boat grounded on the mud near the bank and the three men leapt ashore. One was armed with a gaff - wicked looking pole with a barbed hook used for landing large fish - and another had a long gutting knife. The third wielded the long pole with which he'd been propelling the boat as if it was a spear. It didn't seem a fair match against my sword and seax, even if there were three of them.

'Back to the camp now,' I whispered urgently to the two boys. 'Fetch my warriors.'

Now that they had been given something important to do they nodded and disappeared into the reeds that lined the river; I breathed a sigh of relief and turned to face my adversaries.

'I'll give you one warning, and one only. Get back in your boat, or whatever it is, and go back to the Isle of Athelney. Attack me and you'll all die.'

'A proud boast for a man outnumbered three to one,' the man with the gaff said scornfully.

'If it's boasts you want, I killed my first Dane when I was thirteen and I've lost count of how many I've killed since then. Now, I don't want to kill Saxons, but if you attack me I'll show no mercy.'

'We're not Saxons though. We're Britons. You bastards have driven us out of our lands east of the Sæfern, but these marshlands are ours.'

It explained a lot. They were the same people as the Wealas and they hated both the Saxons of Wessex and the Angles of Mercia equally.

'I'm pleased,' I replied with a grin. 'I don't like killing Saxons or Mercians, but I'll happily kill Wealas or Britons.'

That infuriated them and they charged me as one. I moved to stand with my back to the water so no one could get behind me. The man with the long pole shoved it at my stomach whilst, at the same time, the one with the gaff tried to hook my sword arm. Thankfully the one with the gutting knife held back, waiting for an opportunity.

I twisted sideways so that the pole missed me by several inches. The man holding it had put so much force behind it that he lost his balance and fell face first into the river. Meanwhile I swung my sword around to meet the gaff and sliced the end off. I followed it up with a cut from my seax which wounded the gaff holder's left arm and he howled in pain.

Not waiting to see if he was out of the fight, I brought my sword up to parry a clumsy thrust from the gutting knife. That left its owner's belly exposed and I sliced it open with my seax. I stepped back on guard, wary of any more threats. The pole man was trying to climb out of the water so I gave his head a vicious kick and he fell back into the river, spluttering and waving his arms around as the current took him out into mid-stream. If he could swim – and it didn't look much like it – he might survive.

I turned my attention to the other two. The man with the gaff was holding his arm, trying to stop the blood flowing, and crying like a baby whilst the man I'd sliced open was vainly trying to hold his intestines in place. There was no hope for him and so I cut his throat to put him out of his misery.

Just at that moment the king arrived with a score of warriors.

'I'm afraid you're too late, cyning,' I said with a grim smile. 'You've missed all the fun. We can patch this one up; he might be able to tell us something useful about Athelney.'

I might have known that Bishop Asser would try and blame me for the fight.

'These were good Christian folk,' he protested, spotting a clumsily made wooden crucifix hanging from the neck of the dead man. 'What do you mean by slaughtering them?'

'Am I not a good Christian too, Asser? The difference is these men are Britons who hate Saxons. Their thegn, Brennus, doesn't acknowledge Ælfred as their king and they did the attacking, not me. I warned them it was a stupid idea.'

'It's true,' Æscwin piped up from behind him. 'I heard them deny that the king had any authority over them.'

'Well, whatever the truth of it, it seems the people of the marshes are now our enemies,' Ælfred said sadly.

I was affronted by the implied criticism. I could understand that the king had enough enemies just at the moment without my adding to them. However, I didn't see that I had a lot of choice. Then I had another thought.

'Had I allowed them to go back and tell this Brennus of our presence, then we could have expected an attack when we were least prepared. Now the initiative lies with us. I don't think we have any option other than to attack them first.'

I hadn't expected it to be a popular idea with the clergy, but that evening Ealhswith added her voice to the opposition. However, Eadred sided with me, as did his brother Drefan.

'Very well, I agree that we can't risk being attacked, or betrayed to the Danes, which might also be a possibility,' Ælfred said decisively. 'However, we need to know what we are dealing with here. Jørren, I want you to take a few men and scout out this Isle of Athelney. See how many people there are there, especially fighting men, and what defences they have.'

'Very well, cyning. We'll go tonight.'

✝✝✝

The mist hung close to the water as we poled the strange boat the three Britons had used down the tributary of the River Pedredan. I didn't know what the smaller river was called then but I later learned that the locals called it the Thon. We had waited until the middle of the night before setting out but I had no idea where exactly the island lay, except that the Britons had come from this direction. I was hoping that we might see fires or lights, although I wasn't confident of doing so in such poor visibility.

We had travelled less than a mile when I heard a dog bark. I had brought Erik, Wealhmær and Eomær with me. Four wasn't a great number if we ran into trouble but it was all the little flat-bottomed boat could hold. Wealhmær stopped propelling us and we listened intently as the current started to take us back the way we'd come. He put the pole into the muddy bed of the river but, instead of keeping us where we were, the blunt bows swung around, pushed by the current.

'Head for the right bank,' I whispered to him and a minute or so later we entered a reed bed. We kept going and the craft beached on a mud bank. We got out and struggled through mud a few inches deep before we reached solid ground. We had to have landed somewhere on the island.

The dog barked again, although it was difficult to make out in which direction the sound had come from in the dark and the mist. Then we heard someone shout something and the dog yelped. Presumably whoever it was had thrown something at the animal.

'That way, I think,' Eomær said pointing further along the river bank.

Keeping the reed beds to our left we cautiously made our way across what seemed to be rough pasture until we found ourselves on a narrow track. We followed it for a while and then a hut appeared out of the gloom. It was only a few yards away and as we listened we could hear the sound of snoring coming from within.

Another dog started barking but stopped after a few seconds. We cautiously made our way through the settlement, counting the huts as we went. After a while the ground started to rise and the huts came to an end. At first I thought that was it but Erik gripped my arm and pointed. I looked and could just make out the faint glimmer of a light. As we went closer we could see through the mist that it was a torch but it appeared to float in mid-air. I edged closer and then saw that it was mounted on top of a palisade perhaps fourteen feet high.

We made our way silently around the perimeter of the fortress, being careful not to step on any twigs or anything else that would alert any sentries to our presence but, apart from a man standing near the torch, there didn't appear to be anyone else on watch. When we returned to our starting point I had calculated that the fortress was square in shape with each side being twenty yards long. There was only one gate, and that was facing towards the village. Trees grew quite close to the palisade on the other three sides, which was a mistake. They should have been cleared to a distance of at least a hundred yards.

Satisfied that we had learned all we were likely to, we made our way back down through the settlement heading for the river. Our chances of finding the boat we had come in were slim to non-existent and so I hoped to be able to steal another one to take us home. When we got to the river we found that the inhabitants had built a crude jetty to which a number of the flat-bottomed craft were moored. Most of them were larger than the one we'd come in and I selected the largest to use for our return journey. Half an hour later we moored it back at our encampment.

'This is most unwise, cyning,' Asser told the king for the umpteenth time.

'Be quiet, bishop. I have made my mind up,' Ælfred replied testily.

We were in the boat I had stolen the previous night, together with Eadred, Erik and a few of the king's gesith. Drefan and three more of the gesith followed in the other boat, which we had recovered just after dawn. Later I learned that the strange craft were called punts.

The mist still hung over the water and the marsh in patches but by midday, when we had set out, the weak February sun had burnt much of it off. Nevertheless it was chilly and I was glad of my bearskin cloak.

As we pulled into the jetty at the settlement on Athelney a large crowd gathered but, seeing a dozen armoured and well-armed men disembark led by a man who was obviously a noble and another who was some kind of priest, they moved back to a safe distance.

Ælfred, who had eschewed his byrnie and helmet in favour of a red woollen tunic embroidered with gold wire and a cloak of the same colour, called out for Brennus to step forward. There was movement at the back of the crowd and a large man dressed in a plain tunic and trousers pushed his way through the crowd. He was armed with an axe and was followed by a score of men carrying a variety of improvised weapons ranging from fish gaffs to spears.

'I'm Brennus. Why have you come to my island uninvited?'

'Because Athelney is part of Wessex and I am its king. I go where I please in my own land,' Ælfred replied tersely.

'You are king of nothing, Ælfred; from what I hear the Danes have chased you out of Wessex and it now belongs to Guðrum. Even your ealdormen have submitted to him.'

If this was true, then it was the worst of tidings. I did wonder how Brennus was so well informed, but then I spotted Brother Galan standing amongst the men around the thegn.

'Wulfhere is a traitor but I have two loyal ealdormen with me here and none of the others would betray me.'

'You haven't heard then? Nerian of Somersæte has also sworn to accept Guðrum as his overlord in return for keeping his life and position, albeit as the Danes' puppet.'

It made sense to me. Nerian's hall was at Baðum which was a mere fifteen miles west of Cippanhamme. It didn't mean that the whole of Somersæte was under Danish domination though. It was a large shire and travel over land was difficult at this time of year. All the same, I wondered whether they had reached Glestingaburg and that was the reason that Galan had fled to Athelney.

'You lie! Nerian is not the sort to betray me.'

'You say I speak falsely? No one accuses me of that and lives! Face me in combat, man to man, king of nowhere.'

Calling Brennus a liar had evidently touched a nerve. For one horrible moment I thought that Ælfred was going to accept the challenge. He might be a good commander on the battlefield, but he was no warrior. He was frail of body, caused by a weak stomach, which meant that he had to avoid red meat and anything that came from a cow. I sighed wearily and was on the point of reluctantly accepting Brennus' challenge on the king's behalf when Eadred beat me to it.

'No one speaks to the king like that,' he declared. 'Face me you lying piece of shit, if you dare.'

With a roar Brennus lifted his axe on high and was about to charge at Eadred when Ælfred stepped between them.

'No one is going to fight here today!' he shouted. 'You are both my subjects and I forbid it.'

'I'm no one's man but my own, Ælfred,' Brennus spat at him. 'Now get out of my way or die where you stand.'

'No one threatens the life of the king,' I declared. 'The penalty for doing so is death.'

So saying I nodded at Erik. He was the only one to have brought a bow with him and he now nocked an arrow to his bowstring and, in one fluid movement, drew, aimed and released. The range was not great and Erik was a fine archer. The arrow flew true and entered the middle of Brennus' chest, striking his heart and killing him instantly.

The people of Athelney watched in stunned silence as their thegn dropped his axe and slumped to the ground. With a wail one of the onlookers, presumably his wife, ran to his side and cradled his lifeless head.

'Does anyone else wish to challenge King Ælfred's position as your sovereign lord?' Asser shouted, no doubt feeling brave now that the threat had been removed.

No one did.

I looked for Galan but he had disappeared; a pity. I would have liked to question him to find out exactly what he knew.

The inhabitants were sent back to their huts whilst we explored the island. It covered an area of perhaps three square miles and it was linked to another island called Ēast Hlenc by a causeway made of logs supported on posts sunk into the marsh. The second island was uninhabited, except for a pair of shepherds and their dogs who looked after a sizeable flock of sheep. I licked my lips. Mutton would make a very pleasant change after a month of eating little except for fish.

The fortress stood on the highest point on the island. It wasn't very large and so Ælfred decided that the first priority was to extend it. When finished it would house his hall, a warriors' hall and essential facilities such as a forge and a brewhouse. Later he planned to improve its defences, but that never happened.

Over the next fortnight the improvements were finished and we moved to our new home. However, some elected to stay on our original island and form a monastic community. Ælfred also decided to keep a lookout posted there to watch the approach along the Pedredan from the sea.

We settled down into a semblance of normal life on Athelney. I shared a small hut inside the fortress with the two boys, Cuthfleda, Eafer and our two slaves. With little to occupy my mind now I began to wonder how Hilda and my other children were faring. I was still very much in love with my wife but I was honest enough to know that I found a life of domestic bliss stifling and boring. After a while I craved excitement. I suppose I was the sort of man who liked coming home but who also liked going away again.

I also began to worry about Acwel and Lyndon. It had been six weeks since they had set off to carry my letter to Bjarne at Hamwic. It was a long way and the roads at this time of year were difficult, but it should have taken them no more than a fortnight to get there; three weeks at most. There had been no winter storms recently, or at least none that had made themselves felt near Athelney, and so I had expected Bjarne to arrive with the fleet by now as I'd been told that the river was navigable some way beyond where we were.

Cuthfleda had discovered a passion for hunting and Eomær had been teaching her what he knew. Had she been older, I would have been suspicious of their growing friendship but at her age I didn't worry about it overmuch. However, the Lady Ealhswith took me to task about my daughter. She berated me because Cuthfleda took no interest in appropriate pursuits like sewing and needlework but behaved more like the son of a low-born ceorl, hunting and fishing. I didn't like to tell her that she was very like her mother in that. Ealdhswith had thoroughly disapproved of my first wife. At least Cuthfleda hadn't asked me to teach her how to use a bow or sword yet.

Another thing that annoyed Ealdhswith was the friendship between my daughter and hers. I suspected that Æthelflaed would have dearly loved to have joined Cuthfleda when she went hunting and fishing. However, that was the last thing that her mother would have permitted.

It was whilst out eel fishing with Eomær in one of the punts that my daughter saw the ships coming up the River Pedredan. The two of them raced back to tell me the news. At last, I thought with excitement. Bjarne had arrived. But her next words dashed my hopes and filled me with dread.

'They were longships with carved dragons' heads on the prow.'

It seemed that Guðrum had found us after all.

# Chapter Fifteen

## ATHELNEY

## Spring 878

Thankfully the longships had passed the confluence with the Thon and continued upstream on the Pedredan. Eaomær had counted the ships and told me that there were seven snekkjur of varying sizes from ten oars a side to fifteen. That meant a force of perhaps two hundred Vikings. We had no chance in a straight fight with a mere score of warriors, even supplemented by perhaps fifty members of the fyrd.

I didn't count the Britons because I didn't trust them. They seemed to have reluctantly accepted our presence after the death of Brennus but I doubted very much whether they would fight for us. They might even support the Danes.

I set off in one of the smaller punts with Eomær, Erik and Wealhmær to shadow the enemy ships. We stopped at the smaller island at the junction of the two rivers to check that those who still lived there were unharmed, but the huts were hidden from any shipping on the river and the Danes hadn't bothered to investigate the island.

It was just as well because the settlement was now virtually a monastery, housing as it did Abbot Halig, his monks and the lay people who supported them. They would have been totally incapable of defending themselves.

We pressed on, heading east along the Pedredan, sticking close to the reed beds initially. These petered out as we entered a section of the river where trees lined both banks. Now we went more cautiously as the river began to twist and turn. It would be very easy to come around a bend and find ourselves on top of the moored fleet.

A mile further on the wooded land came to an end and the river entered a section of marshland. The ships were moored either side of the river just before the solid land petered out. We were still in the shade of the tree canopy but any alert man on watch should have spotted us before we could turn and head back the way we'd come.

Thankfully there was no shouted warning, so perhaps they felt secure enough not to bother with sentries, or else they were asleep. We poled our way back downstream, making much better time with the current than we had coming, and an hour later I was back at Athelney briefing the king, Æthelhelm, Asser, Eadred and his brother Drefan. I wondered at the inclusion of the king's nephew. He hadn't formed part of the council before this but, as Ælfred explained, if anything happened to him, his son Eadward was far too young to succeed and Æthelhelm was the eldest ætheling.

'Perhaps they will continue upriver tomorrow?'
Asser said hopefully.

'If so, I doubt that they will be able to go very
much further,' I said. 'The river was already getting
narrower, making it difficult to row as a snekkje
needs a width of at least fifty feet to use its oars.
Furthermore, the river enters marshland near where
they are camped. I can't be absolutely certain but,
from what we saw, the marsh looked to be quite
extensive and they must realise that we are hardly
likely to be living there.'

'So you think they will return and explore the
tributaries?' Æthelhelm asked.

'Yes, most are too narrow for them to explore by
ship, but there is one off to the south about a mile
from the confluence with the Thon. I don't know how
far down it they'll be able to go but hopefully it will
take them much of tomorrow. That gives us a little
more time to plan.'

'Plan? What plan? We must leave as soon as
possible,' Asser said, looking around him in a panic as
if a Dane was suddenly going to appear in front of
him.

'Have a little more courage, bishop,' Drefan said,
trying to hide his contempt for the man, and failing.
'In any case, where would we run to?'

'What worries me most is how the Danes knew
that we were in this area,' Ælfred said, ignoring the
exchange between his captain and his spiritual
advisor.

'Perhaps Brother Galan betrayed us?' I suggested.
'He was with Brennus and then disappeared.'

'But he's a Christian monk, and the only one who knows the route out of here?' Asser said, aghast.

'He's also a Briton born in Athelney,' I pointed out. 'Whether he has betrayed us or not is of no moment now. We need to consider how we can deal with the Danes.'

††† 

We had removed half a dozen tree trunks from the palisade and carried them down on punts to the confluence of the Pedredan and the tributary down which the Danes had just rowed. One of the locals said that the river petered out in marshland after a few miles. If so we didn't have long. Thankfully, we had just finished lashing the last of the trunks together to form a floating boom when the first of the Danes' longships re-appeared.

Reed beds lined the banks of both rivers at this point but the silt in which they grew wasn't deep. We disembarked the archers, composed of my warriors and a few ceorls who had hunting bows, near the two ends of the makeshift boom. Their job was twofold: to stop the Danes from dismantling the boom and to whittle down their numbers as much as possible.

The archers were difficult to spot in the reeds but they had a clear view of the first of the snekkjur as it bumped against the boom. As soon as it came to a halt arrows poured into it from both sides, killing and wounding a third of the crew before they had the sense to disembark and move into the reeds.

My archers withdrew, pursued by the angry Vikings. By now two of the other longships had come up to the boom and their crews joined the hunt through the reeds. What the Danes didn't know was that the reed beds and the waterlogged ground in which they grew only went so far. After a while they reached what appeared to be an open patch of grassland beyond which lay a mound on which a number of the fyrd had been stationed.

As soon as they saw the fyrd, the Danes charged across what they thought was open ground; it wasn't. It was a crusting of slime, algae and water plants lying on top of quite deep and very dank water. The first dozen or so Danes had charged into the morass before they realised their mistake. None could swim and they sunk below the deceptive surface. Those behind them came to an abrupt halt and turned to retrace their steps.

Whilst we had been putting the boom in place, others had been busy trampling down paths through the reeds which led nowhere. The Danes got lost in the maze we had created and those at the rear proved easy prey for those of our men who waited in the reeds at the side of the false trails with drawn daggers to cut their throats.

By now some of the Danes were panicking and a few blundered through the reeds in the direction that they supposed their ships lay. Some made it; most did not. They either fell into deeper water to drown, or they were killed by us.

We knew the area better than the Danes, but it was dangerous even for us and after a while I ordered

Wolnoth to sound the recall on his horn before we lost some of our own men in the marshes. We disappeared back down the Pedredan in our punts leaving the Danes to remove the boom and make good their escape.

We had lost five men in total, all ceorls. Three had been killed by the Danes and two had disappeared, presumably lost in the marshland. Against that, I calculated from the reports which I was given, that the enemy had suffered between sixty and seventy casualties, mostly deaths. That still left perhaps as many as a hundred and twenty or thirty but I hoped that, in view of the attrition rate, they had learned their lesson and would now give up the search.

The next morning my hopes were dashed. Cináed came to tell me that five longships, presumably all the Danes could now man, had turned into the River Tone. Althelney lay less than a mile upstream and so we had very little time to prepare. Unlike the settlement at the junction of the two rivers, the huts here were in full view from the river. We only had one hope: to get everyone inside the fortress before they arrived.

As soon as the horns sounded the alarm everyone stopped what they were doing and made for the gate in the palisade. Women scooped up infants, dogs ran around barking, chickens scuttled out of the way and men dived into their hovels to collect whatever they could find to use as a weapon.

Whilst this was going on I climbed the ladder up to the walkway around the top of the palisade.

'What's happening,' Ælfred demanded to know as he joined me.

His body-servant ran after him carrying his war harness and he proceeded to strap the king into his byrnie whilst I explained.

'Five of the longships are heading up the Tone, cyning. They'll be here in a few minutes.'

As we watched and waited, Æthelhelm, Bishop Asser and Eadred joined us. I was about to take my leave and check that the defence of the fortress was being sorted out when I heard Drefan shouting orders. It didn't need two of us to get the gates closed and the parapet manned and so I turned my attention back to the river.

The first snekkja hove into view around a bend a hundred yards before the jetty and I could hear excited chatter on board as soon as they spotted the moored punts and the huts beyond. A voice bellowed for silence in Danish and the sound faded away. On command the rowers raised their oars and the longship glided into the jetty.

Two of the ship's boys jumped ashore as it came alongside and threw the ropes they carried around two of the upright posts to bring the ship to a halt. The crew jumped ashore and I saw that, unlike at sea, this time they were wearing byrnies or leather tunics and helmets. Each man carried a shield except for three who were armed with big two handed axes instead of swords or smaller axes. I did a swift count and made it twenty eight men. The steersman and the ship's boys had stayed aboard.

The second longship had now arrived but the jarl or hirsir in command of the first snekkje didn't wait for their crew to join him. Instead he led his warriors at a fast trot up the slope. They ignored the huts, although I knew that they would be ransacked later. By the time that the next crew had started up the slope the first had come within range of my archers.

Drefan joined me and asked why I hadn't given the order for the archers to open fire.

'Because the enemy are in line just two deep and holding their shields in front of them; it would be a waste of arrows,' I replied tersely.

I waited until the Danes had reached the palisade. Once there, pairs of men held a shield horizontally so that a third could climb onto it and used it as a jumping off platform to climb over the palisade.

'Now, archers, now is your time,' I shouted.

As one man, they leant over the top of the palisade and sent their arrows down at the men beneath. Some hit the bare area at the junction of the shoulder and neck, some the arms of those supporting the horizontal shields and others the upturned faces of those about to scale the palisade.

It was chaos. Wounded and dead Danes dropped their shields, others fell off the horizontal shields with arrows in their eyes or were wounded in the face. Their problems didn't end there. As the wounded picked themselves up they were struck by more arrows and, at that short range, chainmail didn't offer much protection. By the time that the last of the Danes had withdrawn out of range there were only six of them left standing.

The other crews struggling up the slope towards us halted, looking stunned. I counted ninety men in all. We were still outnumbered, but not by as many, and we had the advantage of being behind stout defences.

I outlined my plan to the council that evening. Asser said that it was foolhardy and Ealhswith said that I was risking lives needlessly. I was surprised that the king let her speak in council but he probably did it to spare him her nagging when she was excluded.

'Lady, what would you have us do? Stay here and do nothing whilst the Danes send for reinforcements? Once Guðrum knows that King Ælfred is here, you can expect him to bring every warrior he has against us. No, we need to prevent word reaching him and that means burning their ships.'

'Jørren's right,' Eadred said, nodding his agreement. 'Let us hope that they haven't already sent him word. After all there are only five ships at the jetty; where are the other two?'

'I think they've probably abandoned them. Taking into account those we killed yesterday, I would have thought that all the rest are here. I think it's very unlikely that they have sent a longship away with enough men to crew her.'

'I agree,' Ælfred said, ignoring the look of anger from his wife and Asser's protest. 'Go ahead, Jørren, and may God be with you.'

The Danes had ransacked the huts but they hadn't set them alight. They had kept them for their use during the siege. That suited me fine because it meant that only a few guards would be left on the longships, probably just a few warriors and the ships' boys.

I chose five of my closest companions – Ædwulf, Wealhmær, Cináed, Wolnoth and Sæwine – to accompany me. Both Cináed and Wolnoth carried burning embers in a clay pot hung from a length of cord. The rest of us carried combustible material – cloth covered in animal fat and dry kindling in the main. It was a clear night, which was far from ideal, but at least it was a new moon so the silvery light it gave off was weak.

We stuck to the shadows as we skirted the settlement and made for the reed beds to the north of the jetty. There were two campfires on the ground twenty yards from the jetty. I counted sixteen boys sitting at one and five men at the other. At first I thought that that was all the watch there was on the ships but then I saw a man stand up on one of the snekkja and piss over the side. Evidently there were guards on the ships themselves.

As we watched two of the warriors and three of the boys got to their feet and made their way to the ships. A few minutes later the five they had relieved made their way ashore. Three boys and two men went to their respective campfires and ladled some pottage into bowls.

We waited an hour and then first the boys and then the men lay down and went to sleep. Another hour or so passed and then the watch changed again. This time those who had been relieved went to sleep. We gave it another half an hour or so before we moved.

Leaving Wolnoth to keep the firepots going, the rest of us crept stealthily towards the moored longships. I took the far one and when I was in position I held up my hand so that the others could see it in the ghostly light of the new moon. When I dropped it we boarded the five snekkjur as one and killed those on watch before any of them could cry out a warning. When I looked down at the one whose throat I had slit, a feeling of revulsion and remorse nearly unmanned me. The Danish ship's boy couldn't have been more than twelve.

'Jørren,' Sæwine hissed at me from the next ship, 'are you alright?'

'Yes, fine,' I whispered hoarsely. 'Let's get on with it.'

We went back and collected the inflammable material and the two fire pots we'd brought with us before returning to the ships. Once we'd piled anything that would burn by the masts, including the oars, we lit lengths of rope soaked in pitch pine from the fire pots and set the ships alight. I waited to make sure that the bottom of the masts were burning well and then we ran for the cover provided by the reed beds.

Flames licked up the masts and the rigging caught fire. I had no illusions that the damage would be enough to sink the snekkjur but, with no mast or rigging and burnt oars, the Danes would have no means of propelling their ships.

Just as one of those sleeping by the campfires gave the alarm, the sound of fierce fighting reached us. It was coming from the fortress and I saw with horror that the Danes were milling about in front of it. Worse, the gates were open. The light wasn't good enough to see any detail but it looked as if our men were trying valiantly to defend the open gateway.

We gave up all pretence at stealth and ran up the slope towards the fortress. As we ran someone amongst the Danes in front of us saw the burning ships and shouted to draw the attention of his fellows to them.

Without their ships the Danes would be stranded here and so most of them gave up trying to take the fortress and hared downhill. They ignored us as they raced past and a few minutes later we reached the fortress. My first thought was for the king but I saw Ælfred standing next to Eadred and Drefan in the gateway.

Suddenly screams rent the air and shortly afterwards a mass of people made their escape through the gateway. I wondered what was going on as they ran towards the causeway leading to the smaller island, the one where the sheep were kept.

'What has happened, cyning?' I asked breathlessly when I reached the gates.

'We were betrayed,' Ælfred replied. 'Some of the Britons killed the sentries and opened the gates to the Danes. Thankfully one of our men managed to sound the alarm before he was killed, but we lost a lot of good men before they retreated to try and save their ships.'

I looked around and for the first time I noticed the bodies lying near the gateway. Many were Danes but a dozen were members of the king's gesith or of Eadred's warband. Then I noticed that one of the bodies was that of Erik. He had joined me with three other Danes when we were all boys; now the last of the three was dead. Erik hadn't just been my captain, he'd been one of my closest friends. I suppose I should have become accustomed to losing my close companions by now but somehow I felt each one as keenly as a knife plunged into my heart. I sunk into a sort of torpor and I knelt by his body and cradled Erik's lifeless head in my lap.

Slowly I became aware of screaming from inside the fortress and I immediately thought of my children. I left Erik and ran to our hut, only to find the door barred. All around me those Britons who hadn't managed to escape were being slaughtered. I banged on the door and eventually Eafer opened it, dagger in hand and looking more like the feral boy he once was rather than my body servant.

'It's you, lord. Thank God.'

I stepped inside and my children rushed to me. I stayed with them until a messenger arrived to say that the king was asking for me.

The way to the king's hall was strewn with dead men, women and children. I didn't have to be told that those Britons who hadn't managed to escape had paid the ultimate price for their betrayal. They had never liked us; after all, we were intruders who had killed their thegn and taken over their settlement, but I hadn't really thought that they would side with the Danes instead of us. Later we found out that it was Brennus' wife and sons who had led the men who had killed the sentries and opened the gates. The majority of the Britons were probably innocent of any involvement, but they paid the price, along with the guilty.

Ælfred asked me to organise the burial of our men. He had negotiated a truce with the Danes and, whilst we dug a pit close to the fortress for our corpses, they came and carried theirs down the slope to where others were busy preparing a pyre. Asser conducted a brief service over the mass grave and I watched as Erik and the others disappeared under the soil. Later the area below us was lit up by the Danes' funeral pyre and the foul smell of roasting flesh came to us on the wind.

The next morning the charred ground where the cremation had taken place could be clearly seen, as could the burnt out hulks down by the jetty. At least no one was going to be able to go to Guðrum to fetch reinforcements now. Nonetheless, we were still under seige and heavily outnumbered. The mood throughout the fortress was one of despondency. Then the lookout on the tower by the gate called down something which made matters ten times worse.

'There's another fleet of longships coming along the Pedredan from the sea.'

Our hearts sank.

'How many?' Drefan called back.

'At least a score.'

Our fate seemed sealed.

# Chapter Sixteen

## ATHELNEY / CIPPANHAMME

## Late Spring 878

'The lead ship is the Saint Cuthbert!' Cináed suddenly exclaimed.

I squinted, trying to make it out. Could it possibly be Bjarne and the fleet at long last? The leading longship was certainly large enough to be her, but I didn't allow myself to hope until I was certain. It would be too cruel if Cináed was mistaken but he wasn't. A few seconds later I could make out the familiar carving on the prow. He was right! We were saved.

The first of the longships didn't land their crews immediately. A few men disembarked from the Saint Cuthbert and cut the lines securing the burnt-out Danish hulks. The ships drifted downstream, making more room on the small jetty.

Of course, the Danes hadn't been idle. They too had thought that the fleet was theirs. When they realised it wasn't, they rushed to oppose the landing of our men. Bjarne and the crew of the Saint Cuthbert scrambled ashore to meet them. As it carried over a hundred men they outnumbered the surviving Danes on their own. As several more longships came alongside and disgorged their crews, the number forming the shieldwall rapidly grew. The Danes hesitated.

Someone – I never did discover who – opened the gates and the warriors inside the fortress ran down the slope to attack the Danes from the rear. Men who'd been besieged and who had been convinced that our days were numbered only minutes before were euphoric at being rescued, and they had a score to settle for the loss of so many of our companions. They were in no sort of formation but what they lacked in organisation they made up for in ferocity.

I was tempted to join them but I stayed with the king and the rest of council and watched from the ramparts. The steadily growing numbers of new arrivals enveloped the Danes like the horns of a bull. Meanwhile the men from the fortress were cutting down the rear ranks of the enemy like ceorls harvesting their crops.

It wasn't long before the Danes were forced into a circle and crowded so close together that they could hardly use their weapons. It was a slaughter. Many tried to surrender but they were cut down. Eventually Bjarne managed to get our warriors to withdraw a few paces. By then there were less than a score of Danes left standing.

I could see that we had sustained a few casualties as well but nothing like the losses the Danes had suffered.

'I think it's time we joined our men,' Ælfred said sombrely.

We followed him down the hill and when we reached the battlefield I anxiously scanned the ground for any of my own warband. Wolnoth was nursing a cut to his biceps and Sæwine had a nasty wound to his thigh, but otherwise my men seemed unharmed and I muttered a prayer of thanks.

Ælfred accepted the surrender of the only hirsir left alive and the Danes were disarmed. They were bound and locked inside one of the larger huts whilst we dealt with the dead and wounded. Our own dead were laid out for burial and the wounded were taken to the hall to be treated. The wounded Danes were killed and their dead were dumped unceremoniously in a heap. Already crows and other carrion birds were circling and diving in to peck at the lifeless flesh. Soon they would be joined by the rats and I prayed that, if I ever fell in battle, I wouldn't be left so that vermin could dine on my flesh.

Someone had the bright idea of loading the enemy corpses onto the charred longships and towing them out to sea, so a couple of our ships went to retrieve the hulks. Once loaded with their grisly cargo, they were towed down to the mouth of the Pedredan and left to sink offshore. So ended our time as fugitives. Now it was time to plan our offensive.

✝✝✝

'Why did it take you so long to come and find us?' I asked Bjarne when the council met that evening. 'When did Acwel and Lyndon reach you?'

'At the end of January, lord,' he replied, looking nervously at Ælfred, 'but I had to gather the crews and that proved far more difficult than I had anticipated.'

'I appreciate that the roads are difficult at that time of year,' the king interrupted, 'but it's now nearly the middle of April.'

'Yes, cyning, but the ealdormen were unwilling to muster the skypfyrd. They said that they were needed to defend their shires against the Danes.'

'So how did you manage to raise the necessary numbers in the end; there must be, what, near on a thousand men with you?'

'I had to send for men from Cent, Suth-Seaxe and Dornsæte, who weren't so threatened by Guðrum's army and, of course, that took time.'

'So Tunbehrt of Hamtunscīr and Anson of Whitlond refused to give you men to come to my rescue?'

'Yes, cyning.'

'But the Danes are in Wiltunscīr and Somersaete, not in their shires?' Ælfred said, looking puzzled.

'Yes, lord,' Bjarne replied nervously. 'But I think that there was another reason that they failed to come to your aid.'

'What? What reason?'

'They, um, they blame you for trusting Guðrum's word and for bribing him to go away.'

He paused, wondering whether to continue.

'They, er, said that giving money to a Dane to go away was a mistake. It only encourages them to come back for more and, at the same time impoverishes your people, cyning.'

267

He stood, licking his lips, wondering if he'd gone too far. Ælfred looked furious but he didn't berate Bjarne for being honest with him.

'Thank you, Bjarne, for being brave enough to tell me the truth. I am grateful to you for your loyalty and for coming to my aid. You shall have a vill of your own when this is all over.'

Bjarne beamed with pleasure and I held him by the shoulders to congratulate him on his good fortune. He deserved it.

'Now, down to business,' Ælfred said. 'We need to muster what forces we can and defeat Guðrum once and for all. As Eadda is God knows where I need a hereræswa; Jørren, you are the obvious man. From now on you command the army on land as well as my ships.'

'Thank you, cyning,' I replied, feeling both elated and somewhat overawed by my new responsibilities.

I never thought much of Eadda's abilities as a commander and that, coupled with the sour expression on Asser's face at this further preferment, banished any reservations I might have had.

For the next week I was busy planning our strategy with the king. We needed to know the whereabouts of Guðrum's army and so my first task was to send out scouts. The problem was there was no one to guide them through the marshes back to Glestingaburg where our horses had been left. Then we had a stroke of luck.

No one had given much thought to the Britons of Athelney who had survived the slaughter and fled to the island on which the sheep were kept. Evidently they had managed to survive there, living on mutton, fish and eels. Of course, we had sent men to collect sheep for us to slaughter over the past few days but the Britons had hidden from them. Now that the threat from the Danes had been eliminated, the king sent men to the island to round up the survivors for interrogation. It didn't take long; there was nowhere for the poor wretches to run to.

Drefan had been put in charge of the operation and he returned at midday with twenty nine prisoners, mostly old men, women and young children. Nearly all the young men and many of the boys had died fighting. I gave them a cursory glance as they passed me, but then I stiffened in surprise. There was one person I recognised only too well, despite the fact that he had exchanged his monk's habit for a simple tunic and bare legs – Brother Galan.

'What are you doing here?' I asked him when he was brought before me.

'I was visiting my sister and her family when you came and murdered Brennus,' he replied defiantly.

'Brennus was a traitor,' I replied. 'He deserved to die.'

'And did all those women and children you slaughtered here in the fortress deserve to die too?' he fumed, a spray of spittle erupting from his mouth.

'You Britons betrayed us to the Danes,' I countered angrily.

'No, it was Brennus' family who opened the gates; his wife aided by his sons and cousins. No one else was involved; they were all murdered.'

There was no point in continuing the argument. Galan had a valid point. Many innocent people did die that night, but it was unavoidable. Our men wanted vengeance for being betrayed and in their anger they killed indiscriminately. It happened in war.

'You say you were visiting your sister and her family? Are they still alive to confirm that?' I asked innocently.

'Yes, all but her husband.'

He stopped, realising I had tricked him. Had he thought about it he would have lied and said that they were all dead. As it was, I now had a hold over him.

It didn't take long to find which of the remaining Britons were members of Galan's family. There was a middle-aged woman and three children: a youth of sixteen, a girl of thirteen and a boy of ten. In return for my promise to not only spare them, but take them into my service and give them a decent life, Galan agreed to guide my scouts back to his monastery.

Once they had departed, led by Ædwulf, the council turned their attention to gathering as many of our forces as we could. The eastern shires were too far away; that left Hamtunscīr, Wiltunscīr, Somersaete, Dornsæte and Dyfneintscīr. Of the five ealdormen, Eadred of Dyfneintscīr was already present, Wulfhere of Wiltunscīr was a traitor and the loyalty of both Nerian of Somersaete and Tunbehrt of Hamtunscīr was suspect. It wasn't a promising situation. Eadred said that his shire reeve was loyal and could be relied upon to gather the fyrd for him, which was a start. We had to assume that Hildenric of Dornsæte would also rally as many of his men to the king's side as he could.

Over the next few days Ælfred wrote a letter to every ealdorman except Wulfhere ordering them to muster their forces for a final battle to defeat Guðrum. He also wrote to the shire reeve of Wiltunscīr, denouncing his ealdorman as a traitor and a turncoat, and asking him to muster the shire's fyrd.

That done we waited. The letters couldn't be sent yet, but at least they were ready.

With time on my hands I took my children fishing once more. Both Oswine and Cuthfleda had the patience and concentration to successfully catch several fish of indeterminate species and a few eels but Æscwin was a daydreamer. Even when his line tugged he didn't react in time and invariably the fish managed to free itself.

Both of the other two asked me about the forthcoming battle, what would it be like? Were the Danes as fearsome as everyone believed? Could they really be beaten? What tactics would the king employ?

I answered as best I could but spared them the awful reality of hand to hand combat. I tried to involve Æscwin but he wasn't interested, saying that to kill another human being was wrong; it said so in the Bible.

'What would you have us do then, brother?' my daughter asked angrily. 'Let the Danes take what they want, pillage our churches and monasteries, kill

271

innocent women and children. Perhaps even rape me?'

I was shocked that Cuthfleda knew what rape was but perhaps she didn't. It was just something she'd overheard. I hoped so. To me she was my sweet, innocent child; time enough for the realities of life when she was a few years older.

'No, of course not,' Æscwin replied, 'but Bishop Asser says we must all pray for deliverance and the Danes will go away.'

'Then Bishop Asser is a fool!' I snapped, annoyed that the man had filled my son's head with such dangerous nonsense. 'The Danes will only go away if we defeat them and kill enough of them so that they don't come back.'

Æscwin looked hurt but he didn't try to argue with me. I sighed. I had now resigned myself to the fact that he wouldn't succeed me when I died. I needed to concentrate on training Ywer to do that when he was older, or perhaps Oswine. He was only my stepson but I liked the boy and he showed promise. In any case, I hoped to live for a few more decades yet.

†††

The scouts returned, bringing a reluctant Brother Galan back with them as well as several more monks. They had found Guðrum's army easily enough as they were still at Cippanhamme. Of course, they had been plundering far and wide but only in small groups.

They also brought the welcome news that Nerian hadn't defected and was, in fact, at Freumh gathering his thegns and his fyrd together.

'We tried to estimate the Dane's numbers, cyning,' Ædwulf told the king, 'but we couldn't get close enough to count them. They had erected temporary shelters outside the settlement and, judging by the size and number of them, I would say that they could accommodate about a thousand fighting men, in addition to their thralls.'

'Thank you, that's helpful,' Ælfred said thoughtfully. 'I wouldn't have thought that the settlement itself could house more than five hundred and so it looks as if we will be confronting fifteen hundred Vikings when we bring them to battle.'

'Provided they are not reinforced, cyning, now that spring is here,' I added.

'I left Acwel and Lyndon behind to watch for exactly that, lord,' Ædwulf added.

'Thank you, you have done well,' I said smiling at him.

I needed a captain of my warband to replace Erik and perhaps he might be a contender. I would have liked to appoint Cei, the captain of the garrison at Dofras and my oldest friend, but he was a Briton and an escaped slave. He was liked and respected but there was an innate prejudice against Britons. They had been the original inhabitants of the island and we had taken it from them; consequently Saxons, Angles and Jutes tended to look down on them as inferior in some way. They weren't, of course, just a different race. We shared a common background with the

Danes and the Norse and so even they were more acceptable as fellow warriors than Britons, provided that they converted to Christianity, of course.

Ædwulf's background was different. He was a Mercian who had been captured by the Danes and made a thrall. My warband had rescued him eight years ago when he was thirteen, along with Hunulf. Initially they had been trained as scouts but when Ædwulf was seventeen he had become a hearth warrior – one of those members of my warband who were closest to me. Hunulf never had the chance. He had died bravely at the Battle of Inglefelle just after he'd turned fifteen. His was a sad loss, one of many over the years.

Now that the scouts were back, and we had several monks from Glestingaburg who knew the path back through the marshes, the letters were sent out. Ælfred had added a postscript to each to say that the muster point would be at a place known as Ecgbryhtesstan - Egbert's Stone – fifteen miles due south of Cippanhamme. The date set for the muster was the seventh of May, three weeks hence. It was a tight timescale to muster a large army and congregate at a point a long way away for most of the shires, but we daren't delay any longer or the Danes might well start their campaign to conquer the kingdom.

As it was there was already a danger that they would have left their base before we could bring them to battle, I was sent with a sizeable force to threaten them, but to avoid a fight. Yet again Ælfred had set me a seemingly impossible task.

I left my children in the care of the Lady
Ealhswith. We might not like each other but I knew
that she was honourable and no harm would come to
them if she could avoid it. I took Ædwulf, Bjarne and
half the ships with me. In the absence of horses the
most sensible way to travel was by water.

It was good to be afloat again. The rowers had a
hard job rowing against the prevailing wind and the
tide but I had the luxury of being able to stand and
watch the land on either side slip past. At first it was
a mixture of reed beds, dank woodland and bog but
then the scenery changed to meadows and pasture.
We passed a settlement at slack water. The place
looked deserted; presumably the inhabitants had fled
when they saw the longships. As the tide started to
flow the other way we picked up speed and reached
the open sea just after midday.

We hoisted the sail and headed north parallel with
the coast. Eadwig, the master shipbuilder from
Hamwic, had accompanied the fleet as navigator as he
hailed from a small settlement on the Somersaete
coast. Once we'd passed a small peninsula our
heading changed to north-east towards what Eadwig
told me was the estuary of the River Sæfern. It was a
clear day and a couple of hours later I could just make
out a smudge on the horizon which Eadwig said was
the south coast of Wealas.

Dusk wasn't far off and I was getting a little
nervous of being caught at sea in strange waters in
the dark. However, Eadwig assured me that we
weren't far now from the mouth of the River Afne.

Shortly after that we turned so that the wind was on our beam and headed towards the land.

I was glad we had Eadwig with us as I could see the sea breaking on a sandbank in the middle of the river mouth. He told the steersman to head for the right hand channel and shortly afterwards we dropped the sail and began to row up the river. I looked behind me anxiously but the other longships were following our course. A little later, as twilight turned to night, we beached the ships and went ashore to camp.

The next day we rowed up the River Afne as far as Baðum before disembarking. It had been a large Roman town and the ruins of their impressive stone buildings were everywhere. Eadwig told me that the ancient baths were a thing of wonder. The water was constantly hot and very pleasant to bathe in.

The Saxon settlement lay to the south east of the old Roman town and was centred around a monastery which had been founded two centuries ago by Osric, King of the Hwicce, or so Eadwig said. The Hwicce had been a Saxon tribe which had long since been absorbed into Mercia. It was also where Nerian, the ealdorman, had his hall.

Seeing the image of Saint Cuthbert on the prow of my longship and the crosses on the other ships, the abbot and monks cautiously approached us as soon as we had moored and disembarked. The abbot offered us the hospitality of the monastery but he was notably relieved when I said that we needed to depart almost immediately. Feeding five hundred hungry warriors was likely to reduce his stores of provisions considerably. He did however arrange for the loan of six horses and promised to look after the ship's boys who we left behind.

Before we left I asked him if Nerian was still at Freumh but all the abbot knew was that he had left Baðum with his warband heading south several weeks ago. He had tried to persuade the abbot to accompany him with his monks but the old man had refused, saying that God would protect them. So far that seemed to be true; the Danes had left them alone.

I pondered the reason for that but the only conclusion I could come to was a superstitious fear of the old ruins. Heathens believed that the Romans were giants whose ghosts still roamed their old towns and cities. It was the reason why our pagan ancestors had built a new settlement at Lundenwic instead of occupying the Roman city. I had wondered why they thought that they must have been giants until I saw the buildings and defensive walls they had constructed. Only giants could have lifted such large blocks of stone and put them in place.

I sent out scouts to watch for any Danish patrols and then led my men eastwards along an old Roman road. From Baðum it was less than ten miles to Cippanhamme and I planned to camp within a couple of miles of the place that night.

We encountered our first party of Danes less than two miles after setting out. We could see the smoke starting to rise into the air ahead of us and five minutes later two of the scouts returned to report. They had seen two dozen Danes leaving the settlement after plundering it and setting fire to it. They were headed our way.

We were in open ground so there was no possibility of ambushing the Danes. Instead I ordered the leading hundred or so warriors to form a shieldwall blocking the road. I had no doubt that the Danes would flee back the way they'd come as soon as they saw us and the last thing I wanted was for them to alert Guðrum to our presence.

The meadow to our right fell away into a fold in the ground which meant that it was hidden from the road. Leaving Ædwulf in charge of the main blocking force, I led fifty men along the dip at a run. If I could get behind the Danes I could cut off their retreat that way. I told Wolnoth to follow me with another fifty and stay in the dip to cut off that avenue of escape. That left the slope to the north of the road. I sent my few scouts up there with instructions to chase down any who fled that way. There weren't many of them but panicking men tend to flee downhill, rather than uphill, so they ought to be able to cope.

I turned to see how many archers I had with me: not many, but they would have to do.

'Jerrick, you and the rest of the bowmen stay with Wolnoth and cut down as many as you can when we spring the trap, but spare the horses. We'll need them.'

'Yes lord,' he said stringing the bow he carried as well as his sword and shield.

It was Jerrick who had first taught me about sailing and sea warfare. He captained one of my ships but it wasn't enough.  When this was over I should make more use of his skills at sea.

We crouched down in the dead ground out of sight of the road.  Soon the sound of horses' hooves and men laughing and talking about the plunder they had taken from the Mercian settlement and the girls they had raped reached us.  Suddenly the sounds ceased as they spotted the road ahead barred by my men.

'Retreat!  Back to Cippanhamme,' a voice shouted in Danish.

'Now,' I told Jerrick and led my men out of the hollow and up towards the road.

Whilst half a dozen archers sent volley after volley into the Danes, adding to their confusion, we raced onto the road to stop their retreat.  Seeing us, a large man on a white horse looked around him and, seeing only a few archers in his way, he charged towards them.  His men streamed after him, leaving half a dozen dead and dying on the road.

Jerrick and the archers made a speedy withdrawal just as Wolnoth's fifty men erupted from the ditch and formed up to cover their withdrawl.  The Danes tried to stop but their momentum carried them into Wolnoth's shieldwall.  Ten more of them died before the handful that were left retraced their steps across the road and headed uphill, the giant on the white horse well in the lead.

Instead of riding to meet them, the scouts up on the hill dismounted and strung their bows.  Their first volley cut down three of the remaining Danes' leaving just four men, all mounted, including the one on the white horse.  They had had enough and they turned to flee at an angle that would bring them back to the road well behind my position. The scouts remounted and gave chase.

Jerrick had seen what was happening and he led his archers past us and along the road for a hundred yards or so. They stopped and took deep lungfuls of air to calm their breathing before taking careful aim at the four Danish riders. It was a long shot, almost a hundred yards, but three of the six arrows hit a target. Two horses were brought down, dumping their riders onto the ground, and another of the Danes pitched from his saddle, an arrow in his chest. That left their leader on his white horse.

Jerrick took careful aim again and let fly. I watched the arrow soar into the sky and thought that it would fall short. The distance was now nearer a hundred and fifty yards. The arrow fell out of the sky and struck the white stallion in the rump. It reared up in shock and pain and its rider fell backwards over its tail.

I watched as the scouts dispatched the three Danes who had been unhorsed and then gave chase to the large Viking, who was now limping towards a nearby wood. I prayed that their leader – Cináed – would have the good sense to take him prisoner instead of killing him. Thankfully he did. They rode around him in a circle, cutting off his escape, and then Cináed barged him with his horse knocking him to the ground. One of the others dismounted and pricked the Dane's neck with the point of his spear. The man let go of his sword and surrendered. It was all over.

†††

The Danish leader proved to be a jarl called Ulfrik who hailed from Læsø. My own family were Jutes who had originally come from Anholt, another island near Læsø in the Kattegut, the sea between Jutland and Swéoland. It was a tenuous link but at least we had something in common. He swore on the Mjölnir, the Thor's hammer he wore around his neck, that he wouldn't try to escape if I spared his life. Whereas Ælfred had trusted the word of a Viking sworn on Christian relics, which meant nothing to them, I was confident that an oath sworn in the name of Thor would be kept.

In return for my word that I would give him a vill in Cent he swore to be my man. When I asked why he would betray his oath to Guðrum, he assured me that he had only recently joined him and had not yet pledged his loyalty to him. He had come in search of plunder but Guðrum's recent failures at Escanceaster and Werhām before that had made him doubt his choice of leader. He had only captured Cippanhamme through the treachery of the Ealdorman Wulfhere.

He added that many Vikings, both Norse and Danes, felt the same and several jarls had deserted him to seek more success in Frankia or Frisia.

This was music to my ears. If his men were deserting him, the morale of those who remained would be low.

'How many warriors does Guðrum have in Cippanhamme?'

'I'm not sure, but I would think that there are no more than fifteen hundred,' he replied, 'and some of those are out foraging as we were.'

'Why is he still in Cippanhamme? I'd have thought that he'd have moved on to raid the rest of Wessex by now.'

'Yes, and most of his jarls would agree with you, but he's fixated about Ælfred. He's waiting for the searchers he sent into the marshes of Athelney to return with news of him.'

I didn't say anything. Although Ulfrik had given me his oath and I liked him, I wasn't so foolish as to trust him. I would only tell him what I needed to in order to get more information out of him.

'How does he know that he's in the marshlands around Athelney?' I asked.

'Because the Abbot of Glestingaburg told him and in exchange Guðrum spared his monastery.'

It seemed that Wulfhere wasn't the only traitor we had in our midst. At least he hadn't shown the Danes the secret pathways through the marshes or told them the king's exact location. I assumed that he had only said what was necessary to protect his monastery. Furthermore, he'd kept our horses safe and allowed my scouts to use them, so he wasn't entirely disloyal.

That night Ulfrik slept in the midst of my camp and I told two of my men to keep an eye on him.

By dawn the next day the weather had changed. It had started drizzling in the middle of the night and we awoke cold, stiff and wet. Eafer brought me a leather beaker of mead and some bread and cheese before helping me into my byrnie. Perhaps the Danes wouldn't yet be alarmed by the disappearance of Ulfrik's group and so wouldn't be alerted to our presence. I certainly hoped so because I intended to intercept as many of the enemy's foraging parties as I could that day.

I divided our men between myself, Ædwulf, Jerrick, and Wolnoth, leaving Cináed with a hundred men to guard the camp. Each of the four groups set off with a mounted scout; the task was to patrol the four points of the compass around Cippanhamme in order to prevent the Danes from gathering any more provisions and to lower their confidence further. If their patrols kept disappearing they would become frightened of leaving the place.

I took Ulfrik with me and we searched the northern sector, but without seeing anyone. The other three groups were more successful. Each had found and attacked a foraging party, but with varying success. One group of Vikings had fought their way clear of Jerrik's group with the loss of six of their number. Ædwulf had killed most of the group he'd encountered but a few had escaped. Wolnoth's band had been the least successful. Not only had most of the Vikings fought their way clear but he had lost two of my men in the process.

The Danes now knew that we were here. However, we had the information that we'd come for and I decided that it was unnecessarily hazardous to remain in the area. No doubt Guðrum would send a significant force to find us and Ælfred needed every warrior he could muster if he was to inflict a decisive defeat on the Danes. There was no point in letting them attack us piecemeal.

We rose at dawn the next day and struck camp. It was then that Acwel, one of the two who were supposed to be watching Ulfrik, came to tell me that he'd escaped.

'Weren't you watching him?' I asked angrily.

'Yes, with another man. We took it in turns. I was asleep when they disappeared.'

'They?'

'Yes, Ajs has vanished as well.'

'Ajs? The man who was Glædwine's steward?'

'Yes, he was one of the skypfyrd from Cent.'

I groaned. He had vowed to get his revenge and he'd evidently enlisted to do just that. I suppose I was lucky. He could have put a dagger in my heart whilst I slept, but perhaps I was too well guarded for that. Ædwulf made enquiries amongst the sentries and discovered that Ajs had taken Ulfrik past them saying that the Dane needed to empty his bowels. Either Ulfrik had gone with him willingly or perhaps he had a knife in his back. I was glad then that I had told Ulfrik little of Ælfred's plans.

'Where will we go?' Ædwulf asked as we left the campsite heading south.

'To Egbert's Stone. It's the muster point the king has decided upon.'

By now it was early May and the trees were all in leaf. We marched through land that should have been under cultivation, the first growth appearing in the tilled fields. Instead the fields were overgrown with weeds and the farmsteads and settlements were either deserted or razed to the ground. Here and there we found corpses, half eaten by animals. We stopped and gave them a Christian burial but my mood and those of the men grew increasingly sombre.

As night approached the sky darkened and rain threatened and so I decided to spend the night at yet another deserted settlement. Plainly the inhabitants had fled and so there were no bodies to bury. It was large enough a place to provide shelter for all of us and there was even a stable for the horses. My hearth warriors and I slept in what must have been the thegn's hall and the rest took over the huts and barns.

The morning dawned slowly. The dark grey clouds kept the light at bay and the rain pattered down incessantly. The dust outside had turned into a layer of mud and by the time I had gone into the woods to answer a call of nature and returned I was soaked and covered in mud up to my knees.

Eafer was trying to get the rust off my helmet and byrnie but I told him not to bother. Within hours it would be covered in the stuff once more. Hopefully the rain would ease off in a few hours and then I could make myself presentable before meeting the king. I changed into dry clothes and donned my bearskin cloak. At least that would keep most of me dry.

As I'd hoped, the rain stopped during the morning and a few hours later small patches of blue appeared in the sky. We stopped and lit fires to dry out and clean our armour. Two hours later we arrived at what had to be Egbert's stone. It stood on the top of a bare hill which afforded views all around. No one could approach without being seen some distance off. However, there was no wood for fires and no water.

We found both to the south of the hill and set up camp there. I wasn't certain of the exact date but I thought it was probably the fifth or sixth of May. The sixth was when Ælfred said that he intended to arrive at the stone so I hoped that he would arrive the following day.

He didn't. No one did. I began to worry that something had happened to him. I tried to reassure myself that he had five hundred men with him and so he was unlikely to have run into trouble. I sent four men up to the stone to keep watch and halfway through the afternoon one of them came down to report that a large warband was approaching from the south west. It was the direction that I expected the king to appear from and so I mounted one of the horses and rode up to see for myself.

I soon came to the conclusion that it wasn't Ælfred. He would have nearly five hundred warriors and a long train of clerics, women and children with him. He wouldn't have left them behind on Athelney without protection. No, this had to be some other warband as it appeared to number no more than two hundred.

I rode back down the hill and collected five of my hearth warriors before riding out to see who it was. If they proved to be hostile, the horses would allow us to get clear as the approaching host were all on foot. I didn't recognise the man leading them but he was attired in an expensive byrnie, a helmet with a gold crest and a red cloak made of the finest wool. The man behind him carried a banner in a leather case over his shoulder. As we approached he uncased it and let it flap in the breeze. It displayed a red dragon on a gold banner – the emblem of Somersaete.

I greeted Nerian warmly. It wasn't surprising that he was the first to arrive as Freumh was a mere eight miles away.

'Is the king not here,' he asked as I walked beside him leading my horse.

'Not yet; he's due today or tomorrow,' I replied, hoping that it was the truth. 'Is this the fyrd of Somersaete?'

'It's all I could muster. Many have fled into hiding, others are too terrified of the Danes to have answered the summons,' he said glumly.

If the other shires produced similar numbers we would be in trouble. We needed to outnumber the Danes, and then by some margin, if we were to inflict a crushing defeat on them. A narrow victory or an inconclusive result wouldn't eliminate the menace from Wessex's soil.

It was shortly before dusk that a rider came down from the hill to report that a mighty host was

287

approaching. Nerian and I rode up to see for ourselves. It was difficult to see much in the fading light but the men on watch were correct. This host was many times the size of Nerian's fyrd. Once more I rode to meet the newcomers with my small escort. I had persuaded Nerian to stay and command our joint forces just in case the new arrivals weren't who I thought they were.

It was with a great deal of relief that I saw Ælfred at the head of the column with Eadred at his side. The king had come to Egbert's Stone.

# Chapter Seventeen

## THE BATTLE OF ETHUNDUN

## May 878

Over the next two days the contingents from four other shires arrived. Ælfred had expected more than there were, a lot more, but there were few from Wiltunscīr or Hamtunscīr. Both were led by their shire reeves; Wulfhere was a traitor, of course, and Tunbehrt made the feeble excuse that he was needed to defend Wintanceaster. I had the feeling that the king would be looking for two new ealdorman after this was all over, not just one.

Thankfully Dornsǣte and Eadred's shire of Dyfneintscīr had sent over a thousand men between them. Of the total mustered, only five hundred were nobles and their hearth warriors. They were the only experienced fighters that we had. The rest were members of the fyrd, many untested in battle. We might have a thousand more than Guðrum but his Danes were all hardened warriors.

On the eleventh of May we left our encampment in the shadow of Egbert's stone and marched north towards a small settlement called Ethundun. Only the warriors and the clerics moved north; the women and the children were sent with the most elderly of the men as escort to Nerian's hall at Freumh.

We now had fifty horses but, of course the king, his gesith, the ealdormen and their captains all expected to ride. That left me with eighteen horses for the scouts. It would have to suffice. I sent six to search for Guðrum's army and the rest were deployed as a screen in front of the column and to the flanks. The weather was warm and sunny, which was better than rain, but it meant we needed to stop more than I would have liked to refill the leather water bottles of our thirsty men.

The settlement of Ethundun lay to the south of a ridge which extended quite some way. It varied in hight all the way along its length but the place where Ælfred chose to make his stand was on a more or less level section of the ridgeline between two wooded re-entrants. I studied the ground carefully before making a few suggestions which the king accepted.

However, all this planning would be in vain unless the Danes came to meet us. It was therefore with some relief that my scouts returned with the news that the Danes had left Cippanhamme and were heading towards us.

'We saw some of their own scouts near here, cyning, so there is no doubt that they know where we are,' one of them added.

It was a relief to know that they hadn't decided to stay behind their defensive works. Had they done so we might have been in for another lengthy siege with the possibility of a relief army of Danes coming to Guðrum's aid from Lundunwic and East Anglia.

We spent that night in the relative comfort of Ethundun's hall and the surrounding huts before trudging uphill just before sunrise to take up our positions. My scouts had been keeping an eye on the Danes since daybreak and two of them came riding in two hours after dawn to say that the Danes were approaching.

'In what strength?' I asked.

'More than a thousand, less than two,' one of them answered less than helpfully. 'I'm sorry, lord, but most of them were obscured by the dust cloud kicked up by those in the lead.'

We continued to stand, eagerly watching for the first sight of the enemy. I urged our men to take their rest whilst they could but most continued to stand and stare to the north. Monks and priests went along the line blessing everyone and giving them absolution for their sins. Bishop Asser came up to where the king and I stood with his gesith and some of my warband to give us the sacrament of the Eucharist. It felt somewhat strange to accept it and be blessed by someone I knew detested me but Asser didn't hesitate and I sensed that even he wished me well on this decisive day.

We saw the dust cloud in the distance before we could make out any details. I sensed the fear and trepidation amongst those around me. There was the faint smell of urine and even faeces in the air. It was the same before every battle. Even the most hardened warriors amongst us wondered whether this would be the day that we were killed or maimed for life.

I swallowed, my mouth parched. I took a swig of warm water from my flask but it did nothing to assuage the dryness at the back of my throat. I thought briefly of Hilda and wondered what sort of a reception I'd receive when – if – I returned to her. She hadn't wanted me to go to Cippanhamme in the first place and she must be worried to death about her only son. It was only then that I realised how remiss I'd been in not sending her a message earlier. My only consolation was that she would have known when Cei received the message to summon the skypfyrd and send the fleet to join Bjarne that we were alive. That didn't excuse me not sending her a personal message and I chastised myself for being so thoughtless.

Such thoughts did nothing to help me prepare for the coming conflict and I tried to banish them from my mind. I could indulge in recriminations later, now I needed to focus on the task in hand.

✝✝✝

As soon as the Danes emerged from the settlement they moved into line some six rows deep and formed a shieldwall. It would be difficult walking up a steep slope holding their heavy shields in front of them but no doubt they had learned from past experience to expect a hail of arrows as they advanced; not this time though. I had kept my archers for a more productive role.

I took my place in the front rank beside Drefan. The king stood on the other side of the captain of his gesith with another of his hearth warriors, a giant of a man called Wulfgar – meaning wolf spear – on his other side. My own captain, Ædwulf, took his place to guard my vulnerable right side. It would be his job to kill the Dane attacking me directly, just as it would be mine to kill Drefan's opponent. A shield could protect your front and left side but not your right.

'Hold steady men,' Ælfred shouted. 'Kill every one of the heathen devils and your women and children will be safe for a generation.'

Then death rained down on the Danes from the wooded re-entrant to their right. I had stationed every archer I could find there, together with half my warband. Men fell in droves on the far right flank of the enemy. Perhaps two hundred died or were seriously wounded before hundreds of Danes broke away from their main body to charge into the trees.

It was a mistake. Those on the right should have changed their shields to their other arm and pressed on. Had they done so they would have been safe from the majority of the arrows and our bowmen would have had to cease fire when the Danes closed with our shieldwall. As it was, our archers disappeared into the wood whilst twenty men from my warband waited behind trees to ambush the Danes who rushed on heedlessly in pursuit of the fyrd's bowmen.

Perhaps a hundred and fifty of the enemy had rushed headlong into the wood; none emerged. If they weren't killed stealthily by my men emerging behind them to cut them down, they ran out of the far side of the wood only to find a hundred archers lined up above them where the ground sloped up to the top of the ridge.

My tactics had reduced the Danes' numbers to about twelve hundred. Now we outnumbered them by two to one. Ælfred and I had chosen this battleground because we could cover the ground between one re-entrant and the next with our four hundred experienced warriors. Behind us stood five rows of the fyrd, the most experienced members of which were in the second rank.

The Danes were forced to spread out more or risk being encircled by us. Consequently they only had three ranks against our six, and they were coming uphill.

The task of the rear ranks was to hold the first few ranks in place. They used their shields to hold us firm, thus preventing parts of the shieldwall buckling and eventually breaking apart.

The man facing me held a large double-handed battleaxe which would have split my shield in two, and probably have cost me my left arm, had the blow landed. As it was Ædwulf thrust his spear into the man's exposed armpit. The spear point sunk in to his flesh and came to rest having pierced his cardiovascular artery. Blood spurted out as Ædwulf tugged his spear loose, soaking my right hand side but I hardly noticed.

I was busy hacking off the point of a Danish spear as its owner jabbed it towards Drefan. I reversed direction and half severed the spearman's forearm. He dropped the useless haft of his spear with a howl of agony and stumbled backwards through his own ranks clutching his wounded arm to his body.

The Danish axeman had been replaced by a boy no older than fifteen clutching a short sword similar to a Saxon seax. He banged his shield against mine and seemed surprised when I wasn't pushed backwards. He raised his sword aiming for my eyes but I lowered my head so that his thrust slid harmlessly off the top of my helmet. Drefan thrust his spear into the boy's side so fiercely that the spear was pulled from his grasp as the boy fell back down the hill, taking the man behind him with him.

It left a gap in the Danish line and I stepped into it, slashing my sword to the left and right as I did so. It cut into the thigh of one Dane and into the upper arm of another. I followed it up with a quick thrust into the throat of each in turn and stepped back into line.

The Danes closed the gap and I recognised the next man to attack me. It was Ajs, the former steward at Cantwareburh and the man who'd helped Jarl Ulfrik escape. He bared his teeth at me and aimed the point of his sword at my right thigh. I brought my shield down to deflect it with the rim whilst making a cut at the man opposite Drefan. The man ducked and my blade whistled harmlessly over his head.

I had expected Ædwulf to dispose of Ajs but my captain was no longer by my side. He'd been killed by a spear which entered his eye but he had quickly been replaced by a member of the fyrd. I didn't have time to mourn Ædwulf's death as the man who now stood guarding my right side was too terrified to do anything except hold his shield in front of him and duck behind it every time he was attacked. That left me very vulnerable.

Ajs saw his opportunity and evidently thought he could make an easy kill but, before he could take advantage of the situation, I punched the boss of my shield into Ajs's smirking face, smashing his nose and knocking out his front teeth. His triumphant grin turned into howl of pain. He was no warrior and he allowed his shield to drop as he stepped back. I took one pace forward and pushed the point of my sword through his throat before stepping back and making a cut at the left thigh of Drefan's opponent. His leg collapsed and Drefan quickly disposed of him.

The timorous man who had replaced Ædwulf was no longer there. One of the Danes had grabbed his shield and pulled him into their ranks where he was quickly killed. Now I had a boy of who looked to be no more than fourteen guarding my right hand side. I groaned in dismay, doubting that he would last longer than a few seconds. I was wrong.

The boy ducked under the axe of a giant of a Dane and the man to the boy's left thrust his spear into the Dane's eye. The giant fell dead, providing an obstacle in front of the lad. A wild eyed heathen was the next man to attack me. If he wasn't a berserker he was giving a good impression of one. To make matters worse my sword was stuck in the torso of a man facing Drefan.

I brought up my shield to defend myself from the berserker but he pulled it down and tried to stab me in the neck with a dagger. My arms were tired and I didn't have the strength to shake his grip so that I could use my shield to protect myself. I thought to myself that this was it and uttered a swift prayer to

God to forgive my sins when suddenly the grip on my shield slackened and the wild-eyed Viking disappeared.

The boy next to me grinned and muttered something about hamstringing him. I didn't have time to thank him before the next Dane attacked Drefan. However, I now trusted the boy to protect my vulnerable side and I could focus my attention on protecting the captain of Ælfred's gesith.

It wasn't long after that that the Danes broke. Two thirds of their number had been killed or badly wounded, which meant the same thing as they wouldn't be allowed to live more than an hour or two. We had our own casualties of course. I'd lost Ædwulf and the number of my original warband was reduced still further but thankfully he was our only loss. Ælfred himself had a couple of flesh wounds, but neither was serious. I was covered in gore and looked like a walking corpse, or so Eomær told me. However, none of the blood was mine.

Our few horsemen chased the routed Danes for the rest of the day and reported killing two score more of them but the rest escaped as darkness fell. Unfortunately, after checking the corpses, we discovered that Guðrum was one of those who had escaped. Wulfhere had been seen on the Danish ranks but he too had managed to get away.

I was bone weary afterwards and I left it to others to search the Danes for plunder and collect our own dead ready for burial the next day. The Danes would be left where they fell as food for the rats and the crows. I was fast asleep in the hall when I was woken by Drefan.

'The king is asking for you,' he said, and then added, 'thank you for saving my life several times today.'

'I was fortunate to be able to do so. Unfortunately Ædwulf, who was guarding my own right hand side fell halfway through the battle and I was lucky to survive after that,' I said grimly, rising wearily from the floor.

Then I remembered the boy who had saved my life. I wanted to offer him a place in my warband in return but I had no idea who he was or where he could be found. All I had was a fleeting image of a round face topped by a mop of wheat-coloured hair.

I didn't have far to go. Ælfred was at the far end of the hall talking to several ealdormen, Bishop Asser and a man I had hoped never to see again: Eadda.

'Cyning, forgive me for sleeping when others were not,' I said, joining the group.

'There is nothing to forgive, Jørren. Your battle plan gave us the victory, and a more decisive one I couldn't have wished for. Moreover you fought like a man possessed. Drefan tells me you saved his life many times over, which meant that he was free to protect me. You have my heartfelt gratitude.'

I was stunned by the king's praise, unexpected as it was. Even Asser smiled faintly and nodded at me. Only Eadda looked sour.

'Lord Eadda, I didn't know you had reached us in time for the battle,' I said pleasantly, although I knew full well from the man's spotless clothes and byrnie that he couldn't have done any fighting.

'He didn't,' Ælfred said tersely. 'He has only just arrived, although he has brought a few welcome reinforcements from Hamtunscīr.'

'Cyning, you know that I would have come to your aid sooner if I could,' Eadda replied smoothly. 'It was my place to stand at your side as your hereræswa.'

'Not any more,' Ælfred said grimly. 'Bjarne has told me that he wanted you to join him when he set sail for Athelney but you declined.'

'Only so I could raise men to come to your side here, cyning.'

'And how many exactly did you bring after having had weeks to do so?'

'Two hundred, cyning.'

Eadda now looked defensive and slightly hurt. He knew that Ælfred was questioning his integrity.

'Two hundred! And you thought it was more important to gather in those paltry few farmers and ploughboys rather than come to advise me as my hereræswa, did you?'

'No, well. I had hoped to raise more, cyning. Forgive me. It was an error of judgement.'

'Yes it was. You are a wealthy thegn and I suspect that they are your ceorls who you kept back from joining the shire's fyrd until you saw which way the wind was blowing. I have no doubt that, had I lost today you would have been amongst the first to bend the knee to Guðrum.'

'You wrong me, cyning!' he protested but his hand went to where his sword would have been had he not had to surrender it before entering the hall.

The only people allowed to carry weapons in the king's presence were his gesith. However, I was also armed but only because I'd fallen asleep in the hall before sentries had been posted to collect weapons at the door.

'I think not. You and others whose loyalty has been tested and found wanting will appear before the Witenaġemot in due course to explain your actions over the past few months. I do not judge you, but they will. Lord Jørren had taken over as hereræswa pro tem and he will continue until after the Witenaġemot has met. I have no doubt that they will confirm the appointment,' he said with a smile, which quickly disappeared as he turned his attention back to Eadda. 'Now you may leave us.'

Eadda walked stiffly out of the hall, his back reflecting the outrage he felt at the way that he'd been treated. His jealousy of me meant that he had been my enemy before this; now he had even more reason to hate me. I strongly suspected that his ill-feeling might well erupt into violence; I would need to be on my guard.

We arrived before Cippanhamme two days later. A grisly sight greeted us: a corpse hanging from the top of the palisade next to the gates. It was impossible to make out the features at this range but I recognised the clothes. It was Jarl Ulfrik; so he hadn't gone willingly with Ajs after all. The Dane had paid for giving me his oath with his life. I was pleased that I had been the one to exact revenge on Ajs.

From what we knew we calculated that Guðrum couldn't have more than three hundred and fifty warriors with him who had survived Ethundun. There might be a few more who had stayed to garrison the settlement but he was unlikely to have more than four hundred in total. We had nearly six times his numbers. Furthermore, his supplies were likely to be low. The Danes would have consumed what there was over the winter and, although we knew that they had sent out foraging parties, they probably hadn't gathered in enough for a long siege. Nevertheless, we needed to bring matters to a swift conclusion, not sit around for weeks waiting for the Danes to surrender.

Of course, we knew where the store huts were and that evening I led my archers around to the opposite side of the river from those huts. At this point the river was twenty yards wide and quite fast flowing. It wasn't possible to swim across but the store huts lay no more than twenty five yards from the opposite bank. It was well within range of our bows.

The fire arrows arced up into the sky and fell down onto the hut roofs. They were made of straw and quickly caught alight in the dry conditions. It wasn't long before the Danes came running in a futile attempt to put out the fires. After the first few had been hit by our arrows they gave up and retreated out of sight. Soon after that the blazing straw fell into the huts and set light to the grain and other combustibles being stored there.

A mixture of smells wafted across the river to us; charred wood and roasting meat amongst them. Satisfied that the Danes now had next to nothing left to eat, we made our way back to camp in a jubilant mood.

It took twelve days but eventually Guðrum sued for peace. This time there could be no suggestion of paying Danegeld. Ælfred's terms were fair but he intended to make it very difficult for Guðrum to ever invade Wessex again.

Apart from taking hostages, something which had proved of little value in keeping the peace in the past, Ælfred insisted that Guðrum and his thirty surviving jarls and hirsirs became Christians and were baptised. It was a clever move. The Vikings were almost universally pagans believing in the Norse pantheon of Odin, Thor and rest of the Æsir. Few Vikings would follow a Christian leader unless they were already sworn to him.

Of course, Guðrum hadn't brought his whole force into Wessex. There were still a couple of thousand Danes spread between Lundenwic, East Anglia and half of Mercia. However, with few newcomers flocking to his banner, Guðrum would be hard pressed to hang on to what he now held without seeking to expand his realm.

The next thirty days were spent hunting and relaxing at Cippanhamme before the king moved to another royal hall at Aller. There was a certain irony in the fact that the nearby river where the baptismal ceremony took place was the Pedredan. The site chosen wasn't that far from Athelney, where we had hidden until fairly recently.

A week of feasting followed in which Guðrum, now known by his baptismal name of Æðelstan, pledged loyalty to Ælfred. In return the king recognised Æðelstan as King of East Anglia. The problematical situation that Mercia found itself in was left for another day, although I have no doubt that Ælfred's dream was to bring that kingdom under his rule. However, it still had a Christian king in the form of Ceolwulf and I knew that Ælfred would do nothing to combine the two kingdoms whilst Mercia still had a king, however ineffective.

In reality it was Ealdorman Æðelred who held the real power over that half of Mercia which wasn't occupied by the Danes: that is, from Legacæstir in the north-west to the north bank of the River Temes near Ludenwic. Even if Ceolwulf died, I doubted that Æðelred would favour a union with Wessex under Ælfred as king.

I found myself longing to return to my shire of Cent and to the arms of Hilda. Life seemed to be in limbo whilst the treaty between the two kings was ironed out and I think I would have gone mad through boredom if it wasn't for my children, of whom I now counted Oswine. The three of them engaged me in different ways. Æscwin, who I had

303

now accepted as being destined for the church, knew enough about Christianity for us to discuss the basis of our belief in God and in Christ. It wasn't a subject that would have normally interested me, but my son had a questioning mind which, whilst not treading on the toes of established doctrine, did make me question some aspects of what I'd been taught.

Cuthfleda and Oswine had learnt the fundamental principles of tracking and hunting small game from Eomær. I now built on that and, whenever the weather and my duties permitted, I took them with me.

It was whilst we were out in the woods tracking a deer that I came across the boy with the mop of wheat-coloured hair again. I hadn't forgotten that he had saved my life. I just didn't know how to find him to thank him and to reward him. He was retrieving a hare from a trap which puzzled me. Most of the fyrd had returned home, leaving the nobles and their hearth warriors to guard the king.

The boy jumped to his feet when he became aware of our presence and for a moment I thought he was going to run. He didn't, however, and relaxed when he saw the two children. He looked uncared for; his clothes were torn and filthy and he was all skin and bone.

'I think you're the boy who stood by me in the shieldwall and saved my life,' I said with a smile.

'It was you, lord? You were covered in blood. You look quite different now.'

'Whereas I wouldn't have recognised you under the grime if it wasn't for your mop of hair.'

'No, I'm sorry, lord. I must look like an urchin.'

'What's happened to you?'

The boy looked miserable and was trying hard not to cry.

'My father and uncle were both killed at Ethandun,' he said, his eyes downcast.

'What about your mother and your other kinfolk?'

'All dead, lord,' he said despondently, 'Our thegn never liked my father and after the battle he told me I wasn't wanted. With no family to care for me I'd just be unnecessary drain on the vill's resources. I could have inherited my father's land had I been older and been able to pay the levy required to inherit the tenancy, but he will now let it to another ceorl. Consequently I've been living in the woods, eating berries and what game I could trap.'

This time he didn't try and hold back the tears and Cuthfleda ran to him and threw her arms around him in spite of the filth and stink. I thought it was a touching sight, especially as Cuthfleda only came up to the lad's shoulders.

'What's your name?' I asked when my daughter eventually let go, although she continued to hold his hand.

'Rinan, lord.'

It meant rain, an apt name considering the tears that now streaked the dirt on his face.

'Well Rinan, I take it that you are a good tracker and hunter?'

'Yes, lord. Both my father and my uncle have taught me since I was quite young.'

'Then how would you like to join my warband as a scout?'

The boy's face lit up and Cuthfleda ran to give me a hug.

'But he stinks, father?' Oswine said, speaking for the first time since he had encountered Rinan.

'Nothing that a bath and clean clothes won't rectify, Oswine. You need to look beyond the exterior and see what's underneath if you want to become a good judge of a person,' I told him.

Oswine didn't say any more but I could tell from the way that he looked at Rinan that he disliked him. At first I couldn't think why and then I realised. It was the compassionate way that Cuthfleda had run to hug and comfort Rinan that had upset him. Even at his young age he was jealous of Cuthfleda showing affection for someone else.

✝✝✝

Whilst we waited for the interminable negotiations to end, the Witenaġemot met and, amongst other matters, confirmed Eadda's dismissal and my appointment as his replacement. Eventually the treaty between Ælfred and Guðrum was signed and the Danes departed with an escort under Drefan's command. His orders were to ensure that they reached Lundenwic without pillaging on the way. To this end the king gave them twelve carts loaded with provisions for the journey. I didn't envy Drefan. Ox carts travelled extremely slowly, even on the best of roads. It would take the best part of two weeks to get there.

The king was returning to Wintanceaster and he expected me, as his hereræswa, to accompany him. I would remain as Ealdorman of Cent, of course, but my brother Æscwin would effectively govern the shire on my behalf as the shire reeve. I wasn't happy at the thought of living at the royal court, especially in a time of peace when there was nothing for me to do, except to supervise the training of young warriors.

Ælfred would expect me to send for Hilda and the twins to live with me. Hilda would hate that. She enjoyed being mistress of her own hall; instead of which she would become one of Ealhswith's ladies. Knowing how Ælfred's wife detested me, I suspected that Hilda wouldn't be well treated. I therefore went to see the king on the eve of his departure.

'Cyning, I have come to see you about my future,' I began nervously.

'Your future? What do you mean Lord Jørren? You are my hereræswa, is that not enough for you?'

'That is not what I meant, cyning. I am also your sǣ hereræswa. With Guðrum defeated our land borders are secure, at least for some time to come. However, Viking raids along the coast will still continue. I feel that I can best serve you and Wessex by concentrating on patrolling our shores.'

'Surely Bjarne is quite capable of doing that?'

'Yes, cyning, from Hamwic he can look after the coast of Dornsæte, Dyfneintscīr and Hamtunscīr; possibly even Suth-Seaxe. However, the greatest threat is likely to come from Frankia where there are now thousands of Vikings. He can't patrol the coast of Cent and the estuary of the River Temes from Hamwic.'

'What about your captain at Dofras, what his name? Er, Cei? Can't he look after Cent?'

I cursed. The king was quite right. Cei was perfectly capable; the problem was his status as a former slave and a Briton. Bjarne wasn't a Saxon, of course. He was a former Viking from Swéoland. However, they were a seafaring people and there were a growing number of Christian Danes, Norsemen and even a few Swéoþeod who had settled in Wessex and had become loyal thegns. He was therefore accepted in a way that Cei could never hope to be.

'Cei is originally from Wealas, cyning, and a former slave. He couldn't command the respect that he would need to become Sæ Hereræswa of the east.'

'In that case I'm surprised that you trust him to hold your fortress for you,' Ælfred said, his voice heavy with disapproval. 'However, there must be someone else you could appoint, or would you have me re-instate Eadda as Hereræswa?' Ælfred said sarcastically.

'Cyning, I do believe that the greatest threat now is from the sea. If we can prevent too many Vikings crossing the sea from Frankia, then that would reduce the threat of another invasion on land as well. What would my role be if I remained as hereræswa? Training warriors? Anyone can do that.'

'That's where you are wrong, Jørren. We need to improve on the present burhs to stop further incursions. You are right when you say that the greatest threat now comes from the sea. I therefore plan to build new burhs, some based on the old Roman forts, and improve existing ones.'

He took me over to a table on which was laid out a map.

'As you can see a string of burhs from Escanceaster in the west to Dofras in the east, coupled with repairs to the coastal roads, will mean that their garrisons can issue forth on horseback from these burhs to deal with any Viking raids speedily.'

'But to garrison even ten burhs, would mean thousands of warriors.' I objected.

'Yes, I'm well aware of that, but that's not all. I intend to build new burhs on the major rivers at places like Baðum, Wælingforde and also at Sudwerca and on an island in the Temes near Cocheham. These will prevent the Danes using the river as a route into the heart of Wessex. They will require garrisons of perhaps ten thousand men.'

'Where will all these warriors come from, cyning? And how will you pay for it all?'

'The ceorls who live there will form the basis of the garrisons. Unlike the fyrd of today, they will be properly equipped with helmets, leather armour and weapons – seax, spear and shield – and trained in their use. It will be a requirement that they are drilled for one day each week.'

'This will be expensive, cyning.'

'Yes, I'm well aware of that but the alternative is allow our settlements and farmsteads to be pillaged and our people killed. Guðrum is no longer a threat but there will be others in the future who will want to take our land from us. I therefore expect everyone to contribute in order to avoid that. I will introduce a burghal hideage. Every ceorl, thegn and ealdorman will contribute to the cost each in accordance with the number of hides that they own.

'You can see now why I want you to continue as my heræswa? You were instrumental in the first phase of creating burhs and repairing roads. I'm relying on you to supervise the new plan as well.'

There wasn't much I could say. If it was successful it should result in a system of defences that would protect Wessex from future invasions. It had its attractions for me as well. It would mean travelling all around Wessex to check on progress. I hated to be tied to one place for too long and this new role would satisfy my wanderlust. My fears about becoming a fixture at Ælfred's court faded away. My only reservation now was Hilda's reaction. However, I couldn't see why she couldn't stay at Dofras, or move back to Cantwareburh if she would prefer that, and I would join her as and when I could.

The problem of appointing a new sæ heræswa remained. After sleeping on it I decided to recommend that Bjarne take over from me but remain at Hamwic. I couldn't think of anyone better to command the fleet in the east and so I decided to ask Jerrick to become Bjarne's deputy and base himself at Dofras in order to oversee the patrols along the coast of Cent and the estuary of the Temes.

Jerrick was the type of man who shied away from power, believing quite wrongly that others were more deserving of being leaders than he was. It was all I could do to get him to accept the captaincy of one of the longships. I therefore decided to say nothing to him in advance; he would only refuse.

I told the king that I had decided that Bjarne should replace me in command of the fleet and he readily agreed.

'Cyning, I would like to return to Dofras and see my wife and other children before I return to discuss the details of constructing the new burhs and collecting the taxes to pay for them.'

'Very well, but don't stay too long. I want you back here by the end of June. The work must begin once the harvest is in and there is a great deal of planning to be done before then.'

I was about to leave when the king spoke again.

'The other matter concerns Wulfhere and Tunbehrt.'

The former had been with Guðrum at the Battle of Ethundun and had reportedly been wounded in the leg but no sign of him could be found on the battlefield, or later after the Danes surrendered. Presumably he had escaped and was a fugitive somewhere. Tunbehrt had also disappeared.

'They must be run to earth and brought back and tried for treason in front of the Witenaġemot,' Ælfred continued. 'Before you leave see Lord Drefan and organise the search for them, would you?'

'Lord Drefan, cyning?'

'Yes, hadn't you heard? I've decided to appoint him as the new Ealdorman of Wiltunscīr. The Witenaġemot will need to formally confirm it, of course, but as he is a son of Lord Odda I can't see that being much of a problem.'

# Chapter Eighteen

## Cent

## June 878

It felt good to be at sea again; my one regret was that I would be able to spend less time on board once I started my new role, although I suppose I could always visit the coastal burhs under construction by ship.

My whole warband was returning to Cent with me, including our newest recruit, Rinan. He might be a good hunter and trapper but he was no sailor. I had put him to work as a ship's boy on the Saint Cuthbert but, once he had spewed the contents of his stomach all over four of my hearth warriors whilst he was up the mast as the lookout, I decided that it probably wasn't such a good idea. He was now sitting against the gunwale at the stern looking miserable, holding his crucifix and praying for deliverance.

He had been thin when we found him but a few good meals had filled him out a little. Now, however, he was thinner than ever and couldn't keep anything down for long. I prayed that he wasn't going to die on us before we reached Hamwic. Bjarne and his half of the fleet would remain there whilst the rest of us continued on to Dofras.

I intended to host a feast for everyone before we left to show my appreciation for their valour. I also needed to divide up our share of the silver and other valuables taken from the Danes, both from those who died at Ethundun and from those who had surrendered at Cippanhamme.

To my relief Rinan recovered quickly once he was back on dry land, although he was sick again on the night of the feast but this time it was due to the mead he'd consumed, not the motion of the ship.

The hall at Hamwic wasn't large enough to hold us all and so we held the celebration outside. Thankfully it was a fine, almost balmy, evening. I wanted to speak to my men but timing was crucial. I didn't want to spoil their eating and drinking by interrupting the flow of banter and reminiscing too early. At the same time, if I left it too late most of them would be too drunk to hear what I had to say.

Eafer filled my goblet up but I left it untouched for now. I needed a clear head and I had already drunk enough. At what I judged to be the opportune moment I climbed up onto the table so that everyone could see me, and Bjorn banged the hilt of his eating knife on the table to attract everyone's attention. As there were nearly a thousand men, and quite a few women, present it took some time and there was a lot of shushing before everyone quietened down.

'Men of Wessex,' I began, 'what we achieved in the marshes of Athelney and at Ethundun has brought peace to this land of ours. Many fought and quite a few died to secure that peace but you played a more important part in the Danes' defeat than anyone. You can be justly proud of yourselves.'

I waited for the cheering and banging on tables to subside before I continued.

'The king has rewarded us handsomely and tomorrow we will all share in the riches we have earned.'

This time the cheering and banging on tables was loud enough to be heard on Whitlond. I waited again before coming to the meat of what I had to say.

'King Ælfred has appointed me as the permanent Hereræswa of Wessex and so I can no longer continue to command the fleet.'

There was a stunned silence, quickly followed by a buzz of conversation and people asked themselves what this meant. I raised my arms for quiet and Bjarne banged on the table repeatedly until order was restored.

'That means, of course, that someone else will need to command our longships.'

The hubbub started again but subsided when I raised my arms again.

'The king has graciously agreed to appoint Bjarne as your new sæ hereræswa and ...' but my next words were drowned out by a bout of cheering and shouted congratulations.

I knew it would be a popular choice but I was far less sanguine about my next announcement.

'He will continue to be based here at Hamwic. He has proved himself to be a most able deputy to me and I am personally delighted by his appointment. Stand up, Bjarne.'

When he had done so I presented him with a seax I had commissioned whilst at Cippanhamme after the battle. It was a beautiful weapon, finely balanced and

315

with a blade that rippled in shades of blue, grey and silver, reflecting the number of times the metal had been folded and re-folded during its forging. The hilt was bound in soft calfskin and, instead of the usual metal pommel, it had a ruby secured in place with thick gold wire.

I could see that Bjarne was overcome with emotion. He took the weapon in his hands and examined it before wrapping his arms around me and thumping me on the back. Thankfully the cheering, clapping and banging went on long enough for him to recover.

He spoke briefly to thank me effusively, both for his appointment and for the magnificent seax. He promised to do his best to lead the fleet to the best of his ability and then he sat down abruptly to renewed cheering.

Obviously everyone thought that was the end of the speeches and chatter started up again. However, I remained on my feet and held up my hands for silence once more.

'I promise you I have nearly finished; then you can get back to the important business of getting well and truly drunk. Whilst Bjarne will take over from me, albeit based here, that leaves the question of who will be his deputy and look after the coast in the east. He will be based at Dofras, as I am at the moment, but he will answer to Bjarne. I have given a lot of thought to who that man should be.'

I paused and looked around trying to look everyone in the eye. Complete quiet reigned, the only sound being the crackle of the fires and the hiss as the fat of the carcasses being roasted on the spits dropped into the flames.

'The person I have chosen has been with me ever since he helped me rescue my brother Alric. He has served me devotedly for the past twelve years and, like me, he's a Jute. He was the person who first taught me about sailing. The man I'm talking about is, of course, Jerrik.'

I waited for cries of approval, or perhaps even of hostility, but there was nothing, just silence. Then Bjarne stood again.

'I cannot think of anyone I would rather have to help me command the fleet,' he said, giving me a broad grin.

It was enough to sway the doubters. More cheers and banging of tables followed for some time but slowly died away as people returned to their drinking and feasting. I looked anxiously across towards Jerrik, who was sitting with his crew looking stunned as they thumped him on the back and toasted him. He hadn't been that happy about being appointed as captain of a longship. Might he refuse this far greater responsibility? Well, for good or ill, the die was cast.

Jerrik came to see me the next morning.

'You might have warned me, lord,' he said reproachfully.

'Would you have accepted if I had?' I asked with a smile.

'Probably not,' he confessed, 'but I am grateful for the opportunity. I only hope I'm up to the task.'

'There is no one better,' I assured him.

After he'd left I sent a Snekkja to Dofras with two letters: one to my wife to tell her that we were all well and were on our way home and the other to Cei, telling him of the situation and asking him to make suitable arrangements for Jerrik to base himself at Dofras. I prayed that both missives would receive a favourable reception.

✝✝✝

The day of our departure from Hamwic dawned overcast and chilly for the time of year. Eadwig, the master shipbuilder, came to find me as soon as I had heard mass and walked with me across to the hall to break our fast.

'Lord, I'm worried about the weather,' he said to me quietly. 'I feel it in my bones that a gale is brewing.'

As we walked through the area where we had feasted the previous evening slaves were scurrying hither and thither, clearing up the debris. I looked up at the sky and, although the clouds were grey, the wind was no brisker than a strong breeze and there were no signs of a storm as far as I could see.

'It's a dismal day,' I agreed, 'but I don't see any indications that danger threatens us at sea.'

I was eager to continue my voyage back to Hilda and I didn't want any unnecessary delays.

'Nevertheless, I caution you against leaving today.'

'I'm sorry, Eadwig, I know you mean well but, unless the weather deteriorates before the time of our departure, we are leaving this morning. I need to get back to Dofras.'

'Very well, the decision is yours, lord. But don't say that I didn't warn you.'

He stomped off, muttering to himself, and I made my way to the hall, eagerly looking forward to eating something that might settle my queasy stomach.

His words did trouble me though and, as I stood on the aft deck of the Saint Cuthbert as she was rowed down the estuary from Hamwic towards Whitlond, I kept a wary eye on the sky. It still looked harmless, if a rather steely grey colour. The other ten longships that were normally based at Dofras followed us in a long line. As I smelt the salty tang of the sea in my nostrils once more I began to relax and, by the time that we reached the channel between the mainland and Whitlond I had forgotten about Eadwig's warning.

I was shaken out of my complacency when Wilfrið tapped me on the shoulder and pointed due south. Black clouds were scudding towards us over the island to our right and the wind had picked up. He had been about to order the raising of the sail but I agreed that it would be sensible to wait for a minute or two to see if this was just a brief squall or something much worse.

'Where can we take shelter if we need to?' I shouted over the howl of the wind.

'There's a large natural harbour at Portcæstre,' the captain replied, pointing to somewhere off our port bow.

I remembered that Ælfred had said something about Portcæstre being an old Roman fort, now in ruins, that he wanted to repair and make into one of his new burhs to defend the south coast. I wasn't convinced that the weather was bad enough yet that we needed to seek shelter but I was curious to see the place for myself and it wouldn't harm to err on the side of caution, so I told Wilfrið to make for the harbour.

I glanced behind me to ensure that the ship following us had seen our change of course. Visibility was poor due to the sea spray and the rain that was now falling quite heavily but I was relieved to see it turn shortly after we had. I hoped that the rest of the ships behind her were close enough to each other to follow our lead.

The seas were now much rougher and it was hard work rowing. Having rowed all the way down the estuary against the tide as well, many of the oarsmen were near exhaustion by now and, when one collapsed, I pulled him out of the way and took his place. I was strong and used to exercising with sword, axe and bow but rowing seemed to use muscles I didn't know I had. After a while I thought that my arms would drop off and my shoulders burned with the effort but at last we entered calmer waters.

I had been concentrating on rowing but now I looked around me. I was thankful to see land quite close to us on both sides. My relief was short lived; moments later we entered a maelstrom of churning water and were swept into the harbour by the incoming tide. We came to a stop in calmer waters and the rowers collapsed over their oars.

'Keep rowing you lazy buggers, or the next ship will crash into us,' Wilfrið yelled in alarm. His shout raised me from lethargy and I gripped the oar once more. We really put our backs into it and slowly the skeid picked up speed. The next longship was borne through the entrance on the tidal rip and came close to our stern but slowed just in time. A few hundred yards further on we stopped rowing again and coasted to a stop. The natural harbour had widened out sufficiently for other ships to pass us if they wished to and I breathed a sigh of relief.

I knew that I would be stiff later on but I felt a deep satisfaction with my efforts as an oarsman. I had rowed before, but never in such conditions, or for so long. I was thankful that we sought shelter; this was no squall but a full blown gale. It had been sheer folly on my part to have ignored Eadwig's advice.

Once I had recovered sufficiently from my exertions, I got up and the rower I'd replaced retook his place with a nod of thanks and sheepish grin. I made my way to the prow and studied what I could see of the harbour. It was almost an inland lake with just the one narrow entrance through which we had come. At its widest point it was probably at least a mile across. The rain prevented me seeing too clearly and so I had Wilfrið take us around the perimeter.

The harbour was lined with reed beds with flat grassland beyond. At the north-western end of the harbour there was a river estuary at the mouth of which lay an island. Further on we came across a natural inner harbour with the remains of the Roman fort that the king had talked about to the left of the entrance. It was quite sizeable and stood on level ground above earthen ramparts. There was a ditch all the way around which was filled with water from the harbour. I estimated that it could hold several hundred men and their families.

The inner haven itself was bordered by a shingle beach with grasslands beyond. It was easily large enough for our whole fleet to anchor there and ships could be dragged up on the pebbles for repairs to the hull and re-caulking.

The fortress seemed to be unoccupied but there was a small settlement nearby with a few fishing boats drawn up onto the sand. We beached the Saint Cuthbert whilst the rest of our ships anchored in deeper water. I was curious about the state of the fortress and went ashore with three warriors as escort to explore. The wind and rain buffeted me so much that at times I staggered, struggling to stay on my feet, however I persevered.

I walked all the way around the old Roman fort. In many places the walls were more or less intact; where they had fallen down the stone lay in heaps and it looked as if they would be easy to rebuild, always provided that I could find a mason. I walked over to the deserted settlement. Obviously the inhabitants had fled when they saw the longships, not realising that we weren't Vikings but Saxons like themselves. There would be time to correct their misapprehension later but I had reached a decision.

Portcæstre would be a much better base for Bjarne; it was much nearer the sea and Eadwig could repair ships here more easily than at Hamwic, where there was only foul smelling mud flats on which to beach ships. Moreover, he could build a watchtower at the outer entrance to watch for Vikings in the channel between Hamtunscīr and Whitlond.

There was another advantage. Garrisons cost money to maintain – lots of it. If Bjarne's warriors and the skypfyrd whose turn it was to crew the ships were based here, it wouldn't need a separate garrison.

Pleased with my neat solution to creating the first of the new burhs, I sent two messengers off on horses we had found in the local thegn's stables: one to tell Bjarne about the proposed move and the other to inform the king of my decision. We stayed the night in the deserted settlement and then left at dawn. I left a small pouch of silver for the thegn to pay him for the provisions we'd used and for the loan of the horses. Hopefully he'd infer from that that we weren't Viking raiders after all.

When we reached the entrance to the outer harbour we discovered that there was one disadvantage to the new base of the western fleet. The current that had borne us into the harbour so swiftly also prevented ships from leaving at the wrong state of the tide.

Luckily we didn't have too long to wait for slack water and, once out at sea, we raised the sail to catch the gentle breeze from the south west that would take us back home to Dofras. The only dark cloud on the horizon was the disappearance of Wulfhere. The man had betrayed the king and nearly caused the death of myself and some of my children. For that there was no forgiveness and one day there would have to be a reckoning.

Jørren will return in the summer of 2020 in the next book in the Saga of Wessex and the Danes

# THE RIVEN REALM

# Author's note

The main events of the years 874 to 878 AD occurred much as they have been portrayed in this novel. The main exception is the Battle of Berncæstre in Mercia, which is completely fictitious. We know something of what occurred in Wessex during this time through the Anglo-Saxon Chronicle and other surviving documents, but far less was written about events in Mercia.

King Ælfred did form a navy to tackle the perennial problem of Viking raids and migration, especially from those who had originally invaded Frankia and Fresia and then saw easier pickings across the North Sea in England. However, the formation of a naval force probably dates from the 880s rather than the 870s.

I am grateful to the following sources which I used extensively during my research for this novel:

**Ælfred's Britain** by Max Adams

**Pauli's the life and Works of Alfred the Great**
Translated from the German and edited by B. Thorpe

**Alfred, Warrior King** by John Peddie

Printed in Great Britain
by Amazon